DAUGHTER *of* XANADU

DAUGHTER *of* XANADU

Dori Jones Yang

EMBER

 Published in the United States by Ember, an imprint of Random House Children's Books, a division of Random House, Inc., New York. Originally published in hardcover in the United States by Delacorte Press, an imprint of Random House Children's Books, New York, in 2011.

Ember and the colophon are trademarks of Random House, Inc.

Visit us on the Web! www.randomhouse.com/teens
Educators and librarians, for a variety of teaching tools, visit us at www.randomhouse.com/teachers

The Library of Congress has cataloged the hardcover edition of this work as follows:
Yang, Dori Jones.
Daughter of Xanadu / Dori Jones Yang. — 1st ed. p. cm.
Summary: Emmajin, the sixteen-year-old eldest granddaughter of Khublai Khan, becomes a warrior and falls in love with explorer Marco Polo in thirteenth-century China.
ISBN 978-0-385-73923-8 (hc : alk. paper)
ISBN 978-0-385-90778-1 (glb : alk. paper) — ISBN 978-0-375-89727-6 (ebook)
[1. Soldiers—Fiction. 2. Sex role—Fiction. 3. Love—Fiction. 4. Mongols—Fiction. 5. Kublai Khan, 1216–1294—Fiction. 6. Polo, Marco, 1254–1323?—Fiction. 7. China—History—Yüan dynasty, 1260–1368—Fiction.] I. Title.
PZ7.Y1933 Dau 2011 [Fic]—dc22 2009053652

ISBN 978-0-385-73924-5 (pbk.)

RL: 6.0

Printed in the United States of America
10 9 8 7 6 5 4 3 2 1
First Ember Edition 2012

Random House Children's Books supports the First Amendment and celebrates the right to read.

For Paul,
who inspired me to try to bridge the gap
between East and West

MONGOL EMPIRE UNDER KHUBILAI KHAN 1275–1276

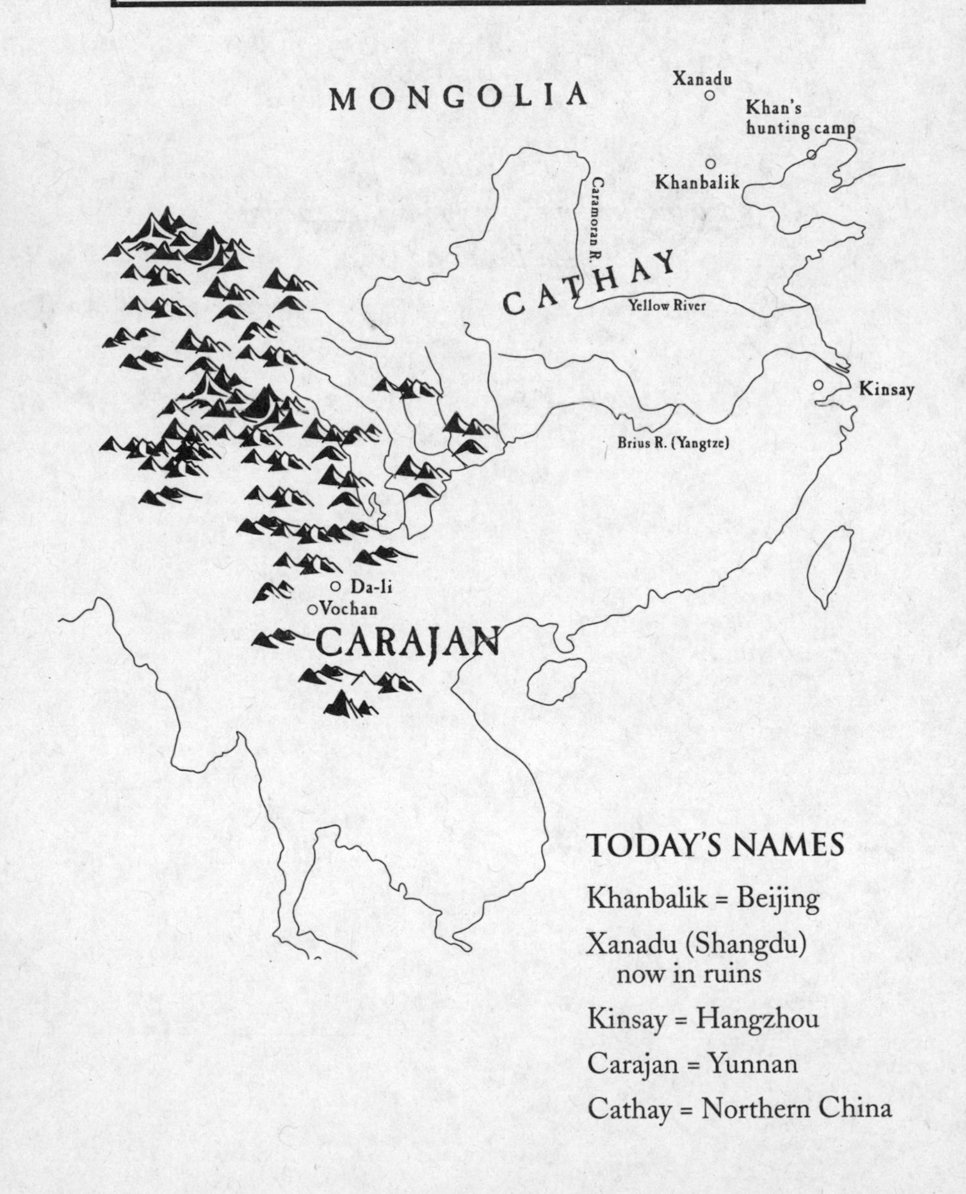

EMMAJIN'S FAMILY TREE

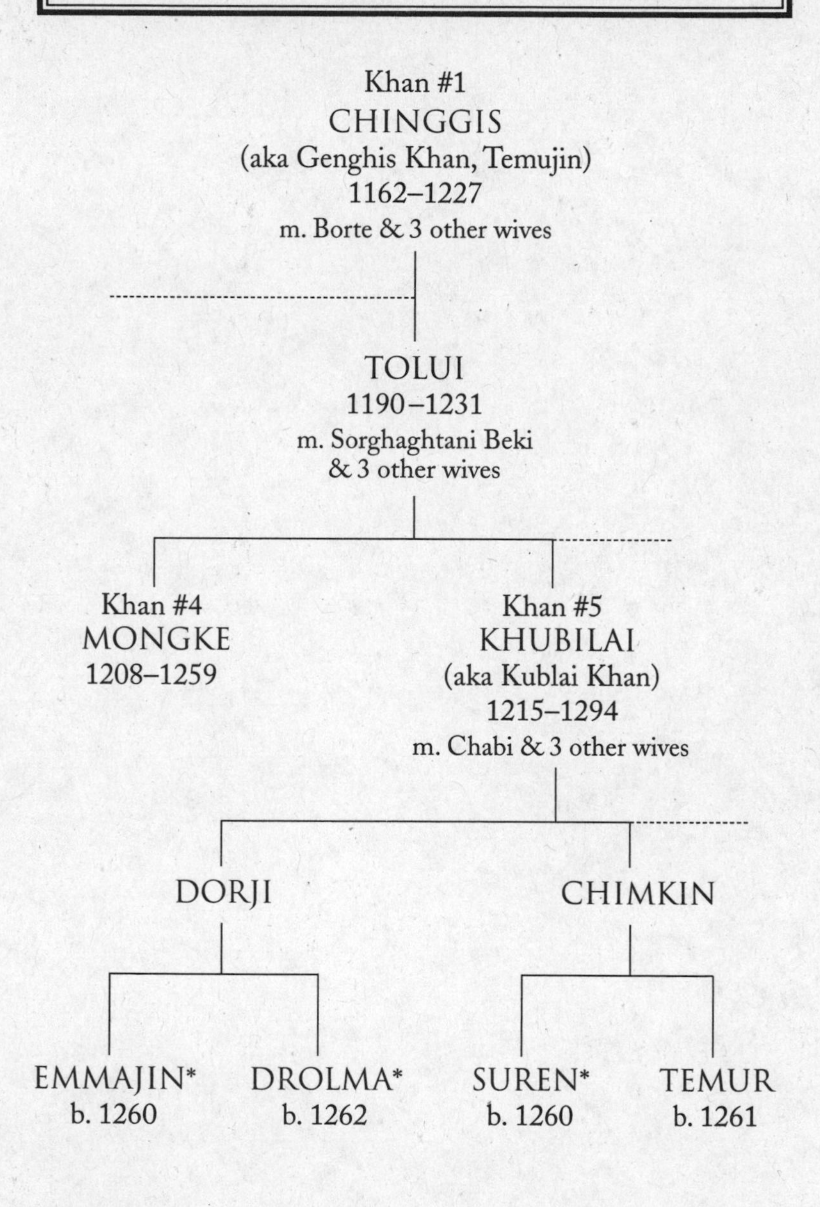

* fictional

FOREWORD

This is the story of two adventurous hearts from thousands of miles and worlds apart: one from medieval Venice and the other from the royal court of the Mongol Empire. A quirk of destiny brought them together, and their tale is revealed here for the first time.

To each, the world looked totally different. For Emmajin, life centered on the court of her grandfather Khubilai Khan. Outside the thick walls of the palace lay the streets of the capital city, and beyond that, land after land that her ancestors had conquered, across the grasslands, over mountains, and through deserts to the primitive kingdoms of the Far West, where men had beards and round eyes of strange colors. The vast Mongol Empire, the largest in history, was at the peak of its power; it controlled most of the known world, and her grandfather was determined to conquer the rest.

Like all Mongolian children, Emmajin had learned to ride horses before she could walk and handled a bow and arrows with ease. She heard stories of brave Mongol women who were her ancestors, brilliant, resourceful, ambitious, and kind. But most of the women at court lived lazy lives of luxury. She preferred action and the outdoors and wanted to gallop off to have adventures like her male cousins, who all expected to join the army.

Beyond the far western edge of Emmajin's grandfather's empire, Marco Polo, at the age of seventeen, left his beloved home in Venice, Italy. It was the High Middle Ages, and many cities in Europe, then called Christendom, were building huge cathedrals. Venice was the richest city in Europe, and its traders brought home merchandise from far lands. But most of Europe was divided into tiny kingdoms that were relatively poor and powerless. When Marco's father and uncle returned from a long journey and told of a fabulous, wealthy empire in the East, ruled by a wise, powerful emperor, with millions of citizens, huge armies, and rare gems, few believed them.

Marco joined them on their second journey to the heart of the Mongol Empire. Because of sickness, bandits, icy mountains, and endless deserts, that journey took more than three years. By the time Marco arrived at the Khan's capital, in AD 1275, he spoke four languages and had many lively stories to tell.

Emmajin and Marco met in Xanadu, the Khan's summer capital, then called Shangdu. Outside the gleaming marble palace stretched a glorious garden, a paradise of brooks and ponds, pavilions and pagodas, winding paths and blossoming trees. It was a land of myth and mystery, where the unthinkable could happen.

Years later, when Marco Polo returned to Europe, he

wrote a book about what he had seen in this marvelous land. Some dismissed Marco's book as falsehood, accusing him of exaggerating. But his writing fired European imaginations for centuries; five hundred years later it inspired a famous poem that begins "In Xanadu did Kubla Khan . . ." Most famously, Marco's book motivated Christopher Columbus to set sail across the ocean to the West, hoping to find the treasures of the East.

The distant land that Marco Polo "discovered" had long been known to the people who lived there. Khubilai's capital was in China, which had developed an advanced civilization with poetry, calligraphy, silk, and jade, and a written history of thousands of years. Khubilai's people, the Mongols, had roamed for centuries across the grasslands of Asia as herdsmen and warriors, living in round tents they called *ger*s, known to us as yurts. Some people called the Mongols barbarians because they had no written language, buildings, or even houses. But they perfected mounted archery and conceived brilliant military tactics that allowed them to quickly conquer much more advanced countries. Two generations earlier, Khubilai's grandfather, Chinggis Khan, and his fierce horsemen had swept across northern China and central Asia, defeating land after land, reaching as far as Russia, Poland, and Hungary in present-day eastern Europe.

By the time Marco Polo arrived, the Mongols had conquered most of the known world. They had abandoned their nomadic lifestyle and were living in Chinese-style palaces, wearing silks and brocades and eating sumptuous banquets in their capital city of Khanbalik, now known as Beijing. Khubilai Khan loved entertaining foreign visitors and debating with them about the merits of their customs and religions.

Admired for his wisdom, he remained determined to fulfill the mandate from his grandfather: to conquer the rest of the world, including Europe.

The young woman in these pages, Khubilai Khan's eldest granddaughter, Emmajin, is purely fictional. But the details about the place and time and events are as accurate as possible, based on historical accounts. Many other people in these pages were real; I have imagined their personalities.

Like a lot of girls today, Emmajin dreamed big dreams. In her culture, the only way to achieve greatness was to prove your military skills on the battlefield. So that was what she set out to do. That is, until Marco Polo came along.

In Xanadu did Kubla Khan
A stately pleasure-dome decree:
Where Alph, the sacred river, ran
Through caverns measureless to man
Down to a sunless sea.

So twice five miles of fertile ground
With walls and towers were girdled round:
And here were gardens bright with sinuous rills,
Where blossomed many an incense-bearing tree;
And here were forests ancient as the hills,
Enfolding sunny spots of greenery. . . .

—"Kubla Khan,"
by Samuel Taylor Coleridge

And when you have ridden three days from the city last mentioned, between north-east and north, you come to a city called Chandu, which was built by the Kaan now reigning. There is at this place a very fine marble Palace, the rooms of which are all gilt and painted with figures of men and beasts and birds, and with a variety of trees and flowers, all executed with such exquisite art that you regard them with delight and astonishment.

Round this Palace a wall is built, inclosing a compass of 16 miles, and inside the Park there are fountains and rivers and brooks, and beautiful meadows . . .

—*The Travels of Marco Polo*,
by Marco Polo and Rustichello of Pisa, circa 1299,
from *The Complete Yule-Cordier Edition,* Volume I

PART I

In Xanadu

1

A Taste of Victory

The fierce Mongol army was riding straight at us.

My cousin Suren and I stood on the balcony of the palace gate, scanning the horizon, our hands on the marble balustrade. In the far distance, on the plain outside the city's south gate, a massive cloud of dust hid the mighty force, advancing toward the city. The sky shone vivid blue on this late-spring day. A cool wind whipped the loose hairs around my face but could not lift the heavy braids on my back.

I leaned over the marble barrier and squinted.

The Mongol army was about to enter my home city, Khanbalik—not to attack us, but for a grand victory parade. I was fifteen, nearly sixteen, the eldest granddaughter of the powerful emperor Khubilai Khan. My blood pounded in my ears, and I could barely stand still.

Finally, my sharp eyes detected the glint of metal armor and the first few horses of the parade as they emerged from the dark arch of the city's south gate. "Look! Is that the general?" I said to my cousin. Suren was the Khan's eldest grandson and my closest friend. His thick neck stretched out like a turtle's as he strained to see, too.

A huge roar of approval rose from the crowds lining the streets, confirming my guess. Shouts of joy echoed from the rest of the royal family, surrounding me on the palace balcony. "Hooray! Hooray!"

I cheered more loudly than anyone else. Victory tasted sweet.

Suren raised his fist high as he yelled. His wide face with its high cheekbones glowed with happiness. In his veins, Suren had a drop of my blood, and I had a drop of his flowing inside me. At the age of ten, we had decided to become *anda*, cutting our fingers and mingling our blood, promising lifelong loyalty, like blood brothers. Now, five years later, we were inseparable.

Suren pointed to the parade. "Emmajin!" he said. "Is that an elephant?"

I leaned forward and focused on the distant archway. Sure enough, a massive gray creature was entering the city, the carriage on its back nearly hitting the top of the arch. We had heard of these beasts but never seen one. "It's twice as tall as a horse!" I said.

"No, three times as tall!"

The general led the army up the broad main avenue of Khanbalik, the Khan's capital, a city known to the local Chinese as Dadu, or the Great Capital. The soldiers rode in neat formation directly toward the palace gate where we stood. I felt the tromp of their horses' hooves vibrating in my body, and I smelled the grit and the sweat in the wind.

These brave soldiers had broken the long siege of a large city in the South, finally conquering it. This victory opened the way for our armies to march toward Kinsay, the capital of southern China. Many battles lay ahead, but now it seemed inevitable that the great Mongol army would eventually control all of China. No one could stop us now.

This general, the famous Bayan, was returning to his Emperor, the Great Khan Khubilai, to get his reward for breaking the siege and winning this historic victory.

Not far from Suren and me, just beyond a clutch of princes and wives and retainers, the Khan of all Khans sat on a raised platform. His massive body was draped in white brocade edged with the finest furs, white with black spots, from snow leopards. His face, wide and normally impassive, seemed to glow in the late-afternoon sunlight. His feet rested on thick embroidered cushions.

On that day, we all wore white, the color of good luck and victory. I had borrowed a silk robe from my mother, because I had grown taller since the last big celebration. I craned my neck until I caught sight of my father, Prince Dorji. As the Great Khan's eldest son, he stood by his side, the first in a row of many sons of the Khan's four official wives. I felt a pang of joy. My father seldom claimed his rightful place at the Khan's side.

Although my father was the eldest, the Khan bestowed his favor on his second son, Chimkin, Suren's father. Chimkin had led armies, fought in battles, and won the respect of all at court. Instead of fighting, my father had run away to a Buddhist monastery. He walked with a limp, dragging one foot. Some of my cousins mocked him.

Suddenly, I felt like running. "Let's go!" I said to Suren. I pulled back from the balustrade and pushed my way through the crowd of onlookers.

"Wait! Slow down!" Though no longer pudgy, as he had been as a boy, Suren was broad-shouldered and sturdy, not able to slip through the crowd as quickly as I could.

I headed for the steps and raced down them two by two. From the high balcony platform above the gate, the staircase curved around down the inside of a stone tower. Suren stumbled after me, his voice echoing in the empty tower. "Emmajin! Where are you going?" Unlike me, Suren never acted on impulse.

Across the courtyard and through the thick tunnel that was a front gate of the palace compound, I ran. I had always loved the most physical of activities: running fast, racing on horseback, practicing archery for hours on end until my arm muscles bulged. Even though I was a girl, I had built up my skills at all three Mongolian "manly arts": horseracing, archery, and even wrestling, the one sport reserved for men only. I loved to compete with Suren and my other boy cousins, the young princes.

In the square in front of the Khan's palace, crowds were jostling, and soldiers rammed them back, to keep the center of the square clear. With Suren trailing behind me, I dashed across the square toward the main avenue. Onlookers buzzed with jubilation, shouting and pointing as the horses, elephants, and soldiers advanced down the avenue toward us. Elation filled my body. I felt I could fly.

With his long legs, Suren caught up to me as I reached the parade route. "You can't see as well from down here. We're supposed to watch from—"

Just then a large man put his elbow in my face, pushing me back into the crowd. Out here, on the streets, royal grandchildren enjoyed no protection. I ducked my head to avoid getting a black eye. A look of consternation crossed Suren's face.

I laughed. "Don't you want to see the elephants close-up?"

I pressed my way south along the avenue, toward the parade. Drums and cymbals grew louder, mixing with the shouts. Guards pushed back small boys who ventured onto the street, trying to keep everyone behind a line of trees on either side. The tramp of hooves intensified. People around me began jumping, trying to get into position to see.

Finally, I found a good viewing spot, and Suren caught up. He flashed me a look of shared mischief, and I smiled. Only I could bring out the more playful side of Suren.

A single rider, richly dressed in silks and furs, led the parade, bearing a tall pole with the white horse-tail standard of the Mongols. Then two riders, and four, and finally eight riders abreast. Thousands of warriors streamed into the city.

My heart beat faster as I saw a strange bulk marching behind the horsemen. The elephant lumbered forward, gray and wrinkled, ten times the size of a horse or a camel, with legs as thick as huge tree trunks and a nose like a long snake hanging from between its tiny eyes. Two menacing white tusks stuck out from the sides of its mouth.

High atop its back, seated in an open carriage decorated with silken banners, sat the general. I stared up, trying to catch a glimpse of his face.

One little boy, dressed in blue, was thrust into the street by the force of the crowd. He desperately struggled to return, but he tripped and fell. Suren dashed out, grabbed the boy's small hand, and pulled him to safety just seconds before the elephant's huge foot would have crushed him.

As the elephant passed, Suren held the boy tightly with his left hand and used his right to shield me. He flashed me an exasperated look I had seen often.

The elephant trudged past me, so close I could have touched it. A sensation rippled through me—not fear, but excitement.

Following the elephant, the general's top commanders rode past, in order of rank. First came the highest, the general's two lieutenant generals; then the commanders of ten thousand men; then the commanders of one thousand. I could tell by their uniforms.

"Is that Emmajin?" One of the commanders of one thousand, riding on the outside of the formation, recognized me. A young uncle of mine known for his big ears, he had left court to join the army a few years earlier, as was the custom.

"Todogen!" I shouted his name as I ran alongside his horse.

Without a second thought, he reached down, and I grasped his hand. He slipped his foot out of the stirrup. I took a few running steps, then put my right foot into the stirrup and jumped up, tossing my left leg over the rump of his bay horse. He laughed as I settled behind him. I hung on to the high wooden back of his saddle. I caught a brief glimpse of Suren's face, which was shining with disbelief mixed with admiration, as we rode past.

On horseback now, I had joined the parade! The thrill nearly took my breath away. People in the crowd waved at us and cheered. The beat of the drums and the horses' hooves stirred my whole body, whipping me into ever higher levels of exhilaration. I grasped the saddle with one hand and waved with the other. People's eyes brightened with delight as they caught sight of me, a maiden, riding behind a soldier.

The sun shone on my face, and the dirt kicked up by the horses got into my teeth. My ears filled with cymbals and drums, the tromping of hooves, and shouts of triumph. Colorful banners flapped in the breeze. I closed my eyes, to capture the moment.

When we reached the square in front of the palace, the mounted soldiers lined up in neat rows, as if they had practiced this many times. The general, on his elephant, faced the central arch of the palace wall, just below the Great Khan. Todogen took his place in the second row, close to the elephant. From my spot on his horse's rump, I could see and hear everything. One soldier frowned when he saw me, but others grinned, as if they wished they had young women on their horses this happy day, too.

High on the palace wall, on the marble balcony, stood my grandfather, the Khan of all Khans. His great bulk made him look larger and more powerful than the thin men around him. Only those closest to him knew that he could stand but not walk.

"Silence!" someone said. Quickly, the crowd quieted. I could not see Suren anymore. He must have been watching from the crowd.

The general stood in his open carriage and shouted, "Long live the Khan of all Khans!" His men echoed him. The general fell to his knees and touched his head to the floor of his carriage in a traditional kowtow of obedience and deference.

"General Bayan, rise! You have served me well!" The Khan's loud voice boomed down from on high. "One hundred taels of gold for you!"

The soldiers roared.

"Fifty for each of your lieutenant generals! Ten taels for every officer! One tael of gold for every soldier who took part in this victory!"

Todogen nearly jumped in his saddle, his fist high in the air. The roar was deafening now, but I cheered so loudly I didn't mind.

The thrill of victory.

The triumph soldiers felt after winning a battle.

This sensation exhilarated me more than anything I had experienced in my life.

I had always loved outdoor pursuits, the wind on my cheeks as I raced on horseback, the tension in my arm as I pulled back the bowstring, the pleasure of hitting the target perfectly. I loved listening to war stories and could recite the tales of all the legendary Mongol heroes. But at that moment, I knew I wanted something more.

I wanted to be a soldier in the Khan's army.

2

A Thirst for Glory

That evening, the Khan's grandchildren flocked to a courtyard to listen to the court storyteller, called Old Master, recount the tale of the army's latest victory. Bundled up in furs to ward off the chilly spring evening air, they sat shoulder to shoulder around an outdoor fire, wriggling and giggling. The Great Khan had twenty-two sons by his official wives and twenty-five sons by his concubines, so there were countless grandchildren.

Suren and I, the eldest of this generation, stood near the back, looking over the heads of the smaller boys and girls. We both loved war stories—the bloodier, the better.

Tales that made my sister squirm inspired my imagination. I especially loved the ones that showed the military brilliance and valor of the Great Ancestor, my great-great-grandfather Chinggis Khan, founder of the Mongol Empire. I remembered with pleasure the story of how he drove the enemy army into a dead-end valley, then pretended to withdraw his troops. As the enemy soldiers filed out of the valley, the Mongol horsemen used their arrows to pick them off, row by row, saving arrows and Mongol lives.

While we waited for Old Master to begin, I tried to remember if I had heard any stories about Mongol women soldiers. One of Chinggis Khan's four wives had gone to battle with him. Sometimes Chinggis Khan had asked Mongol women to line up on horseback, along with horses carrying fake men made of straw, on the ridge of a hill, to fool the enemy into thinking our army was three times as big. A famous Chinese woman, Mulan, had fought against our ancestors, although she had disguised herself as a man.

Of course, many Mongol women had shown great strength. Chinggis Khan's mother had held the family together after his father died. Robbed of all livestock, she had lived by digging up the roots of wild onions and other vegetables until her sons grew up to be fine, daring men. Chinggis Khan's first wife had demonstrated courage and loyalty despite being kidnapped by an enemy tribe. And Khubilai Khan's mother had, by sheer determination, trained her sons to earn the right to take over the leadership of the Empire even though their father, the youngest son of Chinggis Khan, had not been chosen as successor. Although my grandmother Empress Chabi was a quiet and gentle Buddhist, the blood of all these earlier strong women flowed in my veins.

It seemed, though, that the days of strong women had ended once luxurious court life had begun. Now all Mongol women cared about was fine clothing, rich food, and pearls. And finding good husbands for their daughters. At that moment, my sister, Drolma, two years younger than I, was sitting with other girls, exchanging court gossip, which she found more interesting than the battle stories. I wished I had been alive during the early days of the Mongol Empire, when our armies had pushed into unknown territories, and women had enjoyed many opportunities for adventure.

Old Master walked into the courtyard, carrying a bulging bag. Some of the younger boys begged him to say what was in it, but he refused. The children quieted down as Old Master began his tale. I leaned forward, to catch every detail.

This victory was different, he told us. For months, even years, the Mongol army had laid siege to the Chinese city of Hsiangyang. Behind thick walls, the citizens starved rather than let the Mongols win.

Cowards, I thought. In a true battle, two armies, both on horseback, faced each other and fought until victory.

Old Master continued his story. After several years of stalemate, the Great Khan asked his nephew, the Il-khan of Persia, to send him two talented Persian engineers, experts in the secrets of the machines of war. These foreigners designed a machine that could catapult gigantic rocks over the city walls. Outside the walls of Hsiangyang, Mongol soldiers assembled ten of the new machines, bigger and swifter than any previous catapults, and gathered stockpiles of huge rocks.

On the day of the battle, they hurled torrents of rocks over the walls into the city. The army could hear the shrieks of the Chinese citizens. So frightened were the people that they opened the city gates and flooded out, screaming.

I leaned back against a wall and frowned. I disapproved of this new way of fighting, by frightening townsfolk instead of wielding sword and bow. No valor in it.

Old Master continued. The Mongol soldiers, ready with their swords and bows, mowed down the evil people of that city by the tens and hundreds. They showed the bravery and daring of their honored ancestors.

"How many enemies did they kill?" one boy asked.

Old Master smiled, reached for his bag, and turned it over. Out of it spilled what looked like small pieces of leather, the kind used to make armor.

The children shrieked.

Ears. A pile of ears that our warriors had sliced off the heads of the enemies they had killed. By tradition, our soldiers cut off ears to count the dead.

A shiver shook me. Suren recoiled. But many boys jumped forward and grabbed the ears. Some tossed them into the air and shouted with delight. Suren's younger brother, Temur, near the front, shouted more loudly than everyone else. "Victory!"

The horror I felt was weak and girlish, so I shook it off. I drank in the happiness and confidence around me. As the next generation, we would inherit a mighty military more successful than any in history. The Mongol troops had achieved a well-deserved victory. They had fought hard to win each of those ears.

Everything seemed possible. I could no longer contain my secret desire.

"Suren," I said, in a voice only he could hear. "I want to join the army."

Suren pulled away so he could look directly into my eyes. Surprise crossed his wide brow, then a wrinkle of skepticism. No woman had ever served as a soldier in the Khan's army.

But after a moment, Suren shook his head and grinned. I could always count on him to support my wild ideas. Suren planned to join the army in Ninth Moon. He leaned over and spoke directly into my ear. "So may it be! We'll ride off together and fight side by side."

An arrow of joy pierced my heart. I could see the scene clearly. Prince Suren on his bay steed and me, Princess Emmajin, riding my golden stallion, both of us in leather armor, metal helmets on our heads, quivers of arrows at our backs, swords hanging from our belts, riding in a row of gallant warriors, the crowds cheering all around us.

It was unlikely. I knew that. Still, I sighed. What a perfect day.

"Attention, everybody!" Standing next to Old Master, my cousin Temur shouted above the clamor. "Listen!" Although one year younger than Suren, Temur had the commanding voice that Suren lacked, and the young cousins quickly quieted down.

I frowned, annoyed. Temur was always trying to gain attention.

"Who are the future leaders of the Mongol Empire?" Temur shouted. He was well proportioned and handsome, taller than Suren, broad-shouldered yet trim. His eyes were set wide in his face, giving him a distinctive and appealing look.

The younger boys looked at one another, shifting uncomfortably. They were too young to think of themselves as leaders, more used to taking orders than responding to motivation. Suren frowned but didn't stop his brother. Suren, I knew, felt jealous of his brother's confidence. He feared that their father—and the Khan—would choose Temur as eventual heir apparent, even though Suren was the firstborn son and grandson.

"Grandsons of the Khan! We are the future!" Temur continued.

"Yes!" yelled one boy. Then others shouted, "We are!"—still only half convinced. Old Master, rubbing his long wispy white beard, looked on with approval.

Temur stood even firmer. I wished Suren could rally enthusiasm that way.

"Let us prove ourselves worthy!" Temur shouted. "Let us show our skills!"

"How?" Suren asked, with an edge of challenge.

Temur's eyes gleamed in the firelight. "An archery contest. In one of the public courtyards. All the boys of the court. Tomorrow at noon."

My heart leaped. Archery was my best skill. I had spent years perfecting it, both still and mounted. At an age long past that when most Mongol girls gave up, I had persisted. This could be my chance to show, in public, that I was better than any of my boy cousins. But would they let me take part?

The boys greeted the proposal with a cheer. With just a few words, Temur had made it happen. I wondered if the Great Khan himself would watch the contest. I had to find some way to compete in it.

Tomorrow, I realized with a start, would be the day before my sixteenth birthday, the last day of my childhood. If only I could compete, one last time, before whatever awaited me in adulthood.

3

Shame

"Emmajin! You're back!" My mother's voice sounded firm and joyful.

Oh, no, I thought as I entered the rooms I shared with my mother and sister, off a back courtyard in the palace. I did not want to face whatever my mother had to say now.

Mama emerged from the bedroom, her pale heart-shaped face lit by an uncertain smile. Behind her, Drolma had a look of hope mixed with doubt.

"We have good news," Mama said.

"Too good," said Drolma. Short and delicate like Mama, Drolma had once told me she envied my beauty, but to me such things did not matter. Unlike me, she stayed out of the sun and used creams to keep her skin light and smooth.

I did not want to hear Mama's news. My mother had been trying day and night for years to find me a husband. I should have been betrothed long before, but I had managed to sabotage each of my mother's earlier efforts. Although most suitors' parents eagerly sought an alliance with the Khan's family, now that I was nearly sixteen, many of them regarded me with suspicion as a difficult girl, past the ideal age for a betrothal. Each suitor was less appealing than the previous one. Drolma yearned for a betrothal, but by custom she had to wait for me to get settled.

Lately, Mama had been trying harder to make me spend more time with the girls and women, but I hated embroidery, dancing, and music. Drolma loved all that and had already picked out names for her future children. To me, it seemed that the women of the court did nothing but sit and gossip. I had told my mother that Suren's father wanted me to spend time with his sons. My mother feared Chimkin, so she had let me get my way.

My father, Prince Dorji, home from the monastery for the victory celebration, emerged from the shadows behind my mother, dragging his lame foot. As much as I wished he had become a military man, I needed to show obedience and respect.

My father sat down in a Chinese-style wooden chair in the central sitting room between our family's two bedrooms. Like most Mongols of his age, he had grown up in a *ger*, the traditional round white tent with a domed roof. Even though the Chinese were now our subjects, the royal family lived in a Chinese-style palace with raised beds, silken quilts instead of sleeping furs, and chairs instead of stools around a fire. I wondered what the Great Ancestor, Chinggis Khan, would think of that.

I stood before my father, trying to suppress my urge to defy him.

My father cleared his throat. "General Bayan's top lieutenant is an excellent military man named Aju, respected by the Khan. He is back from the wars in the South."

I perked up. I longed to hear more about that campaign.

"General Aju will come here tomorrow with his eldest son, at noon."

I bit my lip to keep the objection from flying out. The timing could not be worse. The archery tournament would begin at noon.

"You must behave properly while they are here." My father's voice was firm. "Dress well, sit quietly, serve us. They will want to see if you can be a proper wife."

I looked at my hands. To me, marriage meant only loss of freedom.

"It's your best chance. A military family." My mother's eyes shifted nervously.

All night, I tossed in the bed I shared with my sister. I wanted to meet this military commander, General Aju, and wished I could ask him about the battle for Hsiangyang. But I also knew that once I was betrothed, my small chance of joining the army would disappear. My dreams would vanish forever.

If only I could show off my skills in the archery tournament, to prove publicly that I could do the extraordinary. Until recent years, I had always been praised for my archery and racing skills. Why should that change now? Perhaps someone, somehow, would realize what a waste it would be for me to marry and leave the family.

The next morning, Drolma braided my hair, trying to make it as smooth and neat as hers. She sang as she worked, in a sweet soprano voice that calmed me. It occurred to me that I would miss her once I left home, whether for marriage or for the army.

When she finished, she bit her lip, facing me. "Please, Emma. Make it happen this time." I hated to disappoint her, to keep her life on hold.

Just then, a messenger arrived, saying Aju would be coming earlier. His son Jebe was to enter the archery tournament. Word had spread quickly, and young Mongols around Khanbalik were arriving at court, eager to compete. My heart leaped. Perhaps these betrothal talks would end early and I could take part in the tournament after all.

At midmorning, they arrived. The minute I saw the young man, Jebe, I knew he would be a disastrous match. His father had the tall, burly physique of a military commander, but Jebe was as skinny and knobby as a winter tree branch.

Both Aju and Jebe stopped when they saw me, dressed in my mother's best blue embroidered robe. "Dorji, you old fox," Aju said. "What have you been hiding?"

Smiling, my father showed them to their seats in the row of Chinese chairs. Mama motioned to me, and I served the men bowls of *airag*, fermented mare's milk. I handed the first drink to Aju, who sat at my father's right, in the guest-of-honor seat.

"I hear she's a spirited one," Aju said after his first sip of *airag*.

"That she is," my father said, nodding as if he had complimented me.

Feeling like a servant, I fetched a plate of Mongolian cheese and brought it to them. I had been through this ritual before. Once, I had dropped the whole plate of cheese into the lap of a suitor's father, but I did not dare do that now. Not to a high-level military commander. I hoped they would talk about the recent battle.

"Emmajin is an unusual name for a maiden," Aju commented.

My father nodded. "I wanted to name her Tara, for the goddess of compassion. But she was born on the day my father became khan, and he chose this name for her."

I lifted my chin and shot a look of pride toward the general, who was nodding as if impressed. My name, Emmajin, a gift from the Khan of all Khans, was the female form of Temujin, the birth name of the Great Ancestor, Chinggis Khan.

"So your son plans to compete in archery today?" my father asked.

Aju grimaced. "His skills are not yet perfected. The Great Khan will be present?"

My father nodded. "I believe so."

My heart pounded. Oh, to have a chance to demonstrate my skills to the Great Khan himself! Then he would see that I was worthy of my name.

My father continued. "I hear your son can read and write?"

"In Chinese and in the new Mongolian script. He spends too much time at it."

"The court needs men who can read. He could serve the Khan well as an official." My father and his brothers were part of the first generation of Mongols to read and write, and he took pride in it. But I agreed with Aju that reading was unnecessary.

Aju shook his head. "Someday, perhaps, after he proves

his worth in the army. His elder brother fought in the battle for Hsiangyang."

At that moment, I was offering a second plate of cheese. My curiosity took charge, and I could no longer remain silent.

"We heard about the battle," I said tentatively. Everyone looked at me in shock. "This new machine, this catapult," I continued, checking Aju's eyes to see if it was all right to continue. "Is that what made us win? It seems . . ." I had never been good with words. "Is it true that— Was it really the idea of a foreigner, from Persia?"

Aju's eyebrows rose halfway up his forehead. I wanted to hear his answers, but he said nothing. My mother started toward me, as if trying to stop me.

The questions kept spilling out of my mouth. "This machine—will it be used in future battles? And did the rocks actually kill enemies, or just scare them?"

Aju put his *airag* bowl on a side table and stared at me until I went silent. Then he looked at my father. "She sounds more like a soldier than a wife," he said. He rose.

My father looked chagrined. The betrothal talks had ended. He had lost.

As my father escorted Aju and his scrawny son to the door, Mama hissed at me, "Now we'll never find you a husband!" I hoped that was true. But I felt a pang when I saw Drolma's pale face twisted with distress.

My father returned, sat down, and called me to him. His thick eyebrows formed a solid line. "You have failed four times now. I don't know what to do with you."

Suddenly, I didn't care what he thought of me. I remembered the feelings of joy, at the parade, and pride, after the victory story. That was what I wanted in my life, not these dreadful betrothal talks. I planted my feet firmly and lifted my chin.

"Here's what you can do with me," I said. "Permit me to join the army."

My mother gasped, and my father's eyebrows shot up. "The Khan would never agree to that. Can you imagine, a mere girl fighting on the battlefield?"

I had imagined it many times. "I can do anything Suren can do," I said.

My father readjusted his body. "That will never happen. It is wrong to kill even an insect, let alone a human being. Our goal should be compassion, not conquest. Here."

He reached inside his cloth sash and pulled out a small square of silver. On one side was a tiny picture, painted on cloth. I took it from him reluctantly. The picture was of a young woman, seated in the lotus position, with a halo of light around her.

"It is Tara, the Great Protectress," he said. "I had hoped to give it to you on the day of your betrothal. It should remind you of good behavior and right thinking."

Although I did not know much about his religion, Buddhism, the idea of not killing even an insect seemed ridiculous—especially for Mongols, who loved meat. How could our ancestors have conquered the world without warfare? The old religion, revering Tengri, Eternal Heaven, had worked well for them. Tengri had decreed that the Mongols should rule the entire world. Why switch to a new religion?

My father's handing me this Tara amulet when I had asked to join the army seemed a mockery. I wanted to drop it on the floor, but he had never given me a gift before.

"I know you wish you had a son," I said, choosing my words carefully. "Let me be that son. I will go to war, and if I fight well, it will bring you honor."

His face darkened. "If you fought in a battle, it would bring me shame."

What more could I say? When he dismissed me, I bowed in deference and rushed to my room to change. If I hurried, I would have time to make it to the archery tournament by noon.

I left the Tara amulet on the floor near my bed, spurned and forgotten.

4

The Archery Contest

The tournament took place in the front courtyard of the palace, a plain of flat gray flagstones between the front gate and the massive main audience hall, with its yellow tiled roof that curved up at the corners. Servants moved a wide thronelike chair out of the hall so the Khan could watch the tournament from the top of a flight of marble stairs.

Each contestant arrived holding a bow, with a quiver of arrows at his back. The high voices of children and the deep voices of men mingled in the cool air, under a cloudy sky. Although this area lay inside the palace wall, it was open to any man with a permit to enter, including selected foreigners.

My mother's objection still rang in my ears, but my father had just shrugged when I had left my family's quarters with my favorite quiver and my bow tucked into my leather belt. I wanted to be the son my father never had, but that was only part of my motivation.

For years, Suren and I had organized tournaments for the

boy cousins in the back courtyards of the palace. No boy had spent as many hours as I had perfecting skills in both still and mounted archery. Recently, as Suren and Temur were becoming men, their arms were getting stronger than mine, but I still could beat them, most of the time. My pride would not allow me to sit and watch them compete—with the Great Khan judging them—knowing that I could win.

Temur stood at the heart of the crowd, gesticulating and barking orders. He organized the contestants into groups. Ages ten and eleven would compete together, then twelve and thirteen, then fourteen and fifteen. This was my last day as a fifteen-year-old.

Suren saw me from a distance as I entered the crowded courtyard. His eyebrows shot up when he saw the quiver of arrows at my back. I made my way through the crowd to where they stood. When Temur noticed me, armed with my bow and arrows, he shook his head. Others stepped aside as I strode up to them. Temur began to object, but Suren cut him off.

"Emmajin will compete with us." For once, Suren's voice sounded decisive.

"No girls," Temur said.

"Only Emmajin." Suren stared him down. The two brothers engaged in a brief power struggle. As a younger brother, Temur was bound to obey, but Suren had seldom insisted. "You're not confident you can beat her?" Suren challenged him.

Temur turned to me, his eyes burning with resentment. "It would be better for you, Elder Sister, if you did not compete." "Elder Sister" was a term of respect, but it did not hide Temur's anger.

His plan was suddenly clear to me: he had counted on defeating his brother in public. And Suren hoped to cling to his superior position by beating Temur. If I won, I would humiliate both brothers, before the Khan. Although I wanted to demonstrate my skills to the Khan, I certainly did not want to humiliate Suren. I hesitated a moment, feeling a flash of compassion for both Suren and Temur. But Temur's defiant scowl justified my decision and strengthened my desire to win. I had too much at stake to turn away.

"Younger Brother," I said to Temur, "I will compete."

Temur's eyes flashed at me. "Good," he said. It sounded like a challenge.

The youngest boys competed first. They lined up close to the targets, which were small sandbags piled neatly into low stacks. The aim was to hit the highest bag in the center of the stack.

I watched from near the back of the crowd, wondering if I had made a mistake.

One little boy became so excited that he wet his pants. Some boys laughed.

I heard from just behind me a distinctive laugh, deep and resonant. As I turned to look, the man behind me had to duck to avoid being hit by the arrows on my back. He was a foreigner, with the thickest beard and largest nose I had ever seen. A fist of fear gripped my throat. I had never stood so close to a foreigner.

The man saw me staring and smiled at me—or at least appeared to. His mouth was invisible inside all that facial hair, which shone with alarming glints of red. His huge round eyes showed delight at the sight of me. They were the strangest color, green like the pond in the palace garden.

"That boy may lead an army someday," he said, pointing to the wet stain.

I was surprised I could understand him; it had not occurred to me that foreigners could speak Mongolian. His eyes looked cheerful and intelligent. But I could not get over his strange appearance. The foreigners in Old Master's stories were always menacing.

I moved away to avoid responding. Many at court said that foreigners brought bad luck.

As I watched the younger boys compete, a thought entered my mind: if I won, perhaps I could ask the Great Khan to grant a special request. I was not sure I dared ask such a bold question in public. But if I did, it could make all the difference for my future.

The sun had lowered to just above the palace walls by the time of the next-to-last contest, for fourteen- and fifteen-year-old Mongols from outside the palace. I recognized several of my former suitors and was glad they would see me compete. Jebe's arrows flew disastrously off course, and he placed last among ten contenders.

Finally, the time came for the last tournament, for the eldest of the grandchildren: Suren, Temur, and me. It would be our last contest as children, since I would be sixteen the next day and Suren would turn sixteen within a month. After that, we would be considered adults.

Temur, with his strong voice, had been calling all contestants for each tournament, and this time, he called for "all grandsons of the Great Khan, aged fourteen and fifteen."

I stepped forward and stood next to him and Suren. The crowd murmured.

Because I was a girl, I was highly visible. Both boys and

girls wore the same clothing, the Mongolian *del,* an outer robe with a high collar, cinched with a bright-colored sash at the waist. But I had two thick braids down my back. All the boys had the distinctive Mongolian male haircut: a bare spot shaved at the top of the head, with a fringe of hair over the forehead and the rest in two long braids pinned up in loops under the ears.

We three competitors stood in a row and bowed toward the Great Khan. Three times, we performed the kowtow on our hands and knees, touching our foreheads to the ground, showing our loyalty and obedience to the Emperor.

After the third kowtow, we waited with our heads on the cold flagstones. Everyone in the crowded courtyard fell silent.

"Rise!" The Khan's voice boomed. "I have only two grandsons this age."

I stepped forward, my head bowed.

"Speak!" the Khan commanded.

I looked up the marble stairs at my grandfather, at his round head and thin, pointed beard, his huge ears and narrow eyes. With his bulky body, he seemed grand and immovable. But I had seen a softer side of him, when he joked with the children of the court in less formal settings, and I knew he symbolized all that was good and wise in the Empire.

I willed myself to speak as boldly as possible. "As the eldest granddaughter of the Khan of all Khans, as one named after the Great Ancestor himself, I beg your permission to compete in this tournament."

My voice sounded thin and high compared to Temur's strong tones. The Khan regarded me in silence. I gathered my courage to continue.

"If my archery pleases you, I beg you to consider allowing me to join your army."

A collective gasp rose around me, and Suren shot me a warning look.

The Khan stared at me for what seemed an eternity. As the most powerful ruler the world had ever known, he reigned over the largest empire in history. What I asked for was far-fetched but not impossible. Had I overstepped my bounds?

Finally, the Khan spoke. "Win or lose, come to see me tomorrow. I make no promises today." His voice sounded deep and ominous.

But to me, "win or lose" meant I could compete. And the next day, on my birthday, I could make my case to the Khan. What a gift. I smiled at him to convey my gratitude.

We three contestants took our positions, lined up, bows in hand. My bow, like all great Mongol bows, curved in a large arc, then curled back at each end. I ran my fingers over its smooth layers of bone and sinew and horn. Its fine horsehair string was so tight that it took great strength to pull it back. My arrows were made of supple bamboo, with vulture feathers and sharp metal tips that could rip deep into human flesh.

As the youngest, Temur went first. He drew an arrow and fit it onto his bow.

"Wait!" shouted the Khan.

We all froze.

"Mounted archery," he said.

The three of us looked at one another in surprise. Temur lowered his bow. Two men left to fetch horses for us, and several others reset the targets farther apart. Mounted archery involved shooting at still targets while galloping past. I felt even more confident about my ability in mounted archery, but my nerves were screeching.

"It's her fault," said Temur.

"It makes sense," I said. "Mounted archery is what matters in war."

"You will never go to war." Temur spit out the words.

"Maybe you will get to go sooner if you perform well today," I told him. Most princes joined the army the year they turned sixteen.

"Emmajin," Suren said. "Participating should be victory enough for you."

I understood. He was asking me to let him win. I had spent more hours than either of them practicing mounted archery. Suren had a powerful arm but often overshot the target. Temur was capable of hitting the center of the target, but not consistently. In recent months, though, both had greatly improved their skills.

I was better, but it was far from assured that I would win. Every contest was different, and I had never competed in a public setting, before the Khan and a large crowd. The delay gave me time to dwell on what might happen if I lost. Or won.

5

Final Round

The horses were led in, and I smiled when I saw that someone had found my horse, Baatar, a golden palomino stallion with a pure white mane. The courtyard full of noisy people made him skittish and uncertain. Normally, I rode him on an open plain outside the north city gate.

I took his reins and put my hand on his warm shoulder. His body was quivering. I stood near his head and looked into one of his large brown eyes, which were the same height as my eyes. "Baatar," I said. His name meant "hero." "Be calm."

We had little time, but he seemed to relax at my touch and voice. I stroked his shoulder. After two years of riding him, helping train him from his youngest days, I loved this horse. I tightened his cinch and straightened his traditional Mongolian wooden saddle, curved high in the front and back. The leather of his bridle, the grassy smell of his skin, the metal of his stirrups, the rough felt blanket under his saddle, all calmed me.

With Baatar here, I could win.

"Mount!" a voice shouted. Suddenly, I realized that Suren and Temur had already mounted and were looking at me with impatience.

I quickly tossed my leg over Baatar's back, and the contest began.

In this type of race, each rider took a turn riding past three targets in a row. In one smooth motion, we were to pull an arrow from our quiver, fit it to the bow, and shoot as quickly and accurately as possible.

Temur went first, starting with a war cry. Riding on a handsome dappled gray stallion, Temur raised his bow and smoothly reached behind him for his first arrow with perfect form. I remembered teaching him that skill, back when he was much younger and looked to me for advice.

His first arrow sank into the top sandbag. The judges were standing close to the target with the assurance that he would hit it and not them. They held out their hands to show the distance between the arrow and the center of the target. All three showed, with hands touching, that his arrow had hit the target.

Temur's next arrow, released just moments later, hit the second target about a hand's width away from the center, an excellent shot.

Inconsistent, I thought, willing him to miss the final shot, the hardest.

But Temur's third arrow struck the third target squarely. The judges' hands came together, and Temur let out a whoop—more like a boy than the sophisticated archer he wanted to be. He acted too young to be a soldier.

Baatar snorted, as if eager to get moving. I flexed my

bow, to ready it, making sure my best arrows were easily accessible.

But Suren was next. He looked nervous, mounted on his bay horse with reddish brown sides and black points. Although an excellent horseman, Suren had only recently begun riding this steed.

With a deep breath and then a yell, Suren started. He reached smoothly for the first arrow, and it seemed to fly straight, but it hit wide of the mark, by about the length of an arm to the elbow. His second arrow struck dead-on, and his third was wide by a hand's width. He had failed to outperform Temur.

As he circled back on his bay mare, Suren shot me a sharp look. I could read his thoughts as clearly as the tracks of a fox in the snow. As the eldest grandson, and possible heir to the throne someday, Suren always had a weight on his shoulders that I could only dimly comprehend. Now his younger brother, Temur, had bested him publicly, in front of the Khan, showing his superiority in the all-important skill of mounted archery. If I did well, Suren might come in third, losing not just to his brother but to a girl. I had everything to gain, and he had everything to lose.

A feeling of guilt crept up my gullet. I craved a win. But should I lose on purpose, to show loyalty to Suren, my *anda*? Prince Suren could not—should not—come in last.

Everyone was looking at me—even, I knew, the Khan, although I did not dare to glance in his direction. Baatar pranced slightly, eager to go, but I held him back for a moment, trying to think straight.

To whom did I owe my loyalty? We had learned from the time we were born that we were all loyal to the Great Khan, of course. I was certainly not loyal to Temur. I wanted to beat him, to put him in his place for embarrassing Suren. But by losing I could not make Suren the winner. With so many strangers watching, could I do my best?

I had waited too long already. I shouted and leaned forward, and Baatar surged ahead. In one smooth arc, my right hand reached back for the first arrow and placed it perfectly against the bowstring. Using my thumb, I pulled back on the string and loosed the arrow just at the right angle and moment as Baatar raced past the first target.

My first arrow hit, and the judges indicated a perfect shot.

By then, my arm was circling back for the second arrow, fitting it against the bow, pulling back the bowstring, releasing. I had done this so many times I could do it blindfolded.

My second arrow hit with a thud. Another perfect shot.

My mind turned off, and my body took over, going through the familiar motions.

Suddenly, for no reason, an image appeared in my mind's eye: that young foreigner's bearded face and his huge round eyes. My hands shook, and my right hand did not catch hold of the arrow soon enough. I had to grasp a second time to get an arrow. By the time I followed through and made my shot, I had ridden past the target. My arrow landed so embarrassingly far from the target that the judges, jumping with excitement, held their hands as wide apart as possible, indicating that the arrow was nowhere near the center of the target.

As if sensing that something had gone wrong, Baatar flinched, tripping slightly before regaining his footing. Off balance, holding my large, heavy bow and not the reins, I felt the top part of my body lunge forward. My face struck the back of Baatar's neck, hard.

With my free right hand I pulled myself back up, just as Baatar was slowing, and grabbed the reins. A horrific pain ripped through me, from my nose through my head and whole body. Bright red blood stained Baatar's creamy mane, then his saddle, then my clothing. Blood spurted out of my nose as if from a demonic spring. A woman screamed, and the boys jumped up and down, pointing at me and shouting.

Somehow I returned my bow to the leather holster hanging from my belt. With my left hand, I touched my nose, to see if I had broken the bridge.

Such humiliation! No experienced rider should have a careless accident. And so many had witnessed it. My ears rang and my vision blurred. The pain was agonizing.

Baatar slowed down and someone grabbed his reins from the side. It was my father. He had been watching after all.

When Baatar came to a stop, I slid down his side to the ground. My father's arm went around me, and he used his sleeve to sop up my blood. He gently covered my nose, to stanch the bleeding. Even that gentle touch sent another surge of pain through me, and I nearly screamed. I pushed his hand away and lightly held my own sleeve over my nose. Blood drained into my throat, making me gasp for air. I could barely see.

Father led me to the side of the courtyard. My head was bowed, but I heard comments from people around me. "She lost on purpose," one man said.

"To make them look good," another added.

But I had not lost on purpose. My hand had slipped, for no good reason. I meant to win. I always competed to win.

"How fine of her," someone said. "She gave face to her cousin, the man who may one day be Great Khan."

I was not used to hearing people talk about Suren that way. No one dared talk openly about who might lead in our generation. But now I realized that others, besides me, understood the deeper implications of the younger brother's very public victory. But at least Suren had not come in last.

The blood kept flowing, soaking through the sleeve and front of my *del.* The only way I could get it out of my throat was to spit in a most unladylike way.

My disgrace was extreme. I had made a fool of myself in public. What chance had I now of convincing the Khan I should join his army? My bravado in making that request now seemed laughable.

In my head, behind that gushing nose, I blamed the foreigner. Sitting on a stool near the side wall of the courtyard, behind the protective bulk of my father's body, I felt besieged, confused, pained, angry.

Suddenly, my father moved slightly, and I could see standing just beyond him, not two feet away, that same bearded young foreigner staring at me. "My lady showed true nobility of spirit today," he said in his odd, accented Mongolian.

His arms were covered with hair, and his beard was so thick I could imagine food sticking in it. This creature was subhuman, I thought. Such beasts should not be permitted to enter the palace, let alone to comment on the nobility of royal family members.

The pressure of the day broke over me. I needed someone to blame. I looked him right in his hairy face. "You're the dregs," I said. It was the worst insult that came to my mind.

He pulled back, clearly confused and chastened. If the Khan allowed me to join the army, I thought, I would one day kill men like him.

I spit at his feet, a big glob of blood. He jumped back in horror.

I would come to regret my gesture.

6

Elephant Ride

The next day, my mother woke me early. My head was pounding. All night I had relived every excruciating detail of the contest, trying to figure out how I could have lost control in such a disastrous way. My future seemed bleak.

"Oh! You can't leave looking like this!" Mama said in an agitated voice when she saw my face.

I felt my nose. It seemed straight, and the small wound at the top had long ago stopped bleeding. But my cheeks under each eye felt puffy and sore.

Drolma grimaced. "It looks like someone punched you in both eyes."

"I'll put white powder on it," Mama said. "Get up at once."

I rolled to face the wall, holding my aching head. "I don't want to get up." Today was the fifth day of Fifth Moon. On this day every year, the Khan, his court, and most of the Golden Family left the capital for the summer palace at

Xanadu. This day was also my sixteenth birthday. I was entering adulthood with a bruised face and pains in my head.

"You must," Mama said. "The Great Khan sent word that you will ride with him to Xanadu. He expects you shortly."

Disaster upon disaster. Normally, such an honor would be a thrill, an opportunity to present my case. Men would pay fortunes for the privilege of spending time with the Khan. But my black eyes and swollen cheeks took away all my dignity. Why on earth would the Khan want me to ride with him after I had failed miserably?

Of course, I had no choice but to get ready quickly.

I had spent many of the happiest days of my childhood in Xanadu, also called Shangdu or "Upper Capital." It was on the high plateau of Mongolia, on the other side of the hills that separated Mongolia from Cathay, or northern China. Xanadu's pleasant weather, sprawling formal gardens, and hunting woods provided the perfect playground for the Khan's many grandchildren. The palace there, though protected by thick walls and moats, was smaller and had a more informal atmosphere. Accompanied only by his family, his closest friends and a few invited guests, the Khan was able to relax in Xanadu.

Soon after my mother roused me, I walked into the rear courtyard of the Khan's palace at Khanbalik, just inside the north gate. The courtyard, wide and leafy, bustled with commotion as everyone prepared for the journey to Xanadu. Men shouted and servants loaded last-minute boxes onto carts, ladies stepped into their canopied sedan chairs, and horses whinnied. My damaged nose filled with the sharp smell of too many animals and men in a confined space.

Fortunately, no one stared at my face. I dodged and ducked and picked my way across, looking down to avoid stepping in horse dung.

Four giant elephants stood at the center of the courtyard. They were lashed together, and one ornate pavilion was strapped on the backs of all four. The Great Khan had decided to try a new mode of travel, inside this pavilion on the backs of four elephants that had arrived with the victorious army. Riding on one elephant would be hard enough; I could not fathom how a pavilion could stay steady on the backs of four such creatures, or how they could possibly walk in unison over such a long distance.

As I approached them, the elephants loomed, ever more massive. What would I say to the Khan during this long day's ride, the first of our three-day trip to Xanadu? What would he say to me, after my humiliating defeat? I began to sweat, even though the dawn air was still crisp and cool.

The early-morning sunlight glinted on the elaborate woven designs of the silk tapestries, trimmed with golden fringe, that hung on the elephants' sides. Each creature had legs thicker than the red columns of the throne room, with rounded toenails bigger than my hand. Standing next to one elephant, I looked up its massive side and saw a turbaned man sitting astride its wide neck. Two huge sharp white tusks jutted out from near its mouth, each tipped with a brass fitting. The creature stood still, as if gentle.

"This way, Little Sister." One of the Khan's attendants gestured to a brightly painted wooden staircase at the side of the creature. As I climbed, my legs shook and jostled the ladder. My mother's *del* felt too tight to move in. She had insisted I wear one of her most beautiful *del*s, the one she had worn as a young bride. The creature turned its head toward me, and its huge round eye seemed hostile.

At the top of the steps, I paused to catch my breath. I rubbed my fingers over the stiff striped tiger skin adorning the wooden side of the pavilion. Above me, the roof had curved eaves in the Chinese style. The four pillars holding it up were painted with creatures of the hunt. Embroidered, tasseled cloths were draped from the sides.

Inside the pavilion, the sun slanted straight into the eyes of the Great Khan, clad in a white ermine cloak. Next to him sat a short, round lady, the Empress Chabi, his chief wife, my grandmother, whose title was *khatun,* "empress."

The pavilion was surprisingly spacious, with two long benches, but too small for a full-body kowtow. So I fell to my knees and bowed, facedown. My forehead nearly touched the cushions where the Khan's feet rested. I noticed that his feet were so swollen that they bulged out of his slippers.

The Great Khan bade me to rise. When I straightened up, eyes still down, I could sense him examining my face. The Empress gasped at the sight. My mother had used heavy powder to disguise the purple lines under my eyes as well as the glaring scab on my upper nose. Just the day before, I had scorned my beauty, but now I felt ugly.

"A Mongol always keeps control of his horse," the Khan said.

I nodded, feeling miserable and stupid.

"Especially a soldier."

I swallowed hard. Why had I made a fool of myself in front of everyone I knew by making such a request? I had to fight back tears.

"You are no ordinary maiden. I have long known this."

I dared to look up at him. Beside him, the Empress had a tiny smile in the middle of her wide, moon-round face.

"I have an assignment for you. Are you willing to serve the Khan of all Khans?"

My heart turned over. "Yes, Your Majesty!"

"Then sit here, and keep silent." He indicated the spot to the left of Empress Chabi, on a tiger skin–covered couch. My grandmother nodded her assent, and I sat down next to her. An assignment from the Khan sounded like a chance to redeem myself.

My bottom sank into a soft cushion filled with down. The view from the Khan's perch stunned me. Lines of snow white horses and soldiers carrying horse-tail banners stretched out along the north avenue in grand parade formation. A rush of awe surged through me. All these men lived to serve the Khan of all Khans, ruler of the world.

Sitting close to my grandfather for the first time, I was keenly aware of his great bulk. My grandmother smelled of flowery perfume, and the Khan smelled of garlic and sour milk. He spoke quietly to me. "I have invited three guests to ride with us today. They are Latins, merchants from a land in the Far West, one we have not yet conquered."

Foreigners! I quaked. Still, I listened with respect.

"In a few years, after we have completed the conquest of China, we will also subjugate their land, though they do not know it. You have a role to play in this mission."

He leaned back, his eyes sparkling, as if he were teasing me about a special treat. I nodded, confused and overwhelmed.

"You will get to know these merchants, and find out

everything you can about their homeland: its kings, its religion, its language, its defenses, what riches it possesses."

Shocked, I stammered, "D-do you mean . . . to spy on them?"

He smiled. "We call it gathering intelligence. This mission would be of greater service to me than any on the battlefield."

Frustrated, I looked at my fingernails, which were rimmed with dirt.

"Khubilai!" My grandmother sounded surprisingly stern. "She is a girl. Think of her safety." It amazed me that she would dare to question his judgment.

The Khan regarded me steadily. "Perhaps she cannot handle this. Can you?"

I had not known any foreigners. My grandfather employed many of them, mainly Muslims and Tibetans and Uighurs, but most children at court either scorned them or feared them. Some foreigners, such as Tibetans, had dark eyes and straight hair like us, but wore distinctive clothing. Others, though, had heavy beards and overhanging eyebrows and thick hair, sometimes wavy like the lines in a sand dune. Farther west, I had heard, the men were ever more hairy, and their eye color ever more deviant. We all understood why "colored-eye" men made good warriors, since their very appearance was alarming enough to scare any enemy.

This assignment sounded awful. But the Khan had honored me despite my defeat. Hearing my grandmother raise doubts made me want to prove I was up to the challenge.

"Your Majesty," I said, "I would be honored."

Just then, I heard someone coming up the steps. When the visitor's shaggy head appeared, I recoiled in horror. Here before me was the frightening foreigner whose image had distracted me during the archery contest. He entered the pavilion and bowed low before the Great Khan, speaking Mongolian with a thick accent.

"Long-a live-a the Kaan of all Kaans." He mispronounced the soft guttural *kh* sound, making it a sharp *k*.

When the foreigner raised his head, I forced myself to look at his features. His eyes, that alarming green, registered concern when he saw my swollen face. He wore a fine blue Mongolian *del* with a high collar and long sleeves. He masked his smell with a perfume of cloves and ginger.

Then the young foreigner did something strange. He bowed to the Empress and me in a peculiar way, one hand behind him, the other swooping in front. Did he not know that no one ever bowed to women, not even the Empress?

"Great Khatun, Empress Chabi," he said. Then he added, to me, "Noble lady. Please forgive me if I caused you offense."

Offense? I remembered with shame the way I had spit at this man, who I now realized was an honored guest of the Khan. Shaking with embarrassment and confusion, I had no idea what to do or what to say to such an unpredictable, outlandish man.

7

A Tale of Bandits

"Young Marco Polo," the Khan said with a smile. "No need to be so formal on this occasion. Where are your father and uncle?"

"I am sorry, Your Majesty. They are ill. Only sickness would keep them from so great an honor." His Mongolian was thickly accented but understandable.

"Just yesterday, in my audience hall, they seemed well. Sit down before these great beasts begin to move." The Khan indicated a seat to his right.

"Your Majesty is too kind. Your ladies are, ah, beautiful."

I looked at him with fascinated curiosity, as one would a monkey on a rope. Normally, no one would mention the presence of women when in the company of the Great Khan. We were supposed to be invisible and silent, mere decorations.

"My chief wife, Chabi Khatun. And this is my granddaughter, Emmajin Beki." *Beki* was my title, meaning "princess."

The Latin did something beyond comprehension. He took off his hat and kneeled before my grandmother and me. "Chabi Khatun. Emmajin Beki. At your service."

Not only did he bow on his knees, but he used the honorific form of "you"—not normally used for women and children. No one had ever referred to me that way. I looked at my grandfather with apprehension. He smiled and shook his head at the foreign manners.

At that moment, we heard a shout, and the elephants began moving with a jerk. The foreign man fell over sideways and grabbed the nearest thing, which happened to be my ankle. Sparks of alarm shot up my leg, and I clutched the arm of my seat.

The Khan reached down to the Latin and helped him up to his seat, laughing.

The foreigner's face turned red, and he spewed apologies. I pulled my feet back under me, but I couldn't help smiling. He looked ridiculous, this man with the strange name of Marco Polo. How could I have feared him? And yet I felt off balance.

"You shall enjoy the view better from your seat," the Khan said to him.

As we rode out of the palace, a servant poured us each a goblet of fresh *airag*. It was frothy and milky, with a satisfying sour bite. But the jostling of the pavilion on elephant back made my headache worse. I was glad to remain silent.

Using half-Mongolian, half-Turkic words, Marco Polo stammered out answers to the Khan's questions. Although respectful, he had a lighthearted manner that surprised me. He spoke about his father, Niccolo, and his uncle, Maffeo, who had visited the court of Khubilai Khan ten years earlier. Apparently, the Khan had treated them well. They had promised to return with one hundred scholars, to explain their religion to the Great Khan.

Marco Polo, along with his father and his uncle, first visited their Holy Land and brought with them some sacred oil. But they failed to bring the hundred scholars. They had found only three scholars willing to travel to the East with them, and all three had run home when they had encountered war. My grandfather, who loved listening to wise men debate about religion, frowned with disappointment as he queried this young man about the details. Marco seemed flustered, trying to explain this major failure of his father and uncle. I guessed he was not used to speaking for them.

Still, the Great Khan showed more consideration for this man than I had expected. "You speak well, young man. If you live to manhood, you will not fail to prove yourself of sound judgment and true worth. How many summers have you seen?"

"This begins my twenty-first summer."

I was surprised. He looked older, though his cheerfulness made him seem young.

"Have you trained as a warrior? Fought any battles?"

"No, Your Majesty. Ours is a noble family in Venezia, but I am a merchant's son." Though not tall, he seemed well built and strong. What a pity he had no training.

"So you came this great distance, yet you have no services to offer me?"

I had thought of this man as a potential enemy, but the Great Khan assumed he came as a faithful vassal. I realized how little I knew about foreigners.

The Latin seemed startled by the question. "I have traveled across many lands, O Kaan of all Kaans." That *k* sound scraped against my ears. Still, the *airag* was causing a light buzz to replace the pounding inside my head, and it helped me to relax.

"Your father spoke only a little of this journey the other day. How long did it take you to get here from your homeland?"

"Three and a half years."

"So long? Yet you carried the golden tablets of safe passage." These tablets, I knew, were issued by the Khan to guarantee safe travel within the Empire. I assumed the Khan had given the tablets to Marco's father and uncle during their previous visit.

"Yes, thanks to Your Majesty. The tablets saved our lives many times. But we also had to pass through freezing mountains, torrents of rain, dangerous deserts."

The Great Khan's eyes grew serious. "And during that time, what was the most challenging obstacle you faced?"

Marco paused. His forehead had an amiable way of smoothing out when he thought. One word escaped his lips. "Bandits." His green eyes sparkled.

I leaned forward to hear better.

"Ah, bandits!" The Khan's face lit up in anticipation. "I would like to hear this story. I command you to tell it to me." A servant refilled his golden goblet, then ours, and the Khan settled back in his fur-covered seat to listen.

Marco began, tentatively at first. "It was a band of . . . Caraonas."

I had heard of these fearful men, Caraonas, bandits born of Mongol fathers and Persian mothers, not accepted in any society. Outlaws.

"We were traveling in a caravan of fifty men, on camels.

We came to a vast plain, in Persia, on our way to the . . . to the . . . big water." He squinted at the Khan as if hoping the Khan would provide the word he was looking for. But the Khan just listened.

Marco swallowed hard and continued. "Most towns there have high walls, built to defend against the Caraonas, who have . . . who have hurt people there for many years."

As he spoke, Marco's manner changed. His posture straightened as his uncertainty dropped away, and confidence took over his voice.

"These Caraonas have a certain magic," Marco continued. "They can bring darkness over the face of day, so that you can scarcely see your comrade riding beside you. They ride abreast, as many as ten thousand of them, spread across the whole plain. Like hunters, they catch every living thing they find. They butcher old men. They capture young men and women and sell them as slaves. Thus the whole land is ruined, a desert."

As he spoke, I thought, *Can I handle this assignment, gathering intelligence from this foreigner?* Like it or not, I had to do what the Khan had commanded me.

Marco seemed to get lost in his story. "One day, as we were crossing the plain, night fell at midday. We could hear the pounding of horses' hooves. The Caraonas galloped at us a thousand strong, in the darkness. Everyone panicked. My uncle, my father, and I were near the back of our caravan. We turned and headed to a nearby village. Our camels, struck with fear, ran fast as horses."

Listening to the foreigner's deep voice, I forgot his odd appearance and imagined myself riding on a camel, beset by sudden darkness, fleeing from murderous bandits.

"The village had locked its gates," Marco continued, "but we pounded, and they let us in. Only when I was inside did I know that my father and uncle had made it, too. Those who came later were not allowed in. They screamed as the bandits butchered them. Of the fifty men in our caravan, only seven of us escaped. We knelt down and thanked God for sparing our lives." He used the Mongolian word for God: *Tengri.*

Marco finished speaking. I had almost stopped breathing during the story. It was a shock to come back to the present. For an unending moment of silence, I wondered if this foreign man had spoken too much. Most people say little in the Great Khan's presence until they are certain where they stand.

The Khan stared at Marco with narrow, piercing eyes. The Empress, who had been listening with interest, looked at the Khan as if curious to see his reaction. Then the Khan beamed. "Well done! You were so quiet at our official meeting yesterday, I had no idea that you have talent as a storyteller."

Marco bowed his head. "I speak your language poorly."

The Khan laughed. "You speak better than many at court. In a few days, I will dine with several of my men. You will entertain us with a story."

The young foreigner seemed flustered but honored. "At your service."

The man's storytelling amazed me. All my life I had looked up to military men. This Latin had no ability in the manly arts. Yet he was an artist with the spoken word.

Intelligence gathering was not a role I had ever envisioned, and I did not excel at talking. But the Khan had entrusted me with an assignment. I would have to try my best.

8

Above Xanadu

On the third day, we arrived at our summer home in Xanadu. A few days after that, I armed myself for my first meeting alone with Marco Polo. I brought my bow and arrows, both hanging from leather straps on my waistband. While I did not intend to use them, I wanted the foreigner to see me as formidable.

My uncle Chimkin told me where to find Marco Polo's tent. I was to treat the green-eyed man as a guest and to see him every day. Without arousing his suspicion, I was to gather information about the kings and princes of his land—how they maintained their dignity, how they administered their dominions, and how they went forth to battle. After each meeting, I was to report back to my uncle.

Overnight, it had rained heavily—the kind of weather that made Xanadu into a garden spot. As I walked across the wet grass, the sunlight angled through the clouds. Still, my hair stuck to my head. The rain had washed much of the white powder off my cheeks, exposing my bruises, which were fading to yellow. A bruised face might protect me against unwanted advances.

The Latin was standing outside his tent, looking toward the low row of hills that surrounded Xanadu. When he heard my footsteps behind him, he whirled around, and his hand reached for his dagger. "Who goes there?" he asked.

My hand rushed to my own dagger, and my heart quickened. I was face to face with a dangerous, armed foreigner. Then I shook my head, appalled at his slow reaction. If I had ill intentions, he would be dead by now.

When he realized who I was, his face broke into a smile of relief and pleasure. "Emmajin Beki. I am honored." He replaced his dagger and bowed in his Latin way, one hand in front, one behind. "What brings you here this morning?"

I took a deep breath. "The Khan has asked me to host you here in Xanadu, to show you the grounds."

He grinned too broadly at this news.

I set my mouth in a firm line, and his smile faded.

"You would prefer not to?"

"I do as the Great Khan asks."

He seemed ill at ease, as if disappointed and uncertain what to do or say.

Not only was this the first time I had had a direct conversation with a foreigner, but it was also the first time I had spoken to a man not related to me without my family present. I didn't even know what to call him. Almost every man I knew was a relative, called uncle or brother. I needed to show him I was in command. "Today, we will ride in the hills."

He bowed his head, appropriately humble. "As you wish."

"Leave your dagger here," I said. He dropped his weapon just inside his tent.

Relieved to be moving, I turned and strode toward the horse pasture. The foreigner hastened to catch up to me, but I stayed one pace ahead. I had decided to take him riding, because it would be easier to keep my distance from him on horseback.

We reached a spot where several horses were tethered to a rope stretched high between two poles. I told the horse boy to saddle up my palomino stallion as well as a tawny mare for the visitor.

The Latin man stood awkwardly by my side, his breath at the level of my ears. I could smell a strange perfume of pungent cloves on his curls. It felt wrong to stand so close to a foreign man. Once I had mounted Baatar, I felt much more comfortable.

But Marco hesitated. "I've never ridden on a Mongolian saddle," he said. How strange. I looked at the wooden saddle, its familiar curved shape high in the front and back, painted red with silver medallions. What kind of primitive saddle did this man use?

He fumbled, trying to mount. I could not fathom how this man had traveled for three years from the end of the world and never learned how to ride on a proper Mongolian saddle. I had learned to ride before I could walk.

Once on the horse, he kicked her in the sides! The mare flinched. Didn't he know it was wrong to kick a horse? I reached over to his steed and steadied her with a hand on her neck. "What are you doing?" I asked.

His weird eyes registered uncertainty.

With the familiar cry of "Tchoo! Tchoo!" I urged Baatar

forward across the grasses, and the tawny mare followed. Baatar and I moved fluidly together, as if he could read my thoughts. I quickly broke into a trot, then a lope, checking to see if the Latin was following. He was hanging on to the wooden saddle and smiling gamely at me. I headed for the foothills and slowed as we started up a well-known trail.

The morning's rain had left diamonds in the grass, and I brushed against wet branches that sprayed me with sparkling drops. I luxuriated in the first warm rays of sunlight on my hands and face.

As we rode, single file, mostly uphill, I silently rehearsed the questions I would ask of this man. If I could get all the needed answers quickly, perhaps the Khan would let me return to my usual life, with hours to spend on archery and horseback. I had hoped Suren and I could begin preparing for military training that summer.

Soon we approached a clearing overlooking Xanadu from the hills just north of the walled city. I jumped off my horse and tied him to a nearby tree. Marco Polo did the same. Then I led him to the edge of the clearing for the best view.

From this vantage point, we could see the whole of Xanadu. The palace sat on a wide plain surrounded by high hills visible along the horizon. Much of the plain was forested, a semi-wild park of trees and grasslands and natural streams. These woods, a hunting preserve for the Khan, contained many deer and foxes. From above, we could see how the thick outer walls of Xanadu formed a huge square. Inside was a small town for servants and guests, as well as the Khan's famous fabulous gardens. Brooks, hillocks, bridges, pavilions, twisting pathways, and artificial lakes all glistened in the intense sunlight.

I sighed. It was like a fantasyland, a place I had longed for during the cold winter.

At the heart of this square was a smaller square, formed by high stone walls topped by turrets. Inside this inner, "forbidden" city were the golden roofs of the palace, a smaller and leafier version of the massive imperial palace in Khanbalik. The main hall, raised on an artificial hill, was pure white marble, shimmering and smooth. It faced due south, as all major doors do, toward the sun, away from us.

Other buildings inside the inner walls were pavilions of painted wood with golden roofs, set amidst tree-shaded courtyards. Each building was positioned carefully on a straight north-south, east-west axis, in the Chinese imperial style. But one large courtyard was dotted with round white tents, our distinctive Mongolian *gers*. They reminded everyone of the old days, when our ancestors were nomadic herders and warriors, traveling freely. The Khan had insisted that the floors of the palace at Xanadu be made of packed dirt, to keep him connected to the earth.

Overhead, an eagle soared. An exhilarating breeze blew my hair about my face. I hoped the magic of Xanadu would make this day go well.

The foreigner gazed at the panorama below, as if drinking in every detail. "My father told me of this place, but I could not imagine it. I thought the Mongols lived on horseback, moving their tents from place to place."

"That's true." I pushed myself to speak. "We Mongols are hunters and herdsmen, with no tradition of fixed palaces. We do not eat plants or dig in the dirt."

He turned back to me, his face radiant with joy. Those eyes looked clear and empty. I wondered if they could see more than dark eyes saw. He looked innocent, but my grandmother had hinted that he was not safe. The time had come to begin my mission.

I led him to a grassy spot and spread a goatskin on the ground. I put my bow in the middle, a clear boundary between me and the foreigner. I sat on one side, and he sat on the other. I kept the sharp-tipped arrows behind me, so he could not reach them.

I got out a leather pouch with dried milk curds in it and offered him some to eat. He tossed a milk-curd cube into the hole in his beard where his mouth was. A frown creased his forehead and he chewed as if trying to make up his mind about it.

"Very good," he said, smiling as if eager to please. He was not good at lying.

Such curds were meant to provide energy on a journey and were not particularly tasty. I ate in silence, rehearsing my first question.

"What do you hope to get from the Khan? What are your intentions?" As soon as I spoke, I knew I had been too blunt.

Marco examined my face before responding soberly. "I will be frank with you, Princess. My father and uncle handed all our precious trading commodities over to the Khan, as is required. If I can gain his favor, perhaps he will give us, in return, goods of great value to take back to our homeland." So this was the way merchants worked. Not buying and selling with coins, but taking their chances with the Khan's goodwill.

"How will you gain his favor?"

"By serving him, entertaining him in the most appealing possible way. Perhaps you can let me know if you hear any reaction to my storytelling?" It occurred to me that Marco Polo was also using me. His success depended in part on his connection with me.

His odd eyes seemed bluish green in this setting. I suspected that they could see inside my mind. It made me uncomfortable. I needed to press on.

"Tell me again," I said "What is the name of your homeland?"

"Venezia," he said.

"Way-nay-sha," I said, trying to pronounce it. I could barely get my tongue around the strange sounds. How could I remember it? "How big and powerful is it?"

Marco laughed. "It is just a city, but with its own army."

"It belongs to a larger country?"

"Well, it is part of Christendom," he said, using a Mongolian word meaning "Land of the Religion of Light." "But Christendom has many countries and city-states."

He picked up a stick and began to draw a map in the dirt.

"This is Italia." The shape he drew looked like a boot with a strange heel. "Here is Venezia." He made a circle near the top of the boot. "Here is Genova, our rival city. They, too, have many ships and merchants, and we compete with them for the best markets."

I noticed that his fingers were long and thin, soft and clean. "They fight?" I asked.

"More like competing in a contest. This, you see"—he scratched the area on three sides of the boot—"is the Middle-of-the-Earth Sea. Up here is France, where the Franks live, and above that is England. Over here, Aragon." He continued drawing and poking in the dirt, naming a confusing array of countries, each with its own king.

I frowned. There were too many foreign names to remember. It was like trying to stuff a month's worth of dried meat into a leather pouch meant for overnight.

I stopped him. "Who is the ruler of these lands?"

He thought for a minute. "We don't have one ruler, like your Great Khan. Some of these lands belong to the Holy Roman Empire. But many do not. They are not united."

I shook my head.

He appeared to smile, or at least I thought so. I could not see his mouth but noticed wrinkles at the corners of his eyes. "We do have a Pope, in Roma. He is the head of our religion. When my father brought him a letter from the Great Khan, he responded, hoping for friendly relations."

"His armies are large and well trained?"

Marco smiled as if this were a strange question. "He has troops to protect him. But he is not a military ruler. You see, all these lands are . . ." He kept talking.

I soon gave up trying to follow what he was saying, with so many foreign words. Behind the big beard was an earnest expression, but his eyes sparkled. His hands moved in mesmerizing gestures when he spoke. What would such a smooth hand feel like?

He had stopped talking and was regarding me intently. I was forgetting myself. I needed to ask easier questions.

"And your people . . ." I hesitated, wondering if I was being too direct again. "They have eyes of many colors? Red? Yellow? Blue?"

Marco laughed. "No. Only blue, green, and brown."

"And your people's hair?" He did not seem to mind my questions. "Also green and blue?" After all, anything other than black hair and dark brown eyes had been beyond my imagination until I saw him.

He smiled. "Some people have yellow hair. Some red. Some brown, like mine."

Yellow hair! I had heard that hair turned yellow only when people were starving.

"Blue eyes are not unheard of in your land, are they?" he said. "I have heard that even your Great Ancestor, Chinggis Khan, had blue eyes and reddish hair."

This comment took me aback. But I remembered vaguely that I had heard such a thing from Old Master. It had seemed impossible, since everyone I knew in the Golden Family had dark hair and dark eyes. We all worshipped the Great Ancestor, so I had never thought of him as a flesh-and-blood person.

"Now I have a question for you, Emmajin Beki." Marco lowered his voice. "During my long journey across the lands of the Mongol Empire, I heard that Mongols drink horses' blood. Yet I have not seen anyone drinking blood at court. Is this true?"

I laughed out loud at the thought of horses' blood in a goblet at dinner. Then I quickly stopped, lest he feel foolish for asking. "It is sometimes true. On very long journeys, if there is no other food, a Mongol soldier might cut a vein in his horse's flesh. He allows the blood to spurt into his mouth, just enough to keep him alive."

Marco's face showed disgust.

I quickly added, "But soldiers do this only when they are starving and have no other source of food. It shows they are smart and resourceful."

Marco shook his head, as if trying to absorb this strange fact. He seemed as relieved as I had been to know that his countrymen did not have green hair. What fears we have of foreigners and their strange ways!

He leaned a little closer. "I truly did not mean to offend you after the archery contest. I only wanted to tell you I admired your nobility."

Conscious of my purple-yellow cheeks, I looked away. For a few moments, I had forgotten my public humiliation.

He persisted. "I have heard that you are an excellent archer."

An excellent archer! What did he know of archery, this man who could barely ride on a Mongolian saddle? "Who told you this?" I asked harshly.

"At the contest, I heard others speak of you. People thought you would win."

Win. My face flushed. All the shame of the archery tournament washed over me, as if someone had tossed a bucket of cold water onto my body.

The foreigner continued. "Many praise your archery skills. Can you show me?"

I picked up my bow. After the awkwardness of conversation, it was a relief to feel its smooth surface and familiar weight.

In the sky, a golden eagle was soaring. Without a word, I stood up. I placed an arrow on my bow and pulled back the string until it was as tight as it could be. My hands held perfectly steady as I aimed at a spot just in front of the eagle. I waited until a precise moment before releasing. The arrow arched high and fast.

The eagle soared on, oblivious to my aim. Some arrows would have fallen before reaching that height, but mine did not.

It hit its target. The eagle faltered and fell in an ungainly arc.

Marco let out a breath of admiration. My chest swelled with pride.

The eagle landed with a thud on the ground. A realization pierced me. Hunting in the Khan's private reserve without his permission was forbidden. I had just broken a rule that was strictly enforced.

I gasped as if wounded. I ran toward the fallen bird. Marco followed me.

The eagle was a beautiful, huge creature, majestic and powerful, as long as my arm. It had light brown wings, a black tail, a golden crown and nape, great curved talons, and piercing orange-brown eyes. This bird of prey was much treasured by hunters. Any man who could bring one back alive would be rewarded.

But this eagle was not alive. Its body was warm, but its heart had stopped. My arrow had broken its wing. The fall had broken its neck.

I rocked back on my heels, in shock. It was too handsome to die from my arrow. I caressed its golden feathers, sorry I had taken its life. I struggled to control my tears.

Marco's smile had faded.

Quickly, I pulled out my dagger and began digging a hole to bury the eagle.

"It is forbidden," I explained. I flailed as I dug. Once, I had seen the head of a decapitated man who had flouted the Khan's hunting rules. Now I had violated not only the law but also the hunter's ethics, killing a fine bird for no reason other than my own pride.

Marco gingerly touched the bird's still-warm chest. He stroked the wing and carefully plucked out one of the longest, most golden of its tail feathers.

I, too, could not help admiring the glorious creature. Even its legs were covered with feathers. I had ended the life of this magnificent bird. Why had I needed to prove my strength to this man? Why should I care what he thought of me?

Gently, I placed the eagle into the hole and covered it with dirt. When I finished, I realized that Marco was standing over me, holding the long golden feather.

My hands in the dirt—*Mongols don't dig in the dirt*—I caught his eye. Perhaps now he would fear and respect me. But he knew about something that he could use against me. Perhaps he would blackmail me. He knew where I had buried the eagle, and he had a feather to prove it. Fear flooded me.

I stood and looked him in the eyes, as threatening as I could be. "Tell no one."

He silently nodded.

As I turned to head toward the horses, Marco Polo lightly touched the back of my shoulder. His fingers sent a startling sensation through my body. I jumped.

He pulled back, aware of his mistake. In his hand, offered to me, was the eagle's splendid feather.

Eyes focused on his, I closed my fingers over the feather, nodding my gratitude. His eyes, somber, sealed our secret pact. I hid the feather inside the front of my *del.*

We mounted our horses and rode back down the hill in silence. That spot on my shoulder tingled.

When we reached the valley and returned to the tethers, I told him I would show him the gardens the next day—in the afternoon.

He bowed his head slightly. "I would be honored."

I had made the worst mistake of my life, and this foreigner knew about it. What was it about him that had distracted me from common sense? He was a mere foreign merchant, and I the granddaughter of the Khan. Now he had power over me but had offered not to wield it. I wondered if I was a fool to trust him.

9

Foreign Menace

The heavy sword wobbled as Suren raised it above his head. He could not control its weight as it crashed down. Its tip hit the ground, far from the spot he aimed to hit.

Suren was preparing to join the army, so he was finally allowed to learn to use a sword. I found him early the next morning in a glade in the Khan's woods, practicing.

My heart fell when I saw that he was sparring with Temur, who also held a sword. I had hoped to confide in Suren about my foreigner, to get his advice. But I could not speak freely in front of his brother. Temur would not be sixteen for another year, so he should not be allowed to touch a sword till his time to join the army came.

"I thought you were supposed to start with wooden swords," I said.

Suren grinned when he saw me. "That's what the sword master said yesterday when we started to train with him. But we couldn't resist."

"Don't tell anyone!" Temur glowered at me. As if I could not be trusted!

I ignored him. "He won't be joining the army?" I asked Suren.

He pressed his lips, which were beginning to show a mustache. "In Ninth Moon."

"But why?"

"The Great Khan awards winners," Temur answered, gloating.

I clenched my fists. It wasn't fair. After the summer ended, when military training began in Ninth Moon, both Suren and Temur would be joining the army. I would have to watch them both receive their uniforms and ride off. After all the years of outperforming them, even training them, I would have to stay at court with the women.

Suren raised his sword, grasping it with two hands, and stood, feet apart, in a ready stance. His broad shoulders were steady; his lips were firm. The girls at court whispered about how good-looking Temur was, but the girl who married Suren would be the lucky one. A princess from a distant tribe had been chosen for him but no date had been set for the marriage. I hoped she would be lively and fun, worthy of him.

Temur faced him and deflected a blow before both sword tips dropped to the ground. Fortunately, both swords were wrapped in cloth. Still, two heavy swords in the hands of untrained boys looked like trouble.

I felt wildly jealous. While all Mongol boys and girls learned archery from a young age, women were never permitted to handle swords. No one would ever train me in swordsmanship. This was my only chance. "May I try? Please?" I asked.

"No," Suren said, heaving to catch his breath, looking embarrassed. Suren usually gave in to my pleading, but I should have known he would not do so in front of Temur.

But he was eager to show off what he had learned at his first lesson. "You need to hold it with two hands at first. You're probably not strong enough."

I bit my tongue to keep from responding. He needed time to gain back his dignity after losing the archery contest.

Drawing attention to himself, Temur grasped his sword with two hands, lifted it high, and plunged it straight down, into the soft earth. This was the simplest move with a sword, the easiest to control. It looked like he was killing a wounded enemy.

I laughed. "One less foreigner to fight!"

Suren laughed, too. "Don't tell anyone, but the Khan has assigned me to get to know a foreigner, to learn about his homeland. Temur has one, too. Do you believe that?"

"Interesting," I said. Suddenly, it seemed more of an honor, this assignment. I straightened my shoulders. "He assigned me a foreigner, too."

Temur sucked in his breath. "That can't be."

Suren looked at me strangely. "He wants you to speak to a foreigner? A man?"

"A young man. At first it was supposed to be three men, but the other two did not come to Xanadu because they are sick."

Suren cocked his head. "The Khan said that this would help us prepare to join the army. It doesn't make sense that he would ask you to do it."

Hope jumped up in my heart. Maybe the Khan was

preparing me to join the army, as well. "Who is your foreigner?" I asked, glad to be on equal footing with them.

Suren lay the sword down and wiped his forehead. He sat on the ground. "He looks so strange. Wears a white turban on his head, with a long tail of cloth hanging down his back. From Arabia. Big thick beard. Eyes a strange light brown."

"My foreigner has green eyes," I said proudly, sitting next to my cousin. "And his hair is brown but shines red like fire in the sunlight. No turban, though."

"Temur's foreigner has a turban, too. He's Bactrian. Fierce-looking."

Temur was still standing, leaning on his sword, regarding us from above.

"These foreigners," said Suren. "What can we possibly learn from them?"

"I told you," said Temur. "The Khan wants us to keep an eye on them."

Suren looked thoughtful. "But others are better suited to getting information from them. Maybe he wants to make sure we can resist foreigners even after talking to them."

"Resist? Hah!" Temur shook his head in disbelief. "Their countries are too weak to face us in battle, so they come here, begging favors and spying on us. They keep trying to weaken our resolve to fight. I can't wait till the Khan bans them from court."

Suren frowned. "Bans them? The Khan would never do that."

"You haven't heard? Some men at court want to get rid of the foreigners," Temur said. "Several of the princes and military leaders are starting an antiforeign movement, trying to convince the Khan that their presence at court is dangerous."

Suren frowned. "How can foreigners be dangerous if they are weak?"

"They are clever. They write in strange script and send our secrets back to their homelands. They manipulate people. The movement is seeking evidence of treachery."

I had never heard of this antiforeign movement. I wondered if Temur was exaggerating. Still, I realized I knew little about the many factions at court.

Suren shook his head. "My foreigner seems friendly enough."

"Of course, they all do," Temur said. "Don't get taken in. They want you to forget about loyalty. We have to show how strong we are—not just our arms but our minds."

This idea made sense. Joining an army of men would take a strong mind. But this antiforeign movement sounded just as dangerous as the foreigners.

Suren looked at me with concern. "Emmajin, you need to be careful."

To break the tension, I jumped up, grabbed his sword, and raised it high above my head. It was even heavier than I had expected, and it wobbled in the air.

"Hai-yah! After the foreigners!" I ran into the woods, holding the sword high.

Suren chased me, to get his sword back. Swords are not meant for lighthearted play. But I couldn't help myself. I did not want to think about dangerous foreigners.

10

In the Garden

To prepare for my next meeting with Marco, I tried to arm myself as if for battle. I didn't want to be naive, as I had been on our first rendezvous. I had already given this foreigner a dagger he could use to threaten me if he wanted to manipulate me: the secret about my shooting down the eagle. I needed to find a way to win back the upper hand.

When I reported to my uncle, he clarified what kind of information he was looking for and asked me to learn some foreign words. He also warned me, "Next time, do not go so far away. Stay near other people." It seemed sage advice.

A drip of sweat traced its way down my face. This time I had arranged to take Marco Polo to the Khan's famous gardens. They were nearby and others would be there, but we would be meeting in the heat of the day, when most people slept. I needed to show confidence and wrestle some useful information out of the man.

That day, Marco looked nervous. "Emmajin Beki, good

afternoon. I was not sure you would come." His hands shifted and his eyebrows twisted.

"Why not?" We had arranged to meet at that hour.

"There are rumors that the Khan is displeased with the foreign visitors at court. I hope no one will advise the Khan against allowing me to entertain him tomorrow."

"I see no reason for that," I said, acting confident but wondering if I had missed something. What had he heard about the antiforeign movement?

He relaxed. "You will tell me, I hope, if I do something to earn his disfavor."

It had not occurred to me before then that this foreign man might feel scared and vulnerable. He was alone, far from home, his life at the whim of the most powerful ruler in the world. That thought should have made me feel more in control, but instead, I was concerned.

We entered the Khan's gardens through a back gate, a round opening in the long red wall that surrounded the garden. Marco's arm brushed against mine as he pointed to the top of the wall, built to curve like the back of a dragon serpent. My arm tingled, and I stepped away, answering his question with stiff propriety.

The minute we stepped over the threshold into the gardens, the air felt cooler, with shade trees everywhere. In Fifth Moon, the gardens of Xanadu sparkled with brilliant colors. The tender green of the willow leaves contrasted with the dark green of the pines. Frothy pink and white blossoms adorned the fruit trees, and the azaleas were just starting to break out in vivid reds and purples.

Marco and I walked along a small man-made lake covered with large pale-pink water lilies. Delicate pavilions and stone pagodas rose at the ends of winding paths. Sparrows and swallows twittered and flitted from tree to tree. Like them, my heart was jittery. How could I act stiff and distant in such a lovely setting?

"Magnificent!" Marco gushed. "I have never seen such beauty." He checked my face for my reaction to his compliments. I tried to keep from looking directly into his eyes.

As we walked, he asked me for the Mongolian names of various trees and flowers and birds. *So this is how you learn foreign words,* I thought. My uncle had asked me to study this man's language, but I needed to find out more than the names of trees and birds.

Looking for a spot where I could question Marco without being heard, I led him up a stone staircase to a small six-sided pavilion, with benches around the inside. A chipmunk scurried away when we entered. The conversation would be like a wrestling match, and it was about to begin.

I indicated where he should sit, then sat down directly opposite him, as far away as possible. My back straight, my demeanor formal and proper, I noticed that his eyes shone, as if he was wonder-struck just looking at me. I struggled to recall the words I had practiced saying to the tent post the night before. Marco's thick chest and arms distracted me.

Envisioning a helmet on my head and set of leather armor on my chest, I began to speak, more smoothly this time. "Latins are rare at the Khan's court. Tell me how you came here from your homeland, so far away."

He clasped his hands over his knee and thought for a moment, as if this were a conversation and not an interrogation. "As you know, my father and uncle came here many years ago, and the Khan asked them to come back." His eyes reflected the greenery of the garden around us. "My father left home on that journey just before I was born, in the year of our Lord 1254. When I was very small, my mother died."

He seemed to have said this so many times he no longer felt it, but I felt a pang. Although many women died when their children were young, I knew that losing one's mother so young was no small matter. It took energy to swallow my sympathy.

"I lived with my mother's relatives. We did not receive letters from my father, so we assumed he had died. When I was fully grown, fifteen years after they had left home, my father and uncle unexpectedly returned. They said they had visited a prosperous land, far to the east, and met an emperor who ruled a vast empire far bigger than Christendom. When they described his riches and power, no one believed them."

"No one believed? The Latins do not know of the Great Khan?"

"No. They know of the Mongols only as 'Tartars,' hordes of horsemen who rode from the East and attacked Christendom during my father's youth. The Great Khan asked my father to deliver a letter to the Pope. The Pope responded with a letter, which we brought with us. We were not allowed to read it, but I believe the Pope demanded that the Khan promise not to invade Christendom again."

It mystified me, why this leader of a small backward land, this Pope, would think he could demand anything of the Khan. This Pope sounded ignorant, tactless, and confused. But Marco seemed to respect him. Marco's arm was covered in light hair.

"My father commanded me to come with them," Marco continued, "on their second journey to the heart of the Mongol Empire, to learn about trading."

A flash in his eyes prompted me to ask, "Did you want to come?"

His laughter surprised me. "Do any of us get to do what we really want?"

"You didn't want to travel, to learn your father's business?" I had envied men because they had more opportunities than women did, but not all men had choices in life.

He smiled ruefully. "The life of a traveling merchant has its appeal, but my aunt often warned me of its dangers. I liked the idea of adventure, but I was a little sad about leaving behind everyone I had known."

"A wife?" He was over twenty, so surely he had at least one wife.

He stopped smiling. "I wanted to marry, but my father insisted I travel instead."

Shifting on the bench, sitting on my hands, I sensed he had left behind a woman he loved. I wondered if he thought about her when talking to me. I chose not to ask.

"I nearly died on the way, from sickness," he said. "We had to stop for a year while I battled a fever. But God did not want to take me yet. So I am here."

Nearly died. Sick for a year. I had never given any thought, when seeing foreign travelers, to the life they had left behind, their difficulties, their loss and grief and fears.

"When will you go back home?" I asked, trying to fight my sense of sympathy.

"Not soon! We just arrived, exhausted after more than three years on the road. My father and uncle are still sick.

I hope they will get better soon so they can come to Xanadu and meet you. It will be months before we can think about traveling back."

So the other two foreigners would be coming after all. I felt strangely disappointed at the idea of sharing Marco with them. At least he would not leave soon.

Our sparring match was not going well. Marco seemed to think we were becoming friends. Why did I keep forgetting that he was an alien, not to be trusted?

Even inside the pavilion, the heat was oppressive. Xanadu summers were usually not so hot. I wiped a bead of sweat from my face. "It's terrible, this heat," I said.

He smiled. "I come from a hot climate, so I like warm weather."

The air between us shimmered in the heat. His manner, relaxed and candid, had a way of breaking down that protective barrier around my mind. I felt disarmed.

A murmur of thunder grumbled in the distance. Startled, I jumped up. I hated thunderstorms. I felt an urge to get out of Marco's presence, lest I do or say something wrong.

"We need to go back before it rains," I said. I strode off down a path along a winding wall. Marco looked surprised but followed.

As we were walking, I remembered my uncle's order to learn some Latin words.

I stopped so abruptly that Marco nearly bumped into me. He pulled back, clearly aware of the need to keep his distance from the Khan's granddaughter, and apologized profusely. He was so close I could feel his breath. I pulled back, too, embarrassed.

We were standing next to a pond covered with brilliant

green lotus leaves. Several flat-topped stones had been strategically placed so it was possible to cross the pond. Normally a popular spot, the banks of the pond were deserted now.

"Teach me some words of Latin," I commanded.

Marco's head tilted. "With pleasure," he said. "What would you like to learn?"

I was tongue-tied. If I learned the Latin words for warfare, Khan, and weaponry, that would suffice for one day. What was it about that smile of his that flustered me?

"Our word for Tengri is *'Deus,'*" Marco began.

"Day-oos," I repeated. "But your Deus is different from our Tengri?" Marco worshiped a different god, and I didn't know what that meant about him.

"Some Christians would say so. But I believe there is only one God. People in each country and of each religion use different words for the same God."

I nodded, trying to understand. It did not seem possible that Marco's Deus commanded Chinggis Khan to conquer the world, but perhaps it was true. "A-a-and Great Khan?" I stammered. "How do you say that?"

"Hmm. We don't have a Great Khan. But in the old days, the Romans used the word *imperator.*" His lips were wet, moving inside his beard.

My lips and tongue could barely get around this word, *imperator.* I was sure I would not remember it. The Mongolian word, *khagan,* was much easier to say.

Marco smiled wryly at my pronunciation. "Let's start with something easier. Try this word: *amo.*"

"Amo." This word was much easier.

Marco nodded. Then he did something that surprised me. He stepped onto a wide, flat stone in the lotus pond. The water reflected the thickening gray clouds.

He gestured to me. "Follow me. Repeat after me. *Amo.*"

I frowned. I hated water. With our roots in the grasslands, we Mongols are people of the earth, not the water. Yet this pond lay still and shallow, calmer than an old mare. And who was he to give me an order? Yet it sounded more like an invitation.

"I will explain. *Amo.*" He smiled, as if walking across water were as natural as riding a horse.

He offered his hand. I looked around, to make sure no one was watching. Such playfulness was improper, a waste of time—and incompatible with my serious mission.

It felt like a dare.

"Amo." Tense and uncertain, I followed him to the stepping stone, trying hard not to take his hand or brush against him. "But I don't . . ."

"Amas." Quickly, he stepped to the next stone. He seemed so enviably free, so naturally open, so unrestrained by rigid rules. Far from intimidating or dangerous.

"Amas." I followed him. Suren and I had played like this, years ago.

"Amat." Marco leaped to the next flat stone, almost losing his balance.

"Amat." My heart lightened. These words sounded ridiculous, almost the same.

Amamus, amatis, amant. By the sixth step, we were safe on the other side of the pond, on firm ground. I had crossed the water without getting wet. Or touching him.

I laughed in spite of myself. "But what does it mean?" This was not a proper way to learn a language, and it didn't sound like a proper language, either.

He bowed to me in his strange style. "It means 'love.' I love. You love. He loves. We love. All of you love. They love."

I squirmed. In Mongolian, there is one word for "love" and "like," so it did not seem an odd word to teach. Still, it was awkward, not something any Mongol man would ever say. I suspected Marco was making fun of me. "All of those words mean 'love'?"

"Listen carefully. I love. *Amo.*" Marco stepped back onto a flat stone in the pond. By then the clouds were darkening. I needed to cut this odd language lesson short and take him back to his *ger* before it started to pour. But I didn't want to.

"I love. *Amo.*" I hesitated, but he refused to go on until I followed him onto the stepping stone. Besides, it was the quickest way to get back. The Latin word sounded soft compared to guttural Mongolian ones. I liked the feel of it on my tongue.

"You love. *Amas.*"

"You love. *Amas.*"

"He loves. *Amat.*"

I repeated and followed him across, feeling foolish and flushed in the heat. On *amant,* as I stepped onto dry land, I almost slipped and he caught my hand. As soon as I steadied myself, I looked at him. He held my hand for a moment longer.

All my senses went on alert. His eyes were shimmering, and his smile, deep inside his beard, was a little crooked. In this garden setting, Marco acted like a perfect gentleman, courtly and well mannered, suave and witty. Not barbarian at all. Still, touching his hand was forbidden, wrong. I looked at our hands and he let go.

He stepped back to give me space, dipping his head in a quick bow, but he regarded me with admiring eyes. "In my homeland, there is a kind of love called courtly love. A warrior offers his services to a royal lady and dedicates his life to her."

This concept was alarming but intriguing. "A lady who is not his wife?"

Again, he bowed his head, as if in deference. "It is love from a distance."

Love from a distance. I trembled. This conversation had lunged off course, into perilous territory. How could I get his mind off love? I licked my lips and tried to think quickly. "How do you say 'God loves the Great Khan'?"

He smiled as if he could see through me. *"Deus amat imperatorem."*

I tried it, but mangled the words. Our joint laughter sounded musical.

"One more word," he said. "*Bella.* It means beautiful. You are beautiful."

My cheeks felt hot. Perhaps where he came from, Italia, such compliments from men were natural. But no Mongol man spoke this way. Lovely. I wanted to look away, but something in his eyes kept me gazing at him. His pupils were black, and the green was deeper now, a perfect ring, flecked with yellow. For the first time I thought them not odd and empty but bright and attractive.

A loud clap of thunder startled us. I looked at the sky with alarm. Thunder meant lightning, which meant danger. Every Mongol knows that when the grasslands are dry, one lightning strike can set off a fire that can kill people and animals for miles.

The first raindrops hit my head. A storm was invading Xanadu.

"Run," I said.

I began sprinting toward the garden gate, and Marco chased after me. The rain pelted us. I was running to escape the rain, but more than that, I needed to flee from the feel of his fingers and the gaze on his face at the pond.

I had let down my guard. Again. I had let him manipulate me. How could I ever hope to be a soldier when I was so weak and naive? I was failing the Khan's test.

But my mind savored this peculiar, perilous concept: courtly love.

11

The Khan's Banquet

The next day, a servant delivered to me a striking green *del* embroidered with floral designs in pearls and gold thread. The fastenings, at an angle from the high-collared neck to the right shoulder, were knots of thick gold thread. With this robe came a pair of green silk pants and a sash of gold brocade.

This luxurious outfit arrived with an order to attend the Khan's banquet that evening. The Khan had invited Marco to entertain him with a story, and he commanded my presence. This request was a great honor, as royal women never dined with the Khan and his men, and they seldom were invited into his banquet rooms at all. It made me worry, though, what the Khan expected of me.

I liked the idea of watching Marco perform and seeing how the Khan and his men interacted with him. The previous night, in bed, I couldn't stop thinking about the touch of his hand and his ideas about courtly love, but that felt wrong, totally improper for someone preparing to become a soldier. The Khan knew how to behave around foreigners, with their strange ideas. I hoped to learn from observing him and lessen my confusion.

My sister could not contain her envy. Drolma and my mother had arrived in Xanadu on the same day I had, and Drolma had expressed horror at my assignment of hosting a foreigner. Now that she saw this elaborate robe delivered to the large *ger* where we lived each summer, her opinion changed. "I wish I could go," she said.

Drolma had never worn such a fine garment, and she tried it on before I did. It was too long for her. My mother, delighted by this honor, took care to dress me like a true princess. She oiled my long hair to make it stiff and arranged it on top of my head inside a royal lady's headdress. From the sides of the hat hung three strands of pearls in a loop across my upper chest, creating the illusion of necklaces hanging from my ears.

I hated all the fussing over my appearance. I preferred to look strong and competent, not lovely and delicate. But my mother insisted on covering the faded bruises on my cheeks with powder and rubbing essence of rose onto the back of my neck.

It was one of the few times the three of us had worked together. "Remember to smile," my mother said. "Show her, Drolma."

Drolma stood in front of me, drew her elbows in, dropped her eyes in false modesty, and blinked, a silly smile on her lips. A laugh burst from my mouth.

"Emmajin!" my mother remonstrated. "It will help you get what you want."

"How would that help convince the Khan to let me join the army?"

My mother sighed. "Hold still," she said, putting a dab of red on my lips.

The banquet took place in a smaller cane palace, erected every summer in the Khan's garden. By design, the cane palace resembled a large Mongolian *ger,* with crisscrossed tent walls made of gilded bamboo rods thick as a man's arm. Instead of being the usual ten paces across, this round palace measured at least a hundred paces across.

As I entered, all conversation stopped. The Great Khan and his men turned to watch me. I walked as elegantly as I could and tried to ignore the pain from my sister's tiny boots, which pinched my toes. Some men grunted in admiration.

"This lady could not be Dorji's daughter, could she?"

The Khan pointed to a seat reserved for me, between him and my uncle Chimkin. My chair was set back slightly, as I was not expected to eat, but I could hear everything the Khan said. I wished I could be invisible, rather than arouse the appetites of these men. I had always tried to hide that I was a woman. Now I was being forced to look and act like a mindless, decorative princess.

The inside of the cane palace was stunning. Its rounded ceiling rose high, covered with a silk cloth dyed light blue like a summer sky. In the center was a large round table made of rosewood. I slid into my seat.

My foreigner, Marco Polo, was not there. For big occasions, the Khan sometimes held banquets for a thousand men. That night, only about twenty men were present, all clad like the Great Khan, in emerald green with gold threads and belts. The table glittered with goblets, bowls, plates, and knives, all made of gleaming gold and etched with designs of wild beasts. The effect of the tableware in the flickering torchlight was dazzling.

The Khan lifted his goblet to drink, and the musicians began playing. As one, we lifted our goblets and held them to our foreheads until he had finished drinking. I took only a small sip, noticing that this *airag* was more intoxicating than usual.

"Where is this famed storyteller from the Far West?" one man asked.

"He probably lost his story inside that thick beard!" Prince Chimkin answered.

"Maybe it popped out of those bulging eyes!" another said.

Marco was keeping the Khan waiting. I could not imagine why. Clearly, some of these men did not share the Khan's friendly feelings toward foreigners. Maybe I would learn more about who supported the antiforeign movement by observing these men.

Finally, a commotion in the courtyard interrupted the banquet. A servant rushed in and announced the arrival of our entertainer.

Marco Polo entered. He was dressed in fine green clothes but muddy and dripping wet. He prostrated himself to the floor and shouted, "Long-a live the Kaan of all Kaans!"

His outrageous late appearance shocked us all into silence.

"Arise." The Khan's voice sounded solemn.

Good! I thought. Maybe Marco's storytelling career would end before it began. If the Khan banished him from court, maybe I could drop this assignment, forget my turmoil, and go back to daily training.

Marco stood up, dripping on the silk carpet. His wet beard and hair were plastered against his face, making his head look small. His eyes went straight to the Khan, then rested on me. He brushed a strand of wet hair out of his eyes, a pitiful attempt to make himself presentable. He looked miserable, and I felt sorry for him. The chance to entertain the Khan was a rare honor, and something had gone terribly wrong.

The Khan began to laugh. We all joined in.

"Behold, our visitor from afar!" the Khan boomed out.

After the laughter softened, Marco spoke. "I crossed many deserts to come here. So when I saw your lotus pond, I could not resist."

We laughed again. Unfamiliar with the layout of the gardens of Xanadu, he had slipped and fallen into a pond. Yet instead of acting embarrassed, he used it to his advantage.

"Are you sure you did not take the sea route?" the Khan asked.

"If I had, I would have flooded all of Xanadu."

I had never heard such hearty laughter. His thick accent, his odd expression, and his wicked smile made us laugh along with him.

"Perhaps you needed to douse the red fire of your beard," said the Khan.

"My beard was black before I crossed the desert. The flaming sun turned it red."

I could not believe it. Marco's wit saved him from a situation that might have been fatal to his hopes. I wondered how Marco could project this air of relaxed, humorous confidence when so much was at stake. Apparently, it was part of his entertaining skills, and very effective. Still, on Uncle Chimkin's face, I noticed contempt.

"Bring our honored guest some dry robes," the Khan said to a servant.

A short while later Marco emerged from a nearby room, dry and dressed in a bright green *del.* A gold belt cinched his waist, making his shoulders and chest appear broad and strong. Richly dressed like a Mongolian noble, he looked almost normal.

From his seat on the far side of the large round table, he glanced at me. His eyes twinkled with relief and mischief, mixed with admiration. *Love from a distance,* I remembered. Would his story be about courtly love? I hoped not.

A servant poured him a bowl of *airag,* and he drank deeply, as if enjoying our favorite drink of fermented mare's milk. Maybe its buzz would relax him.

Soon the Khan said, "Young Latin, are you ready to entertain us? What do you call that city you come from?"

Marco stood up, looking serious and respectful as he began his work. "Venezia," he said. "It is the finest and most splendid city of Christendom."

The men tried to get their tongues around the word and ended up mocking the bizarre sound of it. "Tell us about Way-nay-sha," the Khan commanded.

Marco placed his hands on the table as if to steady himself and control his anxiety. "Venezia—Way-nay-sha—is a city of water," he began.

"It is built on small islands. Its roads are made of water. Bridges of marble-stone cross the . . . the water-roads."

He struggled to find the right words in Mongolian. "We have special boats—long and slender. Men push them with long poles. Sometimes, at night, these men sing songs that are very . . ." He seemed unable to find the right word in our language. "Very pleasant to hear."

I tried to imagine Khanbalik's wide avenues flooded with water. How horrible to have streets made of something as unreliable as water. Marco looked at me, as if for encouragement. My cheeks flushed, and I looked down. He was showing courage, I realized. I could never have stood before a foreign king and told a story in his language.

"No one has been able to defeat Venezia, because on all sides she is protected by the sea," he continued. "In fact, she loves the sea. Once a year, our leader goes out in a boat and tosses a golden ring into the water, to symbolize Venezia's marriage to the sea."

"An excellent addition," said the Khan in a quiet voice, "to our Empire."

My eyes darted to Marco, who did not seem to have heard this comment. But Chimkin nodded to the Khan with a smile, as if accepting the Khan's order.

Something was happening under the surface that evening, and I was part of it. With his big round eyes, Marco apparently had no idea. My skin trembled with a chill.

"We Mongols are men of land," the Khan said, more loudly, to Marco. "And you were raised in a city of water. Perhaps you can never truly communicate with us."

Marco bowed his foreign bow. "I would be honored if you would let me try."

"Entertain us with a story," the Khan ordered.

Marco stood tall and took a deep breath. "Tonight I will

tell you a tale I heard during my travels. It is about a woman named Ai-Jaruk, daughter of King Khaidu, ruler of the western desert and the grasslands beyond."

Marco let his eyes rest briefly on my face, as if implying that he had chosen this story about a woman to please me. I squirmed.

The Khan's faced hardened. Khaidu was his fiercest rival, a distant cousin who claimed the right to the throne. No one dared to bring up his name in Khubilai's presence.

Marco seemed oblivious to the shift in mood. Clearly, he had practiced this tale. "Stunning she was, with a round face and shimmering black hair. Her parents named her 'Bright Moon' in the Turkic language of the western grasslands. Twice as big as an ordinary child, she grew up strong as an ox, swift as a deer, free as a wolf."

Strong as an ox, swift as a deer. I leaned forward, eager to hear this story.

"No Mongolian damsel before or since," Marco continued, "has excelled at the manly arts as did Ai-Jaruk. When she rode, the swiftest horse ran twice as fast. The arrows from her bow flew three times as far." Marco looked at me. "So strong were her muscles that by the age of twelve she could toss her wrestling master to the ground."

The men grumbled and shifted. Mongolian women are free to race and practice archery, but they are not supposed to wrestle. As a small child, I had learned the Mongolian style of wrestling, head to head, but I had stopped practicing in recent years.

Through the eyes of the Khan's men, Marco looked woefully ignorant, if not rude. The admiration I had begun to feel for him wavered. How had I been so weak as to fall under his spell?

Still, I wanted Marco to succeed. This was his big chance. His future, and that of his father and uncle, depended on pleasing the Khan that night. I should not care, but I did.

"When she reached adulthood, Ai-Jaruk's parents beseeched her to let them give her hand in marriage. But she declared that she would consent only if a prospective suitor could defeat her in a contest of strength. Any man who dared to challenge her would forfeit one hundred horses if he could not best her."

One hundred horses! Imagine, a young woman that skilled at wrestling. And she defied her parents' wishes! I thought. Marco seemed to sense that my interest was intensifying.

He smiled. "Noble young men from many tribes came to take up the challenge, bringing horses. One by one, she threw them to the ground. Month after month, they came and she defeated them. Within a few years, she accumulated ten thousand horses."

I sat back, smiling. *Ten thousand horses! Victory after victory! A woman defeating men!* Ai-Jaruk sounded superb. Maybe hearing this story would make the Great Khan want to have a strong, capable woman in his branch of the family, too.

"Finally, one day, a pleasing young prince showed up. He was strong, skillful, and so sure that he wagered one thousand horses. King Khaidu welcomed the prince, son of a wealthy king whom he desired as an ally. He ordered Ai-Jaruk to let this man defeat her so that she might have an excellent husband. 'If he is worthy of me, he will win in a fair contest,' she declared. 'I will not pretend to be weak and grant him a false victory.' "

Fortunately, Marco looked at the Khan, not at me, when he said that. All these men were fathers, and they did not like to hear of daughters who did not obey. But Ai-Jaruk's pride and defiance sent a thrill up my back. How could Marco know me so well?

"Hundreds came from distant pastures to watch Ai-Jaruk's biggest wrestling match. The contest began. The pair seemed evenly matched. They grappled. Each countered the other's move."

I gripped the edge of my seat. I felt as if I were in the crowd, watching the contest.

"The onlookers cheered as the bout lasted three times as long as most. Suddenly, Ai-Jaruk threw the prince to the ground and won! As she danced the eagle victory dance, her parents sat in shock. The prince departed, leaving behind one thousand horses."

Around me, I heard many sharp intakes of breath. But I sat tall, flushed with victory, as if I had earned the thousand horses myself.

"After that," Marco continued, "no one challenged Ai-Jaruk again. Proud of her strength, her father allowed her to accompany him to all his major battles. In recent years, she has often been seen fighting valiantly by his side. In the lands of the West, lands I traveled through, tales are often told of the skill and valor of the Bright Moon of the Desert West, Princess Ai-Jaruk."

Marco stopped. Silence filled the hall. I felt exhilarated. I didn't care what these men thought. This woman had won her freedom! She had succeeded in doing what I wanted badly—to fight in battles! Still alive, she had already become a legend.

From that moment, I wanted more than just the chance to join the army. I wanted to become a legend.

But the Great Khan did not move. The story glorified a woman—a Mongolian woman who disobeyed her father. A woman who defeated men in public. A daughter of Khaidu, a kinsman who defied the authority of the Great Khan. I wondered if the Khan had heard of Ai-Jaruk before. How true was Marco's tale?

The Khan turned to me. "What do you think of this story, Emmajin Beki?"

My face flushed. My enthusiasm had been too obvious. Now the Khan of all Khans was asking me to speak in front of these men, to give my opinion. Could I be as articulate as Marco—and as courageous?

Slowly, I stood up, scanning the faces of the men and finally turning to the Khan. I had never been good with words or good at thinking quickly. So it seemed forever before the words formed in my mind. By the time I spoke, every man was staring at me.

"O Khan of all Khans," I started. "Someday, I . . ." My words caught in my throat. I wanted them to ring out, loud and clear, but they came out soft yet firm. "I would like to be like Ai-Jaruk. I would like to fight."

The Khan threw back his large head and guffawed.

"Like Ai-Jaruk!" he said. "Huge, ugly. Thick arms, wrestling men to the ground!"

The men laughed, too. I felt like a fool. Here I was,

dressed in green silk embroidered with gold flowers, looking slender and slight, with strings of pearls hanging from my headdress. Who could imagine me fighting?

"Ah, pretty Emmajin!" the Khan said with a merry twinkle in his eye. "We don't need any Ai-Jaruks here."

His men roared. Chimkin seemed amused, looking at me as if I were a silly child.

My face burned. To me, Ai-Jaruk was inspiring. To them, she was an abomination, a big-muscled woman trying to act like a man. I felt like storming out of the room. I felt like pummeling someone, preferably the Khan of all Khans.

Marco's eyebrows twisted with sadness and concern. I did not want his sympathy. I wished I could toss a golden goblet across the table and smash him in the face with it.

But I could not. I had to sit there and smile, pretending that I enjoyed the joke, that I agreed with their scornful laughter. Thanks to Marco's choice of story, I had become part of the entertainment.

When the laughing died down, the Khan turned to his men. "The hour is late. This Latin storyteller, has he captivated you? Shall we ask him to return and tell another tale?"

Chimkin nodded. "Yes!" the men shouted.

Marco bowed in the Italian style, one hand before him and one behind. "I am honored," he said, though no one could hear him amidst the noise.

"Next time, though," said the Khan, his voice stern, "tell us a story from your homeland, not one about Mongols."

Marco Polo had been invited back, to entertain the Khan again. Despite several missteps, the evening had been a great success—for him.

But for me, having expected to be a silent observer only, it had been a disaster. Ai-Jaruk had won the right to fight by defeating dozens of suitors in wrestling, with her big thick arms. What could I possibly do, with my strong but slender arms? If the Khan was going to make an exception and let a woman fight as a soldier, he would not do it for me simply because I had asked, or because I was his eldest granddaughter.

After the banquet ended, I rushed home and changed into an old, loose *del.* Then I ran and ran, through the Khan's gardens, out the back gate, to the Khan's hunting woods. My feet pounded my anger into the ground.

Finally, panting, I stopped at the side of a man-made lake. The water reflected the moon, round and white and full, shimmering and bright with cruel promise.

Bright Moon! I thought. *Moon of Xanadu, Moon of the Desert West. Someday they will not laugh at me. Someday I will prove to them that in my own way, I can be as strong as Ai-Jaruk. Yes, even a legend.*

If Marco Polo had aimed to please me, he had miscalculated. Instead, he had exposed me as a weak and foolish girl, a dreamer. How had I ever found him attractive?

12

The Grasslands

The next day, I sent a servant to tell Marco Polo that I was not feeling well and would not meet him in the afternoon. Alone, Baatar and I rode into the hills as far as we could go. We galloped till Baatar frothed at the mouth.

The more his hooves pounded into the ground, the greater my anger grew. The Khan might as well have vowed, in front of his men, not to let me become a soldier. They had laughed at me. It had been Marco's fault. By captivating me with that story of Ai-Jaruk, by playing into my pride and my desire to become a legend, Marco had exposed me. Maybe I was foolish to think I could ever become a legend. But what right had Marco Polo, a Latin merchant, to cast me in such a light? If the Khan closed off this possibility, I had no future. If Ai-Jaruk could go to war, why couldn't I?

I needed to salvage my reputation, to make the Khan think highly of me again. There was only one way: to fulfill the Khan's assignment. To find out something vital and valuable about Marco's homeland, some weakness we could exploit. We would invade his precious Venezia. That would teach him.

So far, he had not said one thing that was useful for military strategy. I suspected he was hiding something. I could not imagine that he had come this far merely to trade. Surely his Pope would not have sent the Polos so far away without trusting them with valuable information. That was what my uncle had led me to believe.

To get him to talk, I needed to regain the upper hand, just like in wrestling. I needed to make it clear that he should not touch me again, on the shoulder or hand or anywhere else. It was not proper. He needed to learn respect, the Mongol way.

The following afternoon, I could no longer delay. It was time to see Marco.

Wearing the plainest *del* I owned, I chose a much different place to walk. Just outside the eastern gate of Xanadu stretches a large patch of grassland, wide and open to the sky. The land had originally been forested. Before my grandfather became Great Khan, when he had been a minor prince, he had ordered the trees felled to build a small palace and walled city there. When his elder brother, Mongke Khan, died suddenly of disease, my grandfather took over as Great Khan. After that, he built a new capital for the Mongol Empire, Khanbalik, and Xanadu became his summer palace.

By the time Marco and I strode out of the eastern gate, the sun had reached its noon peak, but fortunately the sky was overcast. Most Mongols would laugh at the idea of taking a stroll in the grasslands. But this Italian seemed to enjoy it. He remarked on the colorful wildflowers, the fresh green of the grasses, the bees and butterflies.

My mind overflowed with rebukes for Marco. But walking with him made me wonder if it was wrong of me to blame him for my humiliation. It was really my own fault. When the Khan asked my opinion of Ai-Jaruk, I should have said, "Such a strong woman brings great honor to her father." Of course, the right words came later.

Truth be told, I had missed Marco. I wished we could talk about the evening, make sense of it. But I was not supposed to trust him. He was not a friend, after all, but a source of information.

Now, walking close to him in the grasslands, I tried to bring to mind the words I had practiced, the questions that would get him to reveal his secrets.

As usual, he was at no loss for words. "Emmajin Beki, may I ask a question?" he said when we were far outside the city walls. "The topic may be sensitive."

This man had no sense of right and wrong. I stopped and stared at him.

"The Great Khan's feet—what is wrong with them?"

The Khan's feet were swollen and painful. That was obvious to all. He had to be carried everywhere. No one dared to discuss it. Was Marco looking for the Khan's weakness, to report to his fellow countrymen? "Why do you ask?" I said.

"In my country, there is a disease called gout. Only rich men suffer from it. I have heard of a medicine to treat gout, but it is hard to find."

"I know nothing about this subject," I said. I continued walking, wondered if Marco was hatching some kind of plot.

"What are you thinking about, Princess?"

"The story you told to the Khan."

"What about it?"

I stopped walking again and glared at him. "First, you must never—ever!—keep the Great Khan waiting."

Marco blushed. "I lost my way. Then I slipped and fell into a pond."

"You are lucky he didn't send you away forever."

Marco looked down, clearly embarrassed. He reminded me of Suren as a boy. "I was already late. There was no time to go back and change."

I shook my head. I wondered if all foreigners were so careless. "More importantly," I continued, "you should not have told a story about Khaidu. The Great Khan hates him. Khaidu claims that he has the right to be Great Khan."

Marco shook his head. "How was I to know?"

"It's safer if you don't tell stories about other Mongols. We have storytellers to investigate and tell the correct versions of these stories."

Marco picked a long strand of grass and twisted it. "Thank you, Princess. I appreciate your advice."

I had wanted to humble him, to regain the upper hand. But I felt no joy in it. It was too easy. A Mongol man would have fought back if someone had lectured him.

"What made you decide to tell the story of Ai-Jaruk?" I asked sharply.

"I heard it when I was traveling through the desert West. I thought you would like this tale. You showed such courage by competing in that archery tournament."

I tried not to blush at his obvious flattery. "You should tell the Khan a story from your homeland. You do have such stories, don't you?"

"Ah." A small smile appeared in his beard. "I loved hearing stories when I was a boy. The best were stories from France, stories of knights and ladies."

"Knights?"

"*Cavalieri,* warriors on horseback."

This sounded more promising. "Christendom has mounted warriors?"

"They wear metal armor. When they are not fighting battles, they practice their skills in tournaments, called jousting matches. Not archery, but jousting. They use lances, a kind of long pointed spear, and ride straight toward each other, trying to knock the opponent off his horse. It's a test of skill and courage."

Strange. I could not imagine two Mongol warriors doing such a thing. To be knocked off his horse would be the ultimate humiliation for a Mongol. Still, Marco was finally talking about military practices. I nodded, encouraging him to continue.

His green eyes danced as he took on his storyteller voice. "Such matches attract many onlookers, with great excitement," he said. "Colorful banners flutter in the breeze. Shields are displayed, with the symbols of different noble houses. The king and his royal family watch from a grandstand."

He was captivating me, again, with his words. "Do women compete, too?" I asked.

"No. But the ladies of the court play an important role. Before each tournament, a knight will ask a royal lady for her favor. If she wants him to win, she will give him a scarf, and he will tie it to his sleeve when he competes. She will cheer for him to win."

"Courtly love." I had hoped to hear more about this hazardous idea.

"Courtly love." Marco's eyes brimmed with mischief. "In one of our best-loved tales, a king named Arthur is famous for his wise rule, like your Khan. His queen is a beautiful young woman named Guinevere. His finest knight falls in love with her."

"He loves the queen?" That was treachery. "Our Khan would kill such a man."

He lowered his voice, as if telling me something he should not. "It is not like love between a man and his wife. It is more like worship, or adoration, of a man for a lady."

"A man worships a lady who is not his wifc?" Thc idea seemed awful and alluring.

"Yes. The knight watches a royal lady with longing, but he knows he could never have her. One day, he hopes, she will smile at him. Then he will know she admires him."

My insides shivered. I did not smile.

Marco's green eyes seemed to glow. "Of course, it is an impossible love. The knight would never touch the lady unless she wanted him to."

A frisson went up my back. "And if she refused his affections?"

"If he could not see her, he would weep and sigh. He would write poems about her, wishing he had the wings of a dove to fly back to her."

What Marco spoke of sounded both risky and appealing. What kind of place was this Christendom? "He worships a lady."

"Not like he worships God. Very different. But he loves

and admires her from afar. His love ennobles him and inspires him to do great things, to serve her."

"He would serve a lady?" Could love for a woman actually ennoble and inspire a man, rather than weaken him and distract him from his duty?

Marco grinned. "Let me show you how the knights do it."

He looked around and picked a yellow wildflower, long-stemmed and lovely. Then he took off his hat and held it before his chest. He knelt and offered me the flower.

"O noble lady, your beauty and radiance blind me. I am at your service." He looked up at me and I saw a teasing twinkle in his clear eyes, even as his voice took on a serious tone. "Please accept this flower as a token of my love."

I was so shocked I didn't know what to say. A man on his knees before a woman! Professing adoration and willingness to serve her! Women were meant to serve men, not the other way around. Then again, he was a lowly merchant, and I a member of the Khan's Golden Family. Of course, he was just acting, showing me how others did it. Still, it was strange. It was wrong. Terrible, even. But it turned my head.

Marco looked up at me with an odd combination of admiration and playfulness. A butterfly lit on his shoulder. A slight breeze shook the yellow wildflower in his hand.

My heart was bursting in my chest. My ambition had always been to be a warrior, but this foreign notion, courtly love, appealed to something so deep in me I had not known it was there. My cheeks felt hot.

I couldn't accept the flower.

"Very different from the Mongol tradition, no?" He

broke the tension and stood. Then, as naturally as if I were his little sister, he tucked the flower behind my ear.

The touch of his fingertips lit my ear on fire. I looked at him with alarm.

"I mean no harm," Marco said. "You are always safe with me. I am a merchant, not a knight. A teller of tales. I hope I did not offend you."

"You should not . . . ," I began. It took a moment to get my voice back. His eyebrows rose. "You should never, never tell such a story to the Great Khan."

Marco guffawed.

"If you did, he would . . ." I did not want to continue. *He would not trust you to spend time alone with me, ever again,* I thought. Did I trust Marco?

If Marco thought, for even one moment, that he could love me, a princess of the Khan's family, he was making a terrible mistake. A dangerous mistake. A daring, delicious mistake. No, I would have to be firm with him. I was not a lady giving her scarf to a warrior. I was preparing to be a warrior myself.

This conversation had gone too far.

I took off, running.

Marco ran behind me, through the tall grasses speckled with wildflowers. We were like two children, racing across the meadow. I was much more comfortable moving.

Marco caught up with me, ran alongside me, then sprinted ahead. I was surprised to see that he could run so fast. Here was one physical activity at which he excelled.

I veered off toward a little hilltop I knew about, and he followed me up. This hill was a berm, part of the outer defenses of Xanadu. At a strategic spot on it stood a heap of stones, taller than I was. I stopped when I reached the cairn.

"What is this?" Marco regarded the heap with curiosity.

"An *ovoo,*" I told him. "It marks a sacred place." Mixed in with the rocks were blue and white scarves that travelers had left there, to show their respect. "See? You pick up a stone from the ground and circle the *ovoo* three times, making a wish. Then you toss the stone onto the pile."

I picked up a nearby stone and began walking to my left around the *ovoo.* Marco did the same, following me. He remained quiet, respecting our custom.

After three times around, I stopped, repeated my wish inside my head, and tossed my stone onto the heap. Marco did the same.

"What was your wish?" I asked him.

Marco's grin was lopsided. "Should I tell you?"

"Yes!"

"I wished that you would not join the Khan's army."

His wish surprised me. "Why?"

He twisted his mouth. "You could be killed."

I laughed. "That's what makes it exciting."

He shook his head. "I don't like this warfare business. Too much blood. Soldiers are trained to kill. Surely you wouldn't want . . ."

My irritation returned. "Yes, I would. The most highly regarded men are the finest warriors. They are the noble ones who make a difference in the world."

"Ah, yes, sorry. We have it upside down in Venezia."

"Upside down?"

"The noble men become senators, to help govern the city. They get an education. Some buy ships or go off to trade, to bring back precious goods that make life more comfortable. Not as noble as invading countries."

It seemed he was mocking me and my desires and my people, but in such a lighthearted way it was hard to take offense.

"The young men don't wish to train to become warriors?" I asked.

"You saw how slow I was with my dagger!" He laughed. "No, most wealthy young men aspire to go to sea, to take part in trade. But it's not just to gain wealth. We travel to other countries, learn foreign languages, try to understand other people. It's an appealing life, one of adventure. In my homeland, this is considered noble work."

Upside down was right. Who would aspire to go to sea?

Marco grew serious. "Everyone suffers during wars. We traders like stability. During times of peace, we can trade with countries that are far away. This is why I admire your Great Khan. Although your armies are still fighting in China, he has established peace for thousands of miles between here and my homeland. When my father was my age, a Latin could not safely travel this far. We traders prefer peace."

"Peace!" I nearly spit. "The only way you can make peace is through conquest. And the only way to keep it is to suppress rebels and bandits, by force."

"True." Marco smiled. "But I can't help thinking there is a better way."

He seemed so naive. "A better way than conquest?"

He smiled ruefully. "It will probably seem absurd to you. But sometimes there is a role for talking things through. Maybe even a role for storytellers. Once when we were captured by fierce tribesmen in the mountains, I told them tales of our homeland. It softened their hearts and they freed us."

"You were lucky they didn't kill you," I said. "Didn't you tell me that in all those small countries in Christendom, their armies are always fighting one another?"

Marco nodded. "True. Each king has his own army. We believe each country should rule itself. We love our freedom."

"Those countries would be better off as part of the Mongol Empire," I stated. "That's their only chance of achieving greatness."

Marco observed me steadily. "Princess, how can I explain? There is dread in my land, of Mongols, whom my people call Tartars. If my people could see the splendors of Xanadu, they might change their minds. But we hear horrible stories of the hordes that invaded Christendom. Those warriors raped, looted, massacred innocents by the thousand. They cut off the ears of each person they killed."

I remembered the disembodied ears Old Master had showed us. Marco's face reflected his pain and disgust. So this was how our people were viewed in his homeland. This foreigner was cursing our revered Great Ancestor, who gave fair warning to every land he invaded, promising leniency to all who cooperated.

I straightened my back. "Eternal Heaven ordained that the Mongols conquer all lands, from the rising of the sun to the setting of the sun. This is our destiny."

The foreigner backed off, as if I had pulled out a saber. "Again, forgive me, Princess. I am but a simple merchant, not qualified to discuss the affairs of khans."

"True. You are not." I could hear the harshness in my voice. This man was saying traitorous things that could get him hanged. "Let's return," I said.

He nodded. "Emmajin Beki, I did not mean to offend you."

I kept silent. We were ending the conversation where we had begun it, with an apology.

After our walk in the grasslands, I was more confused than ever. Marco was funny and fun to be with. But his worldview and values could not have been more different from mine. Although we were not at war with this man or his homeland, clearly he and I were not on the same side. He claimed to want to serve the Khan, but when he spoke honestly, I could see he was not loyal at all. Our interests would always be in conflict.

That night, I had a vivid dream. In it, a huge army of strangers was galloping toward my house, threatening to kill everyone I knew. Before they arrived, I woke up, my heart pounding and my body covered in sweat.

13

Crucial Information

"Ignorant child!" Chimkin spoke his mind.

My tall, thin uncle sat on a wide, throne-like chair raised several steps above the floor in his own chambers, as if practicing for the day when he would be Great Khan.

It had been hard to decide what to report to my uncle. I told him of the mounted warriors, how they practiced skills by jousting. Of course I had not mentioned courtly love. But I did tell him that the people of Christendom feared our Mongol army, that the little kingdoms fought each other, and that I had told Marco Polo that those countries would be better off as part of our Empire. That didn't sound ignorant to me.

"You might as well have said we were raising an army to invade his homeland."

Were we raising an army to invade Marco's homeland? I dared not ask.

He sighed. "You have much to learn about gathering intelligence. We are looking for the chink in their armor, the best way to take advantage of their weakness."

Uncle Chimkin might as well have been speaking Latin. What was I to look for? He seemed impatient and angry with me, as well as the foreigners at court.

"Emmajin Beki." His voice was calmer now. "I have told the Great Khan that you have provided some useful information, and that you are learning Latin. Suren has asked me to take you with me on my next military venture. I can only do that if you do well."

My heart rose. Did he mean as a warrior?

"The Khan has entrusted me with the task of pacifying the West. His attention now is on the South, on the conquest of China. Once that is completed, I plan to convince him to send several divisions to the West. Working with our fellow Mongols in Russia and Persia, it should be an easy romp to conquer the rest of the Western lands."

My heart clenched. "Including Christendom?"

"Yes. Suren and Temur are learning other languages from that part of the world. I am watching all of you, to see whether you might prove useful to me."

My thoughts tumbled on top of each other. Perhaps there was hope after all. In spite of his judgment that I was an ignorant child, my uncle thought I could play a role of some sort in the army. He was not talking about making me a soldier, but to travel with the army! With Suren! It seemed too good to be true.

Yet how could I take part in the conquest of Christendom, and join a military horde thundering toward Venezia?

Now that I knew Marco, I had begun to question my long-held beliefs.

"I would be honored," I said, bowing my head slightly, to show humility and obedience. What could I do to win his favor?

"Continue with your work. Learn the foreigner's language. Hide your opinions and feelings. Get him to trust you. If he becomes suspicious, he will stop talking to you." I nodded and he continued. "Act friendly, but do not take his side or help him. Probe for that crucial piece of information, the chink in their armor."

"Yes, Uncle."

"Above all, never mention anything about plans to invade his homeland. The Great Khan has not made any final decision."

"I will do as you say," I replied. I left his chambers full of hope and confusion.

Marco was charming and witty, a good friend if not more. He had all but declared his love for me. I knew he was only partly teasing. One word from me, and it could be more than jest. Somehow, he had managed to declare his heart without making me feel awkward or threatened. My feelings for him were jumbled, but I was flattered.

Now my own heart's desire seemed within reach. Chimkin might be willing to intervene with the Khan and let me join the army. Yet at what price? I had dreamed of galloping off with the army. But Marco's words had put doubts in my mind. How would I feel riding off to the West to conquer Marco's homeland? All his talk of peace kept repeating in my head.

What an impossible situation! I had always been loyal to my Khan and my people, but now that loyalty required me to make an enemy of a man who was gradually becoming my friend.

The next time I went to Marco's *ger*, a few days later, he was not alone. Standing with him were two older men, also Latins.

Marco looked uneasy. "Princess Emmajin. Let me introduce you to my father, Niccolo Polo, and my uncle, Maffeo Polo."

I nodded at them. "Welcome to Xanadu. You are feeling better now?"

"Yes, thank you." His father, thin and intense, angular and sharp, had hawkish eyes of dark gray, not green like Marco's. Beneath his neatly trimmed beard, his thin lips tensed in a straight line.

Uncle Maffeo, tall and big-bellied, with pure white hair and beard, coughed so deeply he had trouble stammering out his greeting. "A pleasure to meet you."

Although he was a large, imposing man, I immediately felt sympathy for him. "The journey from Khanbalik was not too hard, I hope?" I said.

"We want come earlier. We send apologies to Khan," responded Marco's father. "We stay rest of summer here." His Mongolian was choppier than Marco's, and his accent much thicker. His manner—distant, formal, dry—contrasted with Marco's charm.

I nodded, sensing that the rest of my summer would be much more constrained. My days of lighthearted fun with

Marco had ended. The Khan had assigned me to get to know all three Latins. Perhaps these older men knew more important information about their homeland than Marco did.

Uncle Maffeo began coughing again. Marco tapped his back with care and affection while I stood awkwardly.

Marco's father ignored the coughing and continued, his voice sleek and oily. "I trust my son has pleased the Khan of all Khans."

"Yes. The Great Khan has invited him back to his banquet hall to tell another tale." I remembered that the success of their trading mission depended on the Khan's goodwill. I suspected that Niccolo Polo thought of little else.

With a pang, I realized that it would no longer be possible for me to see Marco alone. No more talk of courtly love. That should have pleased me. I would have safety in numbers. But part of me, a part I was trying to suppress, felt disappointed.

That first day, I took them into a pavilion in the garden. Marco asked me to repeat to them many of the things I had told him about myself and about Xanadu. In their presence, Marco was more subdued.

"Your son has told me about your homeland, Venezia," I said to his father. "I hope to visit it someday."

His father's eyebrows shot up. But his uncle smiled. "We would welcome visitors from the Khan's court. But is a long journey for a lady."

I smiled at him, practicing hiding my thoughts. "Of course. I have never traveled. But I enjoy hearing about distant lands. Marco tells me you have visited many lands."

After that day, every five days, I walked in the gardens or the grasslands or rode in the hills with Marco, his father, and his uncle. On other days, I was free to spend time as I wished, racing and competing against Suren and the other cousins. Each time I met with the Latins, I looked for the chink in their armor, half hoping I would not find it.

Marco's father was cautious around me, erecting walls of defense, and did not divulge any information about his homeland. His uncle Maffeo, though, seemed more relaxed and told many stories, often humorous. His health gradually improved.

As for Marco and me, our friendship resumed the formal distance it should always have had. Marco, ever talkative, continued to tell me stories of his homeland and of their journey. I asked about the various kings and emperors, trying to remember which had the strongest armies. His uncle patiently taught me many words of Latin until I could stammer out a few sentences, including my favorite, *"Deus amat Mongoliam."* That means "God loves Mongolia." I also asked many questions about the Religion of Light but found the answers confusing.

Marco never again brought up the subject of how fearful the Mongol army looked to his countrymen. Nor did he touch me. But he had already said enough, and I could see admiration and longing in his eyes.

After each talk, I reported to my uncle. One of his men listened to my report and wrote down some of the things I said. No matter how many names of places and kings I memorized, nothing seemed to light up Chimkin's eyes. Even Suren could find out nothing further about how likely it might be that I could join the army.

Every day, I felt torn. In my effort to achieve my own dream, I was collecting information that might someday destroy Marco's beloved homeland. The more I learned of the lovely waterways of Venezia and the grand cathedrals of Rome, the more I realized that conquest by the Khan's troops might harm them more than help them.

Seventh Moon waxed hot, and Eighth Moon hotter. Women sat in the shadiest parts of the garden and fanned themselves with silk fans. Men cursed, hopped on their horses, and rode far afield. This was the hottest summer Xanadu had ever seen.

Marco continued to amuse the Khan with his stories, but I was not invited again. Suren and Temur were sometimes invited. From what Suren told me, it seemed that Marco learned quickly what type of stories pleased the Khan—mostly tales of the lands he had visited on his travels, the quirks and lore of the people he had observed.

Suren began to teach me a little swordsmanship, though we had to do it in secret. He passed on to me what he had learned from the sword master. We arose early each morning to spend several hours practicing, in a small clearing hidden in the woods.

By late in Eighth Moon, I was growing worried. The summer was nearing its end and I had not discovered any information about Marco's homeland that would be useful to our army. I began to despair. How could I find what my uncle had asked for?

One hot day, Marco's father did not come out with us. He had to meet someone about his trading business. But his uncle joined us for a walk in the garden. To avoid the midday heat, we met in the morning and sat near a pleasant waterfall.

Uncle Maffeo was built like a huge bear, but he was far gentler than Marco's wiry, tense father. In his brother's presence, the uncle spoke little, but on that day, he became affable and talkative.

He and I were sitting on a marble bench, chatting about his travels, when Uncle Maffeo mentioned the "Holy Land."

"Tell me more about this Holy Land," I said. "It is in Christendom?"

Uncle Maffeo smiled and wiped his pink forehead, which was streaming with sweat. "Marco, you didn't tell her about the Holy Land?" he asked with a smile.

Marco must have shaken his head. He stood behind me, in the shade of a tree.

"The Holy Land is where our Lord Jesus lived," Uncle Maffeo explained. "All of Christianity is based on his life and teachings. Let me show you where it is."

As Marco had done once before, Uncle Maffeo picked up a stick and drew a map in the dirt at our feet. The Holy Land was at the eastern edge of the Middle-of-the-Earth Sea, and Christendom lay north and west of it.

As he was drawing, I felt a slight touch on the back of my neck, between my braids. Startled, I turned my head. Marco smiled gently, holding up his finger to show a tiny bead of sweat he had tenderly wiped from my neck. I smiled at him.

He had not touched me since that day in the grasslands when he had tucked a flower behind my ear. I sensed he was feeling, as I was, sad that our days together in Xanadu would be over soon.

"We Christians fought hard to take back the Holy Land," Maffeo explained. "But the Muslims—the Saracens, from

Arabia—stole most of it back from us. We've sent armies again and again, for years, to win back the Holy Land from the infidels. Every man in Christendom knows the importance of this duty. It's God's will."

My braids lifted off my back. Marco was trying to help me feel cooler. Each time he touched me, I lost track of what his uncle was saying. God's will, of course, was that the Mongols conquer every land, but I was feeling too good to argue.

"If only the Mongols would help us," Uncle Maffeo was saying.

My attention returned. "Help you do what?"

"Take back the Holy Land! That's what the Pope's letter to the Khan was all about, and we're hoping the Khan will agree. The Pope's fondest dream is that the Khan will form an alliance with Christendom, to retake the Holy Land."

"I'm confused," I said. "How would that work?"

"If the Mongol troops came from the East, from Persia, like this," he said, drawing in the dirt an arrow pointing to the Holy Land, "then all the kings and princes in Christendom would travel from the West to join them, with their finest soldiers." He drew lines over the sea, showing that they would come by ship. "With our combined forces, we could finally drive the Saracens out of the Holy Land!" Uncle Maffeo seemed as thrilled as a Mongol commander planning a battle.

In the meantime, Marco seemed to be drawing a map with a light finger on my back. I felt like shivering with pleasure but did not want his uncle to notice. I had to focus hard to pay attention to Uncle Maffeo's words.

"Wait," I said. "All the kings of Christendom would take

their finest soldiers?" *And leave their homelands undefended?* I did not add.

"Yes. All warriors want to go to the Holy Land to earn glory for Christendom."

"With the best soldiers far away, who would defend the homelands?" I asked.

Marco's fingertips felt delightful, like a cool breeze on a stifling day. But he stopped as suddenly as he had started touching my back. I wanted Uncle Maffeo to keep talking so Marco would touch me again.

"Oh, that would not be a problem," Uncle Maffeo continued. "No one would attack a fellow Christian country during a Crusade."

Uncle Maffeo looked up, and Marco stepped back, away from me.

A thought jumped into my mind. While I had been concentrating on Marco's touch, Uncle Maffeo had given me the crucial piece of information I had been seeking. If all the best troops of Christendom could be tricked into leaving their homelands to fight in the Holy Land, far away, our Mongol troops could sweep in across the northern plains and take over Vienna, Paris, Venezia, Roma.

I stared at the dirt map and imagined a long, sharp arrow starting from Russia and moving overland toward Venezia, even as the ships, filled with Christian troops, left Christendom undefended. If another division of Mongol troops cooperated with the Latins to take over the Holy Land, that could be added to our Empire, too. Surely the Latins could not expect to keep it if we conquered it. The whole West would fall at once, into our Empire. It seemed so neat, so easy.

At last, I had something to report to Prince Chimkin.

Uncle Maffeo stood up, panting. "Too hot," he said. "Shall we return?"

All night, tossing, I could feel a tingling on each spot of my shoulders and neck and back where Marco's fingers had stroked me. It was wrong to think of Marco that way. Forbidden. I knew I had to report the conversation to my uncle, even if it meant the destruction of Marco's beloved Venezia. This was the only path that might lead me to a position in the army and a life of adventure. But my heart felt severed.

14

Overheard

Xanadu, by its very design, was supposed to protect the Khan and his guests from the heat. Breezes blew through the green valley, and shade trees were plentiful in the garden and the surrounding hillsides. Pavilions and halls were designed to catch the wind. But I felt sweat-drenched by noon each day. Although I knew all the places renowned for their coolness, I could not find any place to escape the heat.

One morning in the middle of Eighth Moon, Marco arrived for our walk late—and alone. Both his father and uncle were feeling weak from the heat. It seemed I would have one last chance to see him alone before the summer ended. Yet what would I say?

"Princess, I hope you can help me," Marco said as we walked toward the gardens. "My father is anxious. We delivered all our trading goods to the Khan in Fifth Moon, and we have heard nothing. The Khan continues to enjoy my stories, but he has not rewarded me. We need goods to take back to the West."

"When do you plan to return to the West?" I asked, dreading the answer.

"As soon as the Khan will allow it."

Marco had never before made a direct request. "I will see what I can find out."

"Gratias!" he said, which I knew means "thank you" in Latin.

To find a shadier place to sit, where no one would overhear us, I suggested to Marco that we enter the forbidden part of the gardens, an area only the Khan and his guests could enter. This smaller garden had more trees—willows, pines, and cypresses—and more shade. It was accessible only through a guarded gate. But as children, Suren and I had found a secret way to enter the inner garden from the roof of a small gazebo.

Marco hesitated, but I assured him it would be safe on such a hot day.

Making sure no one saw us, I climbed onto the roof of the gazebo and clambered over the wall into the Khan's private garden. Marco followed. We walked along a pond surrounded by graceful willows and into a pine grove that would have been cool had there been the slightest breeze. I headed toward a midsize pavilion made of gilded cane, thinking to sit in the shade inside.

When we were just behind the pavilion, I heard voices coming from inside. The wooden window shutters, carved with beautiful scenes and paned with thin paper, were open to allow air into the pavilion. I heard the unmistakable booming voice of the Khan.

Nothing could have been more perilous than walking in the Khan's private garden with a foreigner. What had muddled my mind? I ducked below a window, holding my breath. Silently, I eased myself into a sitting position. Marco sat beside me. He pointed back to the grove, as if to say, *Shall we get away?*

I shook my head. The area around us was too exposed, too visible from the Khan's pavilion. We were lucky no one had seen us arrive. Now that I knew there were men in the pavilion, I could not think of any way we could flee without being noticed.

Seeing my fear reflected in Marco's eyes, I stayed put under the window. I hoped the men would go away and leave us free to escape. Why would the Khan hold a meeting on the hottest day of Eighth Moon?

"Good news indeed!" the Khan was saying. "We are winning battle after battle in southern China. If our luck continues, we shall conquer their capital at Kinsay and have a victory parade in Khanbalik not long after the New Year Festival."

Another victory parade? I listened closely. Perhaps I could take part in it.

"After twenty years of fighting, it will be the biggest victory of all," another man said. "Subduing the Chinese has been harder than anyone could have imagined."

"Your Majesty's Empire will stretch from the forests of the Far North to the seas of the South—far larger than any Chinese dynasty." It was my uncle Chimkin's voice. He seemed near the window. I shuddered and ducked my head lower.

"A toast to our great General Bayan and his troops! May

their triumphs continue!" The Khan seldom toasted anyone else. While the musicians played and the men drank, we could have escaped, but my curiosity got the better of me. Maybe I could be sent to the South to help in the final conquest of southern China, instead of to the West.

Marco looked alert as he scanned the landscape for ways to escape.

My grandfather's voice resounded with confidence. "Today is the day I have been waiting for. We begin planning our final conquests, of those parts of the world we have not yet occupied. When this campaign is finished, we shall rule the entire world."

His men cheered. Marco's thick eyebrows twisted.

The Khan's voice grew softer. Leaning closer to the wall, I strained to hear more. I hoped Marco couldn't understand this formal court language. "After the conquest of China, we must be ready to move on the next front. I need to decide which of the three options it will be. Let me hear your reports."

That should have been another signal to run, but my muscles were frozen as stiff as those of a deer standing still to avoid the detection of a nearby hunter.

A man began speaking. I recognized the voice as that of one of the Khan's generals. He recommended invading Zipangu, Land of the Rising Sun, a set of islands east of Korea. This would require an enormous fleet of ships, and it might take two years to build them.

Another man reported on a huge land called India, famous for rubies and spices, elephants and tigers. To get a large army there, though, would require sending troops over the highest mountain ranges in the world. On the other side lay a country called Burma. Burmese soldiers had recently clashed with Mongol troops in the mountains. The king of Burma had threatened to invade China, and our army had to stop him if he did.

The names of these faraway countries meant little to me.

Finally, Chimkin spoke. I shut my eyes to listen, afraid of Marco's reaction. "Many lands in the West remain unconquered. Our Mongol kinsmen control Persia and Russia. But now we know that many small countries lay behind that—in Christendom."

Inches from my side, Marco flinched. My eyes flew open.

The Khan spoke up. "Why Christendom? As we have heard from our storyteller, these countries are weak and poor, with no good sources of gold or gemstones."

"Certainly, Your Majesty," said Chimkin. "We also know they have many skilled artisans, a useful addition to our Empire. More important, our spy has come up with a simple, elegant solution."

I closed my eyes tight again, hoping Marco did not know the Mongolian word for "spy."

Chimkin continued. "Those Latins have long been obsessed with one goal: taking back their so-called Holy Land. If we offer to cooperate with them to remove the Saracens from their holy city of Jerusalem, they would quickly send their finest troops to the Holy Land. That would leave their homelands undefended. Our Mongol troops could easily sweep in from the north and east, from Russia, conquering all of Christendom in a matter of months. Then the Mongol Empire would stretch from sea to sea."

Marco gripped his forehead. I thought of the countries he had described, their kings and queens, their languages and history, their churches. They could soon be destroyed, because of me. What Marco thought was a charming friendship with a Mongol princess could turn into the defeat of all the lands of Christendom.

"Sea to sea," said the Khan, as if he liked the sound of it.

"Your choice of a spy turned out to be excellent, Great Khan," Chimkin said. "At first she provided little useful information. But I give her credit for this brilliant strategy she picked up from talking with the foreigners. They revealed too much."

This was what I had dreamed Chimkin would privately report to the Khan, to prove my loyalty and competence to join the army. But I had never imagined that Marco would hear these words. This was a living nightmare.

I felt as if a saber had sliced through my head and body.

15

Betrayal

Marco nearly stood up, but I pulled him down. If he made his presence known, we could both be killed. His eyes burned with angry disbelief. He grabbed my arm and squeezed it hard, with more strength than I had thought he had. I winced in pain and closed my eyes. With an easy wrestling move, I could have pushed him away, but not without making noise.

"Airag!" shouted the Khan. I could hear servants shuffling to refill goblets, and a lone musician, a flutist, struck up music as the Khan likely took a drink.

That was the signal I had been waiting for. When the men drank, they would probably not look out the window. Awkwardly, I started to run, nearly dragging Marco. We raced across the open space to the pine trees.

Panting, we ran without stopping until we reached the section of wall where we had entered. I quickly found a foothold and pulled myself up to the top of the wall and over to the other side, landing with a thunk on the pavilion roof. Wincing with pain, I reached my hand down to help Marco, who was heavier and less agile.

He wavered, as if unwilling to touch my traitorous hand. But it was his only way to get out. His hate-filled eyes cut into my heart. He reached up and I tugged with all the arm strength I had developed in my years of wrestling. His body lurched over the wall. He landed on his side on the roof and slipped out of my hands. He slid down and rolled off, landing on a rock with a crack.

Sure that I heard a sound of pursuit on the other side of the wall, I jumped off the roof and ran toward the far side of a hill, leading Marco into a small grove of trees not visible from the inner wall.

I dashed behind a pagoda, jumped across a stream, and ran to the edge of the garden's outer wall, then dove under some thick bushes. Finally, I found what I was seeking—a spot under a sprawling evergreen where Suren and I had hidden as children. Even as I crouched on the ground, the branches hit my head, but this spot was protected and hidden.

For a long moment, I could not hear Marco following me. Had he been captured? What was taking him so long? Then I heard a stumbling noise in the woods.

"Over here," I called in a loud whisper. He was moving slowly and awkwardly. "Quick!" I called out again.

Marco crashed into the site and collapsed, breathing heavily. He grabbed his ankle and grimaced in pain. I put my hand on his, with a surge of concern, but he pushed it away. I could well imagine his thoughts.

We stayed there, silent, until our breathing calmed down.

I listened and could hear no shouting or sounds coming after us. Marco moaned for a while, then stopped.

When I finally dared look at him, he was staring at me.

"Well. An excellent spy," he said, shaking his head. "What a brilliant strategy we revealed to you, a way to trick us into leaving our homeland undefended so that the Mongols could invade and conquer. How could I have trusted you so?"

My first reaction was defensive. "You know I serve the Great Khan," I said. "That is my highest loyalty. Does that surprise you?" My words felt cold and hard.

"From the beginning, then, your purpose was to gather information about my homeland, so the Great Khan could decide how best to invade and conquer it."

I looked away, watching the bushes for signs of movement. That had been the Khan's purpose in assigning me to this task. I had succeeded. Now it felt wrong.

At what point during the summer had my feelings changed? During that elephant pavilion ride with the Khan, my choices had appeared clear and simple: Loyal without question, I had wanted to prove myself capable by gathering the information the Khan had requested. Then, gradually, meeting by meeting, in the gardens and grasslands, I had learned to see the world through Marco's eyes. Now loyalty to one man felt like betrayal to another.

Those jade eyes bored into me, and I needed to defend myself. "It was my assignment, before I knew your name, Marco Polo. If I do well, I will be allowed to join the Khan's army. That is my dream." Even as I said the words, I thought, *What have I done?* This man had never harmed me, never tried to control me. He had trusted me. Now I had sown the seeds of the destruction of his homeland.

Marco rolled over onto his back, still clutching his ankle. "What a fool I've been."

I looked again at his thick curly beard, his reddish hair, his delicate lips, his well-formed eyebrows over those deep-set eyes whose color changed in every light. How often had he made me laugh and forget my worries? Just as I had shown him the sights of Xanadu, he had introduced me to the wonders of the world beyond, painting verbal pictures. I blushed as I remembered the map he had traced on my back.

I reached to touch his shoulder. "Marco, I . . ."

He rolled his head in my direction, and I cringed at the deep disgust in his face. I hated the person he saw.

"Marco. I wanted to tell you. But what could I say?"

His face darkened with anger.

Marco laughed bitterly. "Ah, Emmajin Beki. My noble lady." His sarcasm dripped like acid onto burnished metal. "We Latins are people, like you. We love our homeland as much as anyone."

My face burned. When I had told my uncle about the strategy, I had felt torn. But I had assumed that Marco would never know of my role. Now it seemed possible, even likely, that the Khan would send me on a mission to invade Marco's homeland. Instead of triumph, I felt shame.

Venezia was far away, and Marco was here, glaring at me. Now that I had lost his friendship, his admiration, I realized how much I cared for him. My heart felt stabbed.

Once we knew we had not been followed, Marco leaned on me and limped back to his *ger.* His anger and resentment weighed heavy on my shoulder.

He did not say good-bye. I was certain I would never speak to him again.

16

Commission

Finally, it rained in Xanadu. A heavy storm one night blew branches off trees and watered the parched grasses of the meadows. The thunder and lightning woke me. At first, it seemed a punishment by Tengri, Eternal Heaven. But no lightning struck in the valley of Xanadu, so we took it as a good sign: God's anger was directed elsewhere.

The next morning, the grasses shone greener and the world seemed made afresh. A cool breeze softened the air, chasing away the heavy humidity.

Suren and I grabbed our swords and headed for our secret clearing in the woods. We began our daily practice, slashing cloth-wrapped sword against sword. Thunks and whaps rang out, instead of clangs of metal. The slices and blows were a wonderful way to vent my anger and confusion.

We had not been practicing long when we heard the sounds of horses crashing through the trees to our secluded site. The entourage was hidden until the last minute.

Entering our clearing was the Great Khan's palanquin, carried by six servants. When they had pushed up the last twist of trail, they carefully lowered the carriage, draped in imperial yellow silk covered with dragons.

Suren and I froze. We had no time to run or hide the signs of our forbidden activity. We bowed low, heads to the ground, swords laid out before us in the wet grass. When we heard the cloth pulled aside, we shouted, "Long live the Khan of all Khans!"

The Khan's servants lifted him out, wooden seat and all, and carried him to a high spot of ground.

"Arise."

We rose and faced our grandfather. Apparently, my training was not a secret. Suren and I stood with spines stiff, he stocky and thick, and I lanky and thin. I heard Suren take a sharp breath. Would the Khan punish him for teaching me swordsmanship?

"Prince Suren, Emmajin Beki, I have heard that a woman is learning swordsmanship in these woods."

We bowed our heads. I should have sought his permission. Now I was getting my beloved cousin in trouble.

"I have come to watch you practice."

Suren glanced sideways at me, clearly apprehensive. He had made progress, working with the master, but still we handled our swords like beginners.

I spoke. "Our skills are meager. We have little to show to one who has watched the greatest swordsmen in the world."

The Khan laughed deeply and switched to his familiar tone of address, used only within families. "Show me what you have learned so far."

Suren glanced at me, and I smiled to put him at ease.

Maybe now I could show the Khan directly that I was worthy of becoming a soldier, not just a spy.

I picked up my cloth-wrapped sword, and Suren did the same. We took our stances. I made the first thrust, and Suren parried. Thunk. Whap. Our muffled swords crossed and thrust. I focused hard, trying to remember all I had learned.

Suren made an error, exposing his left arm. I could have pretended to cut it off, but I did not. Instead, I thrust to his right, and I saw realization in his eyes at the last moment. I did not want him to look bad before the Khan.

Although it was practice, the swords were heavy, and we were soon out of breath and sweating.

"Hah!" I shouted. It was the sound we used to end a fight. Suren stopped, his sword high against mine. We froze in that pose for a moment, then dropped our swords to our sides and bowed again to the Khan.

The Khan smiled. "You do not want to kill each other?"

Suren again looked at me, uncertain.

So I spoke: "We are both Mongols and kin. No need to kill today."

The Khan laughed. He tried to stand, and two servants rushed to his side. He wobbled, and his swollen feet would not hold him. He sat again, hard, but on the edge of his fur-covered seat. "You have learned much in a short time."

Suren spoke with fervor. "We are eager to cut down the enemies of the Khan."

The Khan smiled. "Suren, son of Chimkin, you will make a fine soldier."

Suren breathed relief. The Great Khan had not reprimanded him.

Then our grandfather turned his eyes toward me. "Emmajin Beki. Come."

I approached him, my head bowed. The Khan knew everything and did nothing by chance. Did he know I had overheard his military strategy?

The Khan spoke. "You handle a sword better than I expected. But you are more woman than warrior."

I stiffened, then summoned my courage to speak. "I can be both."

The Khan smiled, looking surprised and indulgent. "I have been watching you all summer. Your uncle Chimkin thinks you have grown strong. He says you have carried out your assignment well. Much better than anyone expected."

I nodded but did not smile, remembering Marco's pain.

"What did you learn from the foreigner?"

"Christendom seems defenseless," I said. "It is divided into many countries."

He nodded as if asking me to continue.

I paused, trying to think of the right words. I needed to sound both wise and loyal. Yet I spoke from the heart. "I have learned that the world is large. That every land has good people as well as bad. That no decision can be taken lightly. That the Khan's wise rule can"—my voice faltered—"*will* unite all the peoples of the world and bring peace and prosperity." It was not exactly what Marco had taught me. But I wished it to be true.

The Khan's thin eyebrows rose.

"The foreigner, Marco Polo," I continued, "wishes to return to his homeland, with goods to trade." The Khan's eyebrows joined. "If that is the Khan's wish," I added.

"My plans for the young Latin are up to me," he said.

I gulped and nodded. Why had I risked my future by asking a favor for Marco? Still, I could not help adding, "He has served you well, and pleased you as a storyteller."

The Khan tapped his finger on his armrest. "I am considering an invasion of the Latin's homeland. Your uncle Chimkin says your Latin words and your knowledge could prove useful. Would you be prepared to join this expedition?"

Suddenly, I had the choice of betraying Marco or my homeland. I knew the Khan was testing me, to see if I sympathized too much with the foreigner. If I said the wrong thing, I would never be able to join the army.

"I would like to fight against enemies of the Empire, but not in Christendom."

Suren sucked in his breath, and the Khan stared at me. While I knew this was not the right answer, something had changed inside me during the summer in Xanadu. If given a choice, I would not take part in the invasion of Marco's homeland.

"You must face a hard truth, young Emmajin," the Khan said. "All enemies are people, like Marco. Every man you kill in battle has a father, an uncle, a homeland, some skill, perhaps a sense of humor. Everyone who joins the army must learn that."

The Great Khan was right. It had been weakness that had made me identify with that foreigner. Soldiers needed to show strength. But finally the Khan had said the words I had ached to hear: "join the army." I had already betrayed Marco. It was time to be loyal to my dreams.

Calm confidence flowed through me. I no longer felt confused or angry, embarrassed or humiliated. I regarded him steadily. "If the Great Khan gives me the honor of being the first woman soldier in his army, I will strive to bring you glory."

He cocked his head, as if not understanding. "But you would not obey my orders to invade that man's homeland."

I straightened my back. "I obeyed your orders by reporting what the foreigner told me about his homeland. As a soldier, I will obey any orders the Khan gives."

"Good," said the Khan. "Then I will let you train with the army, in Ninth Moon."

I bowed my head and closed my eyes, flooded with relief and gratitude.

At last I had resolved the battle in my heart. Face to face with the Khan, I had spoken up for what I thought Marco wanted. Against all odds, the Khan had allowed me to join the army anyway.

My blood pounded so fiercely that my head felt light. I was ready to leave my childhood behind. I was prepared to venture into the real world of battles and conquest in the Khan's army. Now I had to forget about Marco and prove myself a good soldier.

PART II

Journey to Carajan

17

The Army

On the last day of Eighth Moon, the Great Khan and his court left Xanadu and returned to the capital in Khanbalik. This time, I rode with Suren, and we were high with enthusiasm. My joy about joining the army the next day helped me to bury my still-simmering regrets about Marco. My independent adult life was about to begin. Temur, too, had been permitted to join. Good-hearted Suren did not seem to mind.

When I arrived home, I found on my bed a fur-lined military-style coat, a fur cap with ear flaps, thick felt leggings, a new pair of leather riding boots, and a set of leather armor. Beside them lay a white *del,* embroidered with the insignia of the Khan's army, made of smooth, firm silk. Clearly, someone from the military had delivered them, at the Khan's orders. I held the *del* to my face, feeling its texture against my cheek.

This type of silk, I knew, was a special fabric used only for the army. It was famous from the stories of Chinggis Khan's conquests, a layer of silk worn under the leather armor, so tightly woven that arrows could not pierce it. Mongol soldiers astounded their enemies, because when an arrow struck them, they could pull it out of their armor, toss it aside, and continue fighting. A surge of gratitude overwhelmed me as I held the first tangible sign that I was truly to become one of those soldiers.

I ran my fingers over the leather armor, a cuirass designed to cover the front and back of the torso. It was made of overlapping strips of lacquered black leather and laced with rawhide thongs, and it had flaplike sleeves. The flap that protected the right arm had no laces. That made me smile. The right arm needed to be free for shooting during battle.

I tried on the armor. It was remarkably flexible but still it made my body feel stiff and masculine. I tucked my braids inside and pulled the cap over my head. I wished they had given me weapons, as well. In my room, I pretended to wield a curved saber.

"Why are you doing this?" My mother was standing outside the bedroom door. At her side, Drolma had twisted her face into a look of disgust.

I walked over to my mother and gave her the gentlest expression I could. "You know me. I have always loved archery. I can think of no greater honor."

She looked up at where the wall met the ceiling. "I tried to discourage you."

"No more need to worry about my betrothal. The next suitor will be for Drolma."

Drolma sighed. "No one will want to marry me now."

"If I bring glory to our family, every general's son will want to marry you," I said.

Now my mother sighed. I thought I saw her blink back a tear.

"This is only training," I said. "I will be at a camp south of the city. I am not going far away." But no soldier trains for long. Ultimately, I would go far away.

Early the next morning, the first day of Ninth Moon, filled with exhilaration and apprehension, I donned my military garments and packed a bag of belongings, enough to last several weeks. Clad in full armor, I looked like a soldier in every way, except for my hair. My chest under bulky clothing was flat enough that I could pass for male.

Suren smiled when he saw me. We were overdressed for that late summer day, and no one wore armor within the city limits. But we couldn't help wearing every item.

"You look intimidating," I said, teasing him. "Where is Temur?"

"My father decided he should train with a different battalion."

Good, I thought. Temur would not be competing with us as we learned new skills.

I wished Marco could see me outfitted as a soldier. He had returned to Khanbalik with his father and uncle, I had heard, but I did not know his plans. I wondered if the Khan had given them enough treasures to enable a return journey. Thinking of Marco made my heart hurt. I wished I had been able to say a proper good-bye.

Suren and I rode together to the camp where we would begin training. We were to be among three hundred new recruits for the Khan's personal guards, the *kashik.* This was the elite of the army, a roster of ten thousand men. It included many of the Khan's close relatives, as well as select

Mongolian noblemen and sons of high commanders. The rest were chosen on a competitive basis, the best of every battalion. These soldiers remained near the Khan, so they seldom went to war as a unit, but the Khan selected men from this group for special missions.

When Suren and I arrived, most of the recruits had already lined up for inspection. Each holding a bow, they were standing in rows, in three companies of one hundred. All were dressed, like us, in full armor.

For his personal guard, the Khan chose Mongols from many different clans, mixing them so no one clan could conspire against him. Cathayans were not permitted, since they outnumbered us and could not be trusted to support the Khan's rule. But other foreigners, such as Turks and Tibetans, were allowed to join in small numbers if they were from clans allied to the Golden Family through marriage. They were called in-laws. I recognized only one face, that of Jebe, General Aju's son.

It was a crisp fall day with a high, clear blue sky and a slight breeze. It had rained overnight and the ground was muddy. Most of the training would be done by a lower officer, but that day the Khan's son, Chimkin, stood before them, tall and handsome.

I struggled to suppress my doubts. Earning the Khan's permission might have been easier than earning the respect of my fellow soldiers would be. Suren and I tied up our horses, took our bows, and walked toward the troops. We stopped at a respectful distance. Many of the men glanced at us, so Chimkin followed their looks. I stood as straight as I could.

I detected a look of annoyance on Chimkin's face. Suren and I had felt certain that we were on time, but instead, we had disappointed him by arriving late. We advanced and stood beside him, facing the troops. I heard murmurs of surprise when they realized I was a woman.

"Soldiers of the Great Khan!" The recruits stood stiffly at attention when Chimkin addressed them in a loud, firm voice. Chimkin held his arm out toward my cousin. "You have the honor of training with my son, Prince Suren, eldest grandson of the Khan of all Khans! Show your respect."

The men fell to their knees and put their foreheads on the ground. Suren looked embarrassed. No one had ever kowtowed to him.

"Rise!" Chimkin continued. They did. He pointed to me. "We also have a woman from the court, Emmajin Beki." No mention of my father, Prince Dorji.

The men stayed silent. Some soldiers, I suspected, would consider it bad luck to have a woman soldier in the army. But these were recruits, eager to please. "The Great Khan has honored us with the command that this girl be allowed to train with us."

I gazed into the sea of faces, trying to seem more confident than I felt. I saw curiosity but not hostility or alarm. Could I keep up with them?

Chimkin did not ask the soldiers to kowtow to me, of course. No one bowed to a woman, except that Latin Marco Polo. Why was I thinking of him now?

"Make room for the new soldiers."

Two of the men in the front row moved out of the front ranks. Suren and I took these spots, front and center, and turned to face our commander, General Chimkin. I held my bow at exactly the same angle as the others and matched the stance of the other men.

I had done it! I stood among the soldiers of the Great Khan's army. A dizzying rush of excitement rose from my gut to my head, and a huge smile spread inside me, hidden behind the stern mask on my face. I was a part of the great Mongol army, which had conquered most of the lands of the world.

"Soldiers of the Great Khan!" Chimkin was referring to me as well as the others now. "Let us practice how we will kowtow to the Great Khan. Imagine you have just marched into his illustrious presence."

"Long live the Khan of all Khans!" we soldiers shouted, in precise unison. We put our swords to our foreheads, fell to our knees in the mud, and kowtowed three times. I matched the movements of the others, anticipating the moment when I would do so in front of the Khan himself, as part of his personal guard. I was no longer powerless. Although I was a woman, I had served the Khan by gathering intelligence. I had proved myself both loyal and worthy. Face to the mud, I was exactly where I wanted to be.

18

Training

My first day of training started well. Chimkin explained that we were to spend at least half our training on archery, mostly mounted archery. That was my strongest skill, and I looked forward to competing with these soldiers. But what made my blood rush with excitement was to hear that we would also be trained with weapons used for close combat: hatchets, maces, lances, lassos, and especially swords.

The large group was split into companies of one hundred soldiers, each under the command of a centurion. Suren and I were assigned to a sergeant called Chilagun, who seemed to be in his thirties. Chilagun had sun-darkened skin and bowed legs from riding all his life.

He immediately began barking out orders. His job was to break us as one breaks a wild horse, molding us so that we would work together as one. He said we were raw and untested, spoiled by too many years at court. Many of us were members of the Golden Family or pampered sons of high officials. None of us had ever taken orders from a commanding officer. I craved the discipline of military life.

Although we would ride as mounted archers, Chilagun immediately began teaching us how to march in formation. He held a whip and flicked it at us occasionally, just missing. When he made us race on foot, something I was not used to doing, I immediately fell behind. After a short distance, a cramp in my side made me double over with pain. Chilagun rode up from behind me on his horse and cracked his whip.

"Keep moving!"

"I . . ." I was puffing heavily, holding my side.

"So, you cannot keep up with the men, even on your first day?"

I stood straight, willing the pain to go away. He expected me to fail. They all did. I began running again.

That afternoon, we were given blunt sabers for practice. Many of the new soldiers had never used a sword before. Suren had taught me the rules for practicing with swords—how to thrust and parry without hurting your opponent. Some soldiers did not know those rules and drew blood, hitting arms and legs of their opponents not covered by armor. One nicked Suren in the lower arm.

At first, no one would practice fighting me. Finally, one of the smaller men, egged on by his comrades, shyly agreed. "Don't make her look bad. Let her win," I heard one say to him. Within a few minutes I had pinned the short man down with my sword.

A large well-muscled man swaggered up to take his place. I could tell by his stance that he expected to humiliate me. I heard someone call him Bartan. I bowed to him before the practice fight. This time, the match went on a little longer, but I defeated him, too, using a swift, dexterous move Suren had taught me. A small group of men gathered around us. Bartan rose from the mud. He looked at me with narrowed eyes, as if I were the enemy. When he walked away, others went with him. "She cheats," I heard one say.

After that, the men were reluctant to fight against me. Suren saw this and challenged me. We fought a good fight, using the skills we had practiced in Xanadu, each of us carefully avoiding a victory so that the other would not be humiliated. When the other soldiers saw how skilled we were, some stopped to watch.

Distracted by the attention, I missed a move, and Suren won the match.

"Ah, see? She's human," I heard one man say. Had they thought me a goddess?

After that, it was easier to find men to fight during practice. There always seemed to be others watching, offering advice for my opponents. Some liked the novelty of clashing swords with a woman.

Chilagun wandered the field, observing us without comment. When I felt his eyes on me, I put in extra effort, hoping to win his respect. The exertion and sun built up heat under my armor, and lines of sweat dripped down my face.

At the end of the day, my arms ached but I had held my own. Chimkin commanded us to stand at attention in rows once again. He was joined by a white-haired portly man, whom he introduced as General Abaji, one of the Khan's top military advisers. I recognized him from the Khan's banquets. He outranked even Chimkin, as I could tell from Chimkin's deferential manner toward him.

"Soldiers of the Great Khan's army!" General Abaji's

voice was firm and loud. He was still vigorous despite his age, which must have been over fifty years.

"Listen well. On the first day of Tenth Moon, we will divide you into three groups. Most will stay in Khanbalik for further training. A company of thirty soldiers will travel with me on a reconnaissance mission, to gather intelligence. Another thirty men will go with General Chimkin on another journey, in a different direction. Learn well and prepare for the day when we select the best among you for these two missions."

My heart pounded. Surely, Chimkin's journey would be to the West. Even though it was only for reconnaissance, I now wanted to avoid it. It would be easy for the generals to insist that I stay safe in the capital. I assumed that Marco, his father, and his uncle had also returned to the capital from Xanadu. So if I stayed, I might be able to see Marco again before he left for home. But that assignment would be humiliating. The best option would be to join Abaji's mission, whatever that was. I had one month to prove myself.

After Abaji finished, Chilagun led us to our quarters. We were to stay at the army's training camp every day of Ninth Moon, with no more than half a day's rest every ten days. The soldiers were to sleep on pallets in long, low wooden buildings surrounding a courtyard of hard-packed earth. Where would I sleep?

When we arrived in the courtyard, Chilagun took me aside. "My orders say you are to be treated like the other soldiers," he said gruffly.

"Yes, Sergeant." My muscles ached so much it was hard to stand at attention.

"But we have had to make separate sleeping arrangements for you."

I nodded. He marched me to a small room on one side of the courtyard and left me there. I was expected to sleep alone, something I had never done. Of course there would be no maidservant to help me. What was more, this was a drafty square building made of wooden planks, not a *ger* covered in felt and designed to withstand the wind. I took off my leather armor and propped it in a corner. Standing in that small room, I felt more exposed than I had in the company of the other soldiers. I sat on my pallet, exhausted, head in my hands.

At dinner, I sat with Suren and met several other recruits. A few avoided me, but some came to converse with us. Suren chatted easily and made friends quickly. No one knew what to say to me, but I didn't mind. I sat quietly, listening to their chatter.

Once, one man used a crude word, then caught himself, looking in alarm at me. Suren laughed. "Don't worry. She's heard it all." After that, they didn't censor their words in my presence. I enjoyed the illusion of being an ordinary soldier.

Not long after dinner, though, I returned to my small room, alone. I had my own privy, but I suspected that some soldier might be tempted to look through the wooden slats. To my horror, I discovered that my monthly courses had arrived, several days early. My body had slapped me, reminding me that I was, after all, female. How could I wash my monthly cloths here? At court, a female servant took care of this annoying task.

I emptied my bag, looking for something I could use. At

the bottom, I found several clean white cloths. Apparently, my mother had packed them.

Later, without removing my clothing, I snuffed out the candle and lay down. After feeling hot all day, my body felt stiff and cold, and a heavy weight tugged at my belly. In the darkness, I could hear every sound from the men's barracks across the courtyard. From this distance, their easy laughter seemed mocking. In my loneliness, I imagined that they were talking about me, a young woman by herself, sleeping across the courtyard. Would Suren stop them from saying rude things about me? They had joined the army to protect women and children, and having a female soldier in their midst confused that view.

That night I barely slept. After the sounds died down in the courtyard, the quiet seemed more ominous. I watched the faint light under the door flap, imagining shadows of feet outside. Once, I heard a loud cough that seemed to come from just outside my door. I sat upright, clutching my sleeping fur around me. My insides went cold as I sat frozen in place, listening to phantom footsteps.

What would I do if some man came into my sleeping quarters? Would I scream? Soldiers were supposed to be courageous, yet I feared my fellow soldiers. How could I show valor in battle when I was quaking in my own bed?

By daybreak I had made a decision. At the morning meal, I sought out Suren and told him I could not sleep alone. He searched my eyes as if trying to read my thoughts. "Shall I arrange a guard for you, to sleep by the door?"

My eyes said yes for me, even though the request betrayed weakness.

"I will arrange it." His voice took on a tone of authority

I had never heard before. He saved me the embarrassment of asking myself.

That night and every night afterward, a guard kept watch outside my door. My nighttime fears were eased.

I had never worked my muscles so hard, day in and day out, morning, afternoon, evening. We raced on foot and on horseback and practiced standing archery, mounted archery, and swordsmanship. We also learned how to wield hatchets in battle, against enemies made of straw.

The other soldiers, all sixteen to eighteen years old, were at the peak of their physical strength. In many ways, I could not match them. I surprised them with my endurance and could beat most of them in archery. But no matter how hard I worked on swordsmanship, most of the men surpassed me quickly once they received proper training. And I was always one of the last in foot races.

I was frustrated, since as a child I had been on more equal footing with boys. Now they were far taller and stronger than I was. Their muscles had continued to develop, and despite my efforts, I could no longer make mine stronger than theirs. By bedtime each day, my arms and legs ached so badly I had trouble sleeping although I was overcome with fatigue.

After the first few days of euphoria, my mood dropped. The sheer exhaustion drained my spirits. Training was more routine and less exciting than I had expected. On the surface all was well. I was treated with respect yet pushed hard to my limits.

I could not understand my moodiness. I had promised myself I would be tough, and I refused to complain. But sometimes when Chilagun shouted an order at me, my instinct was to shout back. I had to keep reminding myself that

I had achieved my highest dream. Coping with the reality of military training was much harder than dreaming of it.

Some days I didn't perform as well as I knew I could, even in archery. When my arrow was far off target, I imagined the men laughing at me. This increased my anger at myself. When I tried to channel that rage into my performance, my arrows flew farther but did not hit center. I began to get headaches. Often I wished I could escape to a quiet place by the side of a lotus pond in the Khan's garden in Xanadu.

I missed Marco. I thought of him often, especially at night, in the solitude of my room. When I looked up at the green trees, I thought of his eyes. A horse's date red mane reminded me of his beard. One soldier had Marco's deep laugh, and whenever I heard it, my head turned quickly. I was always disappointed to see the wrong face. I regretted my betrayal.

After dinner, the soldiers would sit in the cool night air, drinking *airag* and talking. Many expressed disappointment that they could not immediately join the main army in the final conquest of southern China. That would be the big victory.

The soldiers had heard rumors about the intelligence-gathering missions. They all assumed that my uncle Chimkin would lead a mission to the desert lands of the West. Abaji's mission would be to the Southwest, to subdue the king of Burma and prepare for the invasion of India. Many men had heard that a battle against the king of Burma was likely. Most of the men wanted to join this mission, to have their first taste of war.

* * *

Early in the morning of the first of Tenth Moon, the leaves on the maple trees had begun to turn red. All three hundred of the recruits lined up in the same field where we had met a month earlier. Only sixty soldiers would be selected to go—thirty on each fact-finding mission. I stood with Suren in the front row, awaiting judgment.

Sergeant Chilagun read out the names of the thirty soldiers who had been selected to go with Prince Chimkin to the West. I held my breath, hoping I would not be among them. Suren expected to go with his father, but his name was not read. The men selected marched off behind Chilagun.

My name was not called. I sighed with relief. Perhaps my words to the Khan about Marco's homeland had influenced this decision. But why had Suren not been selected? Maybe Chimkin wanted us both to stay in Khanbalik. Suren and I exchanged nervous looks.

General Abaji came forward to read the list of the thirty soldiers selected to go on the other mission, under his command. Again, I held my breath, this time hoping to hear my name. The first name read was that of Suren, son of Chimkin. He closed his eyes and raised his eyebrows with a relieved smile. But my name was not next. As Abaji read the rest of the list, I stiffened my back and reminded myself that I would do whatever I was assigned.

"Soldiers, follow me!" General Abaji said.

Suren started off, then turned as if expecting me to follow. "Emmajin!" Suren's voice sounded incredulous. "Come on!"

I looked at him, not understanding. General Abaji had said my name, and I had been so certain I was not selected that I had not even heard it. Not until Suren called me did I realize what had happened.

I would be going on the mission to southwest China, as a soldier. Even as I breathed out in relief, I wondered: Could I find a chance to say good-bye before Marco left? Even my happiest moments now had an edge, because I kept thinking of him.

19

Departure

Ten days later, when we left Khanbalik, I could barely contain my excitement. We were headed to Carajan, a mountainous region just this side of the border with Burma. Troops from Burma had been crossing the border and clashing with our Mongol soldiers, and the Mongol commander in Carajan had urged the Khan to send a much larger army. Abaji's mission was to assess the gravity of the situation and make a recommendation to the Khan. We would need to invade and subdue Burma before moving on to the bigger prize, India. My fellow soldiers, especially the recruits, hoped we would have a chance to engage in battle with the Burmese. I had packed and repacked my bags for a six-month journey, but I did not feel ready.

When Suren and I reached the south gate, after saying good-bye to our families, fifty soldiers—thirty recruits plus twenty experienced soldiers—were rechecking their horse packs and getting ready to leave. Traveling with us would be another twenty people: cooks, horse boys, servants. The supplies went on a caravan of pack mules tended by a group of mule boys. Everything seemed chaotic.

In the half-light of dawn, I heard horses whinnying, mules braying, pots clinking, men swearing, leather belts creaking. Clearly, the caravan would not be ready to depart at cock's crow. I left Baatar in the area where the soldiers were assembling and ventured into the area where the mules were being loaded. What possessed me, I'm not sure. Maybe curiosity, maybe a premonition. There, among the mules and mule boys, was a foreigner rearranging his wares in heavy saddlebags on the side of a mule. He wore no hat, so I easily recognized the reddish curly hair. He was clearly swearing in some silvery foreign tongue that seemed familiar.

Marco Polo.

I stayed still, watching him until he turned slowly. A shock shot through my body as I saw the familiar face. What was he doing here?

He smiled coldly and bowed his head. "Emmajin Beki. You look different as a soldier. I had heard you were assigned to this mission." His voice, so close, washed over me like cool water on a hot day. I had not expected to see him again.

"And *you* are assigned to this mission?" Why would a merchant, storyteller to the Great Khan, go on our reconnaissance mission?

"I am on assignment to the Great Khan."

"Because of me?"

He laughed ruefully. "Not everything I do is related to you, Princess Emmajin. The nature of my duties is secret; only General Abaji knows."

That piqued my curiosity. A foreigner who knew

something I was not allowed to know? "And your father and uncle?"

"They are to remain in Khanbalik. My uncle's illness has returned."

"I am sorry to hear it. I see your ankle has healed."

He nodded. "Mongolian medicine. Your ways of treating broken bones are far superior to ours. The doctor massaged and pressed my leg and foot daily, and somehow the break is healed. It works better than my father's prayer."

"Perhaps you were cured by your father's prayer."

He laughed in spite of himself. I had missed hearing that sound.

A horn blasted, and I returned to formation.

My mind spun. What would it mean to travel with him? As delighted as I was to hear his voice, I dreaded his presence, a reminder of both how easily I had fallen for his charms and how bad I felt about betraying him. How could I focus on my duties as a soldier when Marco was nearby? Just being near him confused me and made me conscious of being a woman. I had worked hard to toughen myself into a soldier.

We rode out of the city's south gate in formation, in full uniform, with helmets. A small crowd gathered along the roadside to watch us, just as I had done as a child. I scanned the crowds, hoping that my parents or sister would come to wish me farewell, but I did not see their faces. I held my head high, remembering the military parades I had watched.

In my sixteen years, I had never left Khanbalik heading south. As the houses grew farther apart, I felt increasing exhilaration at the unknowns of the journey ahead. We traveled southwest, along well-paved roads lined with willow trees. It seemed a time of fresh beginnings. I resolved to maintain my soldierly demeanor around Marco.

Less than an hour outside the city gates, we came to a marble bridge over a large river. As we crossed it, I could see that Abaji and Marco had dismounted to examine the bridge. I wondered how the two of them had met. The bridge was exquisite, made of stone, with marble columns. Each column stood on a base shaped like a lion, and a second beautifully sculpted marble lion sat on top of each pillar, gazing at another lion across the road. There were hundreds of lions, and each was unique.

"Beautiful sculptures," I heard Marco comment to Abaji. "What is the name of this bridge?" I rode past them, averting my eyes, before I could hear the response. I imagined that Marco looked up and watched me as I passed.

I enjoyed the pleasures of travel familiar from my yearly journeys to Xanadu: the snorting of the horses, the sun on my back, the breeze on my cheek. I loved watching the countryside, and the new views from each hilltop delighted me. I was riding straight into the heart of Cathay, where Mongol soldiers were obeyed but not necessarily welcomed.

The first day was a relatively short journey—only thirty miles to the city of Cho-chau. We arrived at a hostel and rubbed down our horses. We were called to gather in formation in the courtyard, and Abaji addressed us.

"Most of you know Captain Todogen," Abaji said. "He will be in charge of our group of fifty during this trip. He will name the sergeants."

It was my young uncle, the one who had let me ride in the victory parade. I wanted to wave at him, or grin, but I knew better.

A tall man with the biggest ears I had ever seen, Todogen quickly named five men who would be sergeants, each in charge of a squad of nine men. It was the way the army was organized, in groups of ten, one hundred, one thousand. I had not expected to be chosen as a leader of nine, and I was not.

But Suren was chosen, and I was assigned to report to him. Suren had been promoted after a month's service, and I still ranked at the bottom. Yet what Mongol soldier would report to a female sergeant? It strengthened my resolve to work harder than Suren did, to earn the respect of the men and the officers.

By dinnertime, I was hungry. For each meal, we were expected to sit with our squad of ten. That night, my squad and I sat at a table not far from General Abaji. As I had entered the hostel's dining room, I had noticed that Marco, having no rank, sat with Abaji and Todogen. I was no longer the royal granddaughter but a low-ranking soldier.

The other men in my squad seemed honored to be associated with two members of the Khan's family. They were not men I had known well in training, except for Bartan, the man who had challenged me on the first day. Bartan ignored me, but the others talked to me eagerly. I could see Marco and Abaji by slightly turning my head. I was too curious not to overhear part of their conversation.

"I am glad you speak Mongolian," I heard Abaji say to Marco. "You Latins look like Persians and Saracens, with your yellow hair." Abaji had a plump face and spoke in a pleasant tone that made his words seem welcoming. I knew that Marco considered his hair brown, but most Mongols called any hair that was not black "yellow."

Marco smiled in response to his goodwill. "We consider ourselves very different from Persians and Saracens."

"You all worship the same god, no? Muslim religion?" Clearly, Abaji had no knowledge of Marco's people.

"Our religion is different, older. It is called the Religion of Light."

Abaji laughed. "Yes, yes. The Khan is fond of you colored-eye people. You have a great reputation for storytelling. Perhaps you can entertain me during this trip."

"You are too kind. I am hoping to learn more and talk less during this trip." I loved hearing that deep voice with its lilting accent.

The first dish served was *mian-tiao,* a favorite of the Cathayans. It was a bowlful of long strings made of millet flour, flavored with beef broth, and eaten with bamboo sticks. The soldiers at my table laughed as they tried to use these sticks. Marco, too, seemed confounded by them. I watched as he fumbled the sticks and tried to get the *mian-tiao* into his mouth. The strings kept plopping back into his bowl, spraying his face with hot broth.

Abaji laughed. "It's easier if you hold the bowl close to your face, like this." Abaji picked up the bowl with his left hand and shoveled the *mian-tiao* into his mouth with the eating sticks in his right hand, slurping loudly. He had traveled widely in Cathay and was familiar with their customs.

Marco tried it that way but splattered his face with broth again. Suren picked the strings out one by one and held them over his face, dropping them into his mouth. I laughed.

Abaji asked Marco to compare the women of the West with the women of our country, and Marco said the women of his country had rounder breasts and bottoms. I felt rather than saw Marco's gaze dart involuntarily toward me, so I deliberately picked up a big wad of *mian-tiao* and shoveled it into my mouth with my fingers. The men at my table laughed at my antics, and I could not hear any more of Marco's conversation.

Before long, I heard Abaji say the name Chinggis Khan, and the men around me grew quiet. "You have not heard that tale?" Abaji was saying.

"Tell me, please," said Marco. "How did he use fire to capture the city?"

Abaji laughed a deep, pleasing laugh. "Chinggis Khan's troops were besieging Volohai, a walled city in the Tangut kingdom of Western Hsia. The siege had gone on for many months, but the king had prepared enough food and supplies. Our men could not break the siege and enter the city. One day the Great Ancestor sent a message to the Tangut king: 'We will stop attacking if you deliver to us all your cats.' "

"Cats? You mean, the kind that chase mice?" Marco seemed perplexed.

"Yes, cats. Useless, right? So the king rounded up all the cats and let them out at the front gate. The Mongol soldiers gathered them up, as best they could . . ."

"Herding cats is no easy task, even for Mongols!"

Abaji laughed. "Yes! Not like sheep. Chinggis Khan did not kill the cats. Instead, he commanded his men to tie an oil-soaked rag firmly to the tail of each cat. Then he set the rags on fire and let the cats loose." Abaji smiled at the Great Ancestor's cleverness.

Many of us who were listening laughed in delight at this familiar story. Marco looked sick.

"When cats are frightened, they always run home," Abaji said. "These cats all found ways to run through that city wall, through small holes none of the Mongol soldiers knew about or could fit through. Within hours, the city was aflame. The citizens threw open the gates and ran out. By nightfall, Chinggis Khan's troops had taken the city."

"Good! Good!" the men shouted, and a serving woman from the hostel brought more *airag*.

Marco's mouth twisted. Maybe he was imagining the city of Venezia burning. But that was absurd, since its streets were made of water. For the first time, hearing that story, I thought about the cat owners in the city, the people whose homes were burned. Watching Marco's face, I thought the story sounded brutal.

At least Abaji did not tell the story of the capture of Nessa. When our army took that city, our troops herded the inhabitants together and ordered them to tie one another's hands behind their backs. As soon as they were bound, the Mongols surrounded them and killed them with their arrows—men, women, and children, without discrimination.

Now that I knew more about Marco, I would have instead told him about the *Yasa,* the Supreme Law written by the Great Ancestor, and about his high moral standards. But my chance for private time with Marco was over. I was not sure when, or if, I would find a chance to talk with him again. I decided I should try to stay away from Marco. But the more I tried to put him out of my mind, the more I thought of him.

20

Archery Lessons

The next morning we set off early. It was the first day of a twenty-day journey west to the former Cathayan capital of Kenjanfu. From Baatar's back, I could see that the land was fertile and carefully cultivated, with frequent towns and villages, but the people seemed poor and tattered. The once-rich land had been devastated by earlier wars. The Khan was trying to rebuild prosperity in this region. How would Marco view this poverty?

The journey was easy at first, a ride through farmland and woodlands and over rolling hills on well-tended roads, with excellent hostels in most towns. Marco rode at the rear, near the pack mules. He seemed to be deliberately avoiding me. When I tried to catch his eye, he looked away.

Each night at dinner, Marco sat with Abaji. The soldiers quieted when Abaji told inspiring military stories about the brave exploits of our predecessors. I could not read Marco's reaction. I wanted him to understand our history from our perspective. I wished he would charm Abaji with his storytelling, but he remained quiet.

At the end of each day, our troops held exercises so we would stay fit. Before dinner, we raced and practiced archery, and after dinner, we practiced swordsmanship. Occasionally, Marco watched, and I could feel his eyes on me. But he never approached me. Although I understood why he was avoiding me, I missed the way he had been during the summer, so deferential, so charming, so solicitous of me. This silence felt like a grievous loss.

During the long daily rides, I tried to remember Latin words. I reviewed each of the places in Xanadu where we had talked. Without considering the consequences, I tried to think of ways to talk to him, to overcome the barrier between us. If he had pursued me, I would have rebuffed him. By holding himself aloof, he challenged me to win back his esteem.

One night, less than ten days into the journey, an idea flashed into my mind. Captain Todogen raised his eyebrows when I told him of it, but he gave his permission. So I invited Marco to join our archery practice. I liked the idea that he might develop the manly skills that mattered to Mongols, but mostly I wanted a chance to interact with him. By reaching out to him and including him, perhaps I could make amends. My conscience still bothered me.

Marco refused, insisting he knew nothing of archery.

"Surely your people have bows," I said in front of my squad mates.

"Not curved ones like yours. And merchants are not trained to shoot them."

But I insisted, and the other soldiers seemed to like the

idea. It would provide entertainment on what had quickly become a routine journey. Suren agreed to the plan. One afternoon several soldiers went to get Marco, and suddenly there he was, standing before me.

"We found him *writing*," said one soldier, laughing, as if that were the most ridiculous thing a man could spend time doing. Marco seemed embarrassed.

I showed Marco where to stand, at a precise distance from the target, next to me. He hesitated, then stepped into place. He was so close I could feel the air vibrating between us like a newly released bowstring.

"You hold it like this." I demonstrated with my bow. "Then pull back, aiming up. Then bring the bow straight down, like so." I shot an arrow, which hit the target but not perfectly. Marco's closeness had again distracted me. The soldiers acted as judges, gathering around the target and showing with their hands how far my shot was from the center.

I handed Marco my bow. "Try."

Marco caught my eyes with a slight frown, as if saying, *Why are you torturing me?* But he turned to the soldiers watching him. "My friends, I am a merchant, not a soldier." In a kindly way, they urged him on.

Finally, he took my bow and fitted the arrow onto it. The arrow kept sliding down. I pointed to the spot on the string where it should go.

He pulled the string back with his forefinger, and the men laughed. I showed him the correct way, using the thumb to hold the string. He held the string with his thumb, but it looked awkward. I pushed his arrow up the bowstring. He shot me a look of warning, but I merely nodded approval.

He pulled back on the string, holding the arrow firmly in place and aiming at the sky, as I had done. He lowered the bow slowly, but it wobbled. I steadied his hand, touching him for the first time in months. He kept his eyes focused on the target.

He lowered his aim, squinted at the target, and let the arrow fly. It fell a few yards in front of him. The soldiers laughed affably.

Marco shrugged without smiling. "It takes greater strength than the bows used at home. Ours are longer and heavier, but not so tightly strung."

I did not laugh. "This is the short bow, which we normally use on horseback."

I handed him another arrow. I wanted him to win the admiration of these Mongol soldiers I had been trying to impress. Besides, he might need these skills where we were going. "Pull back harder. Bring your right hand all the way back to your cheek. Look straight at the target."

Marco held the arrow and examined it. "Your arrows are lighter, too. They seem to fly farther than ours. Hollow reeds?"

I nodded. I didn't want to discuss arrows. He held the bow properly this time, with the taut string digging into the flesh of his thumb. He pulled harder and aimed up, then lowered the bow. He let the arrow go and it fell sideways. The laughter was more boisterous this time. I felt a flash of anger toward the soldiers; I had aimed to make a man of Marco, not embarrass him. "You can do better. I know it."

He shook his head but tried again. I could see the bow trembling as he drew the string taut. I put my hand lightly on the bow to steady it, then stood back. This time the arrow flew true, straight toward the target, and hit the ground directly in front of it. The judges jumped forward and spread their arms as wide as they could, indicating he had missed by more than that distance. He looked at me for approval.

"Much better! Doesn't our Latin friend learn quickly?" I looked around at my colleagues, hoping they had not noticed the attraction between us. The soldiers murmured assent. Suren's face showed concern, but he did not stop me.

Marco stepped back, preparing to leave, and I turned to him again, addressing him so that others could hear. "I hope you'll keep practicing with us, Messer Polo. You will not find it difficult if you practice every day. You may need these skills for defense."

Marco nodded as if trying to sense the will of the men. I looked him straight in the eye and dared to give him my most charming smile, despite the onlookers. He seemed distrustful. He looked at Suren. "I do not wish to interfere with your training."

Suren was too much a gentleman to deny him. "You are welcome to join us," he said, though I suspected he felt otherwise. Marco bowed to us and went to his tent.

From then on, as we traveled, Marco joined our squad for a short time every afternoon for archery. His skills improved, though no one would ever mistake him for a Mongol archer. Each afternoon, I stood close to Marco, showing him how to hold the bow, showing him how to be a manly man any Mongol woman would admire.

Still, I did not talk to him alone. It was unseemly, and there was no need.

One afternoon, as I watched him miss the target arrow after arrow, I realized that I had been foolish. Marco did not have the heart of a warrior. None of the soldiers could talk to me about distant lands and cultures as Marco did; none had much to teach me, except Abaji. Instead of appreciating Marco for what made him unique, I had tried to mold him into a Mongol man.

Suren, my loyal, lovable cousin, saw what I was doing and could not fathom it. One evening, after dinner, he took me aside.

"Elder Sister, have you noticed? The other soldiers accept you now. Don't lose sight of your target. That foreigner may be dangerous." My body tensed. "When you look at him, all the soldiers are watching your eyes. They can see it."

"See what?"

"You know what I mean. You have worked too hard to become a soldier."

Suren's words hit their mark. I had been fooling myself into thinking I was being kind to Marco. In reality, I was feeding my attraction to him. I was playing with fire.

That night, I again willed myself not to think of Marco. But my reveries had gone too far. What would the hair on his arm feel like? Was his beard soft? Was his chest hard? Such thoughts were wrong. My heart and my mind battled against each other, neither one able to win decisively.

One night, Abaji told us the story of how Chinggis Khan's two great generals, Subedei and Jebe, led the army westward around the Caspian Sea, using clever tactics to defeat the princes of Russia. Once they diverted a river and flooded a city. Often they would start a retreat and lure the enemy forces into a river valley surrounded by cliffs, only to block the enemy into the valley using a hidden rear guard of Mongol soldiers.

Marco's face showed little emotion as he listened to General Abaji tell his stories. One night, though, when other men were not paying attention, he spoke. "When I was a boy," he told Abaji, "everyone in Christendom feared the Mongol hordes. They were known for rape and murder and pillage."

Abaji laughed. "How little you knew! We had only a few hundred thousand troops, yet we conquered lands with millions of inhabitants. Fear was our best tactic."

"Surely some kingdoms resisted with great force?"

Abaji leaned forward, his face serious. "Every kingdom was given a choice: Cooperate, and we will spare you. Resist, and we will destroy you. Once people saw how fiercely we destroyed our enemies, they gave up without a fight."

"So that is how so few men could conquer almost the entire world?"

"Ah. That is the miracle, isn't it? Chinggis Khan and his commanders were the most brilliant military men in history. They hired local men to gather intelligence before entering each land. They sent the information back to headquarters quickly, using a highly organized system of horse riders. Mongol soldiers were well-trained archers, extremely disciplined. They used clever strategies to outwit much bigger armies. There has never been a leader like Chinggis Khan, and our army continues that tradition."

When Abaji spoke, Marco seemed fascinated. Who would not be? The story of Chinggis Khan's conquest of the world was the best ever told. Surely now Marco could understand why I had wanted to join this army, why the Great Khan deserved to rule the entire world. But remembering Marco's preference for peace, I began to have doubts again.

All those afternoons in the sun in Xanadu had gradually reshaped my view of the world, polluting my Mongolian idealism as surely as a cow pollutes a streambed. Even if I had not watched Marco's face during Abaji's stories, I probably would have heard them with different ears. But with Marco's foreign face before me as he tried hard to remain polite despite his distaste for our tactics, I was robbed of my central faith—faith in the absolute glory and wisdom of Chinggis Khan.

I began, despite myself, to look at all the familiar stories from the point of view of the vanquished, a dangerous angle of vision. I tried to resent Marco for opening my mind to this, but could not. Instead, I often found myself imagining his thoughts and feeling his emotions. It was as if an invisible rope linked us together.

Each night, when my thoughts became untethered from military discipline, I thought of Marco. My fingertips caressed the skin of my arms and belly as I remembered each moment he had touched me, on the shoulder, on the hand, on the back. At first I tried to banish such thoughts, but gradually I came to savor them. What harm was there in imagining something that could never happen? My nightly forbidden thoughts became ever more vivid.

21

Bamboo Fire

Each morning, I reminded myself how lucky I was to be a soldier on a mission, traveling ever farther from all that was familiar. Perhaps it was my Mongol heritage, but in the open air, I felt taller, stronger, wiser. In my memory, the Emperor's court became more closed-in and narrow. If only those people could get out and see how vast the sky was, and how the land stretched on and on. They would have a whole new sense of life.

Yet I also felt unsettled. I was a soldier at last, one of the few recruits chosen to go on this distant mission. I knew Abaji was watching me, to see how well I would withstand the rigors of travel and army life. This travel seemed easy. But I had doubts about my courage and preparedness. Was I tough enough for battle?

In North China under the Great Khan, the region known as Cathay, the Empire was at peace. The roads were wide, smooth, and well maintained, slightly raised and bordered by drainage ditches and trees. Sturdy stone bridges crossed numerous streams and rivers. Excellent hostelries with clean rooms and passable food were located a day's journey apart. The autumn weather was pleasantly cool, and the red leaves sparkled in the sunlight and sprinkled the hillsides with color. Traveling was much less taxing than daily military training. I could feel my muscles growing lazy. Once, I even envied the soldiers left behind in Khanbalik; they were improving their skills daily.

Every time our troops passed a small town, vendors crowded around, eager to sell us whatever we might need. In these towns, I saw for the first time the merchant in Marco. He always sought out the town's marketplace. At dinner each night with Abaji, he would describe the unusual local products. He particularly praised the excellence of the silk cloth, gold thread, taffetas, and brocade. I had been raised to have disdain for merchants, who live off the labor of others. But gradually, I could see the appeal of his life.

After traveling through hilly country, we crossed a huge roaring river called the Caramoran, "Black River" in Mongolian. Chinese call it the Yellow River, because it carries silt from the yellowish soil of nearby hills. We loaded our horses and mules onto ferries, which took us across the wide river.

Eight days later, we arrived in Kenjanfu, the ancient capital of Cathay. Called by the Chinese the City of Eternal Peace, it had once been a great and fine capital, noble and rich, the most populous, cosmopolitan city in the world, home to powerful emperors for ten dynasties. A massive gray wall surrounded it, with four huge gates pointing toward the four cardinal directions. I wondered if it had been difficult to conquer. Parts of the city wall were in disrepair, with bricks lying about. It had fallen three hundred years earlier.

It was common knowledge that the Cathayan empire had collapsed when its later emperors grew lazy, spending too much time with women. One famous Tang dynasty emperor had fallen in love with a great beauty, his concubine, and spent so much time dallying with her that he neglected his duties. His generals colluded to have the lady murdered so that the emperor could focus his attention on ruling. Not until after death could the two lovers reunite. It was one of Cathay's greatest love stories, and it ended in tragedy. I could not think of any love stories that ended happily.

Shortly after we left the city, heading south, we entered a rugged mountainous region. Our caravan followed rivers, but many times the hills were so steep that the road had been hewed into the sides of cliffs, held up by poles. Everyone had to walk, leading horses and mules along the narrow road. Every time I heard a loose rock slip into the canyon, I turned to make sure Baatar had not lost his footing. I tried not to look at the roaring river below. One day it rained, and a servant boy slipped off the path to his death. I had longed for danger, but not this sort.

We heard stories of lions, bears, and lynxes in the surrounding forests. The road became a crevice between walls of red sandstone several hundred feet high. I looked up to the ragged ridges that cut into the sky, where I caught sight of an eagle. As we climbed higher, the air grew colder, requiring everyone to bundle up in fur-lined coats. When it rained, my coat felt twice as heavy and I had to wear it wet the next morning.

Despite the wild environment, we passed numerous towns and villages and even two cities where the valley widened into a small plain, in a land called Szechwan, or Four Rivers. The food was zesty, flavored heavily with hot peppers and garlic, which locals claimed would prevent illness. Between cities, we camped under the stars. While the scenery was stunning, the travel was wearisome; I was disheartened to hear it would take a month through such rugged terrain to reach the region of Carajan.

In Szechwan, we stocked up on all the food and provisions we would need. We were preparing for a journey through wild, uninhabited country and then through a mountainous region called Tibet, a friendly part of our Empire. Marco traded one of his silk carpets for salt, which Tibetans used as currency.

Before we reached Tibet, the land became even more rugged. This part of Szechwan, Abaji told us, had been sorely ravaged in the battles led by Khubilai Khan to control the area twenty years earlier. Abaji, who had served under Khubilai, told us many stories about the battles they had fought in this part of the empire.

One town, by a rushing river with mountains at its back, had been burned to the ground by Mongol troops. The crumbling bricks of the town's wall still stood, but the houses inside were charred remains. We stopped to water our horses, and Abaji told us how the town leaders had resisted, feigning surrender at first but then surprising the Mongolian horsemen by attacking with arrows from hideouts on cliffs and blocking the way with boulders. I looked up and shivered, imagining a torrent of arrows coming from those cliffs. It had taken three days for the Mongol troops to break through. When they did, they killed everyone in the town and burned it to the ground.

I noticed something half hidden behind a boulder and pointed to it. Abaji led the way, and several of us followed, including Marco. When we rounded the boulder, we saw that it was a stack of human bones and skulls, piled higher than the roof of a house. Most of them had been bleached in the sunlight and half rotted during the wet winters. Twenty years earlier, the stack must have been twice as high. Someone had placed all those bodies in one spot after the Mongol troops had left. Who? Wives or mothers?

The eyes in the skulls were empty holes, staring at us from the past, filling me with horror. I remembered that Marco had told me of seeing similar stacks of bleached bones many times during his journey from the West. But seeing them with my own eyes was far worse than hearing about them. Some were small, children's bones. It seemed impossible that brave Mongol soldiers would kill so many. That the great Khubilai Khan, with his good humor and intellectual interests, could have ordered it. That fat, good-natured Abaji himself had helped carry out such atrocities.

"They resisted," Abaji explained. "Now the land is at peace, and we can pass safely, without fear for our lives."

I tasted bile in my throat and looked away. Marco closed his eyes and turned, walking away without looking back. Yet without such killings, we Mongols could not have established wise rule and peace in these wild places.

I had often imagined fighting in a battle between two armies, and I had dreamed of killing armed enemy soldiers by the dozen. But a village of ordinary people, including women and children? In resisting the Mongols, they had merely been defending their homes. No wonder Marco wanted to prevent this from happening in Christendom.

That night, we camped under the open sky. Abaji picked an open area along a stream that flowed into the river, near the edge of a forest. "Few people remain in these parts," he told us. "The biggest danger is wild beasts. Lions and bears are hungry and often attack travelers. But I know an excellent way to keep them far away—a technique they use in this part of the Empire. Let me show you."

Abaji ordered several of the soldiers and servants to chop down tall trees called bamboo. The stems were hollow, divided into sections. The long, slender leaves, I learned, were the favorite food of the gentle white and black bear the Chinese called a bear-cat, or panda, with black patches around its eyes and small black ears. "No danger from them," explained Abaji. "Pandas are large but shy, and we're unlikely to see one."

While the others cut down bamboo trees for a giant bonfire to scare off the wild beasts, I helped tie up the horses and mules. As Marco was tying up his horse, a handsome bay mare he had purchased in Khanbalik, I heard him call her by name.

"Your horse has a name?" I asked, laughing. We Mongols do not have the custom of naming animals, and I had always been careful never to speak my horse's name, Baatar, aloud. I had thought I was the only one to name my horse.

"Yes." Marco looked embarrassed. "I call her Principessa."

That long foreign name meant nothing to me. It didn't seem to fit this wiry Mongolian horse.

"It is our word for *beki*, princess," he added, watching for my reaction.

I laughed again. How odd to give a horse a title—my title. Had he named her for me?

We gave the horses long leads so they would enjoy what grasses they could find in early winter. I hoped the servants could get the fire going soon, as I was hungry.

Abaji strode over to where we were tying the horses. "You will need to tie those horses tighter. Tie all four legs together and peg the ropes down strong."

It sounded like a strange way to tie horses.

"A bamboo fire makes sounds louder than you have ever heard, a deafening noise that makes men swoon or die of fright. It scares off the lions and bears, but it frightens horses, too. We have to ensure they can't run away."

I looked at all the horses and mules. "I fear we don't have enough rope to tie all four legs of every creature."

"We're likely to lose those we don't secure well."

I did as I was told, but I wondered if Abaji was showing the mental confusion of old age. What noise could possibly be so loud as to scare horses and men to death?

Principessa stomped and kicked, and I tried to hold her still while Marco tied her legs. But he took pity on her and tied the knots loosely, and only on the front two legs. I could see from the way he stroked her neck and spoke softly in his own tongue to calm her down that he had a soft spot for that mare. I blushed, remembering Marco's fingers stroking my back.

The soldiers stacked up enough bamboo for a huge bonfire, but Abaji insisted they not light it until after dinner.

Night fell early, and the stars shone clear in the wintry air. Instead of bantering as usual, we all ate our roasted venison quietly, listening for sounds of lions and bears in the nearby woods. Once, we heard a loud crack of a branch behind us, and everyone started. Captain Todogen jumped up and strapped his bow and arrows to his back, to be ready. The rest of us followed suit. I also felt for my dagger at my waist. Marco sat still, fingering his own knife. We hadn't traveled this far only to be attacked by wild creatures in the forests of Szechwan.

After dinner, Abaji stuffed his ears with bits of fabric and wrapped a cloth around his head, covering his ears. "Everyone will need to do this."

Suren and I looked at each other in disbelief. How could this general, who had slain hundreds of people, fear some popping noises from a wood fire?

To humor our commander, we all tore off bits of fabric to stuff into our ears and wrapped our heads with excess clothing. Suren wrapped his head loosely, whispering to me that he wanted to hear the full effect. Marco said we looked like oriental Saracens. Instead of endangered, we felt lighthearted and curious.

Finally, a servant brought over a burning branch from the other fire to light the bamboo. At first, there was no loud sound—only the muffled noise of wood catching fire. I was ready to take off my silly head wrap but knew we had to show deference to Abaji.

Suddenly, I heard a huge explosion, a bang so loud I felt my head would crack open. Suren grabbed his ears. Then came another explosion, and another, each louder than the last. Some men started running away.

"Stay near the fire!" Abaji shouted. "It is safer here." Through the muffle of earplugs and cloth, as well as the explosions, I could barely make out his words.

I noticed Suren pointing at the horses and shouting. "Marco, your horse!"

Suren pointed upstream. The other horses were stomping and trying to run, but were unable to, since their four legs were tied tightly. But Marco hadn't tied Principessa's legs tightly enough. Now he began running toward the woods.

"Marco! Stop!" I shouted. I ran after him.

"Emmajin! No!" Suren tried to stop me, but I tore loose from his grip and ran after Marco. Suren chased me.

My ears, still wrapped in cloth, were relieved when I moved away from the explosions of the fire, but I knew Marco was heading into danger. The woods loomed, dark, damp, and menacing.

For a fleeting moment, I could see his horse's shape ahead of us in the dark, but then it disappeared into the forest. What a fool Marco was! Did he consider his horse's life more important than his own?

The cold night air bit into my cheeks, but Marco kept running, and I ran after him, Suren at my heels. My side ached and I remembered how fast Marco could run.

Suddenly, I heard a roar and then a squeal from the horse. In the darkness, I could barely make out a tangle of struggling animals. I halted, uncertain, as growls and yelps filled the air, drowning out the noise of the bamboo fire. Principessa had been brought down by a beast.

My body trembled. I wanted to flee, but my legs were like stumps of wood. Any minute, I was certain, the creature would thrash too close to me and sink its fangs into my flesh. I breathed in thin gasps. It was too dark to see the creature or how close it was.

I reached back for an arrow and fitted it to my bow,

trying to take aim at the thrashing animals. Marco reached for his knife and lunged forward.

Something large jumped onto Marco and knocked him over. He screamed and flailed. My heart nearly stopped beating. I hesitated about letting the arrow fly. What if I aimed for the creature and hit Marco instead? For a long, fearsome second, I tried to focus on the flailing. I loosened the bowstring, and my feet started to turn. This terrifying creature could kill all three of us.

I heard an arrow whiz past me. Would Suren save Marco's life as I hesitated? I took a deep breath and steadied my arm. I drew back my bowstring and let my arrow fly.

The wild creature let out a yowl, flinched, and then turned toward me. Closer now, I could see a huge cat's eyes, big gold circles surrounding a thin line of black. Rage filled me. I let another arrow fly, straight at one of its glittering eyes. It landed true, in the lion's left eye. The beast fell back, struggling with its paws as if to extract the arrow.

"Marco! Run!"

Marco scrambled to his feet and stumbled toward me. I grabbed his hand, but he yelped in pain. He held his left arm with his right hand. But he could run. Suren urged us on. Abandoning the horse, we ran like lightning away from the wounded creatures, stumbling on roots, toward the camp area near the stream.

When we got back, Abaji was furious. "Why did you run into the woods? I commanded you not to!" Abaji pulled me toward the fire, examining me. "You're not hurt? And Suren? You're all right?" Losing either of the Great Khan's grandchildren would have been the end for him. The life of a foreigner mattered nothing by comparison. "You were to look after her!" he raged at Suren.

I pulled away and hastened to Marco's side. His arm was covered in blood, hanging limply at his side. His manservant quickly set to dressing the wound, forcing him to sit close to the exploding fire.

"I'm sorry," Marco kept saying, his accent suddenly thick and his words slurred.

The other soldiers stood looking at us with fear and curiosity. "Stand guard!" Abaji shouted at us. He meant me, too. With the other soldiers, heads wrapped in cloth, we turned away from the fire and watched the moving shadows, our bows at the ready. I wanted to go to Marco, but I had already stepped far out of line.

I found my hands shaking. In my whole life, I had never killed anything larger than an eagle. Now I might have killed a great beast of the forest, a lion. I wondered if it was still alive, thrashing in pain, possibly even approaching our fire to attack again. Or was it feasting on the meat of Principessa?

I had not expected such a strong, nearly paralyzing surge of fear. Was that how I would react in battle? Suren had not hesitated to shoot. I worried that Marco might bleed to death. Would someone have to amputate his arm?

Finally, Marco's servant came up to me with a whispered report. "The wound is not too deep. I have treated it. The foreigner is lucky. He is resting." I was relieved but still could not take my eyes off the menacing darkness that was the forest.

After a silence, when Abaji had gone away, the other soldiers began talking.

"Suren said she killed a lion," one said.

"With one shot," said another, who could not possibly know.

The soldiers gazed at me with awe. I looked away. I welcomed their admiration, but it was not the reason I had shot the beast. My motive had been to save Marco.

After a time, we took turns guarding as others slept. Captain Todogen told me to rest. I went straight to Marco, who was lying on a sleeping fur on the far side of the popping fire. I squatted next to him and his eyes fluttered open. "Are you all right?"

He tried to smile. "I will live."

"Your horse is gone," I said, unable to think of better words to say.

"I owe you my life."

I wanted to tell him how frightened I had been, not of the lion, but of losing him. Why had I thought it so important to keep my distance? But words failed me. "You should not have run off like that," I said instead. "And I should not have followed you."

He smiled. "But you did. God bless you."

My words of response got stuck in my throat, so I put my hand on his good shoulder. I cherished the feel of his warm body, and I didn't want to take my hand away, not ever.

He gave me a lopsided smile. That moment I knew: He had forgiven me. He had not stopped thinking of me. The distance between us was false. He had known all along about that invisible rope. We were closer than ever.

Suren called for me to take my rest, but I stayed a long time at Marco's side, watching his eyes close, first in pain, then in sleep.

O-mi-to-fu, I called out in my mind, using the Buddhist term I had heard from my devout father but never used myself. *O-mi-to-fu. Let him live. Heal his wound. Don't ever take him from me.* I had never prayed before.

I learned something about courage that night, in the wild woods of Szechwan. Courage is not an attribute some people have and others do not. It comes when you fear losing something valuable. I wondered about the other Mongol soldiers around me, and about other soldiers in history. How many of them had been brave in battle simply to defend themselves or comrades they loved? No storyteller would relate this side of valor.

The next day, some soldiers went into the woods, well armed, and found the body of a full-grown female lion, its powerful jaws slack yet stiff in death. Next to the creature, Principessa lay dead, her mouth and eyes wide in terror, but no flesh consumed. A Mongol soldier shut the mare's eyes. My arrow had lodged deep in the eye of the lioness.

After that, my fellow soldiers treated me with deference. But I still wondered how I would react in battle. If an enemy soldier threatened me in the darkness, as the lion had, I could kill him. But what about face to face, in daylight? I could not yet be sure.

22

Tibetan Village

Marco's arm was not as sorely wounded as I had feared. He rode one of the packhorses, using his right arm to hold the reins. He rested his left in a makeshift sling, and within a few days, he could use it almost normally. His servant, who had applied a mysterious white balm to the wound, predicted that his remedy would work.

For the first time, I rode beside Marco. By now I did not care what people said. I wanted to make up for lost time. Still, I could not speak of emotions. I noticed that Marco had strapped to his saddle several long tubes of green bamboo. I asked him why.

"Have you ever heard such a frightening noise?" he asked me. "I think it is because the bamboo branches are hollow. They could prove valuable."

Marco's mind worked in amazing ways that I was only starting to appreciate.

Suren rode up from behind and separated us. He seemed

determined to keep me away from Marco. Now that we were camping, Suren slept each night in my tent, near the entrance, as if keeping guard, though against what danger he did not say.

During the next five days, we passed through increasingly rough terrain. We had to climb on foot up ever more arduous trails and descend so steeply that my knees became wobbly. The higher we rose, the more I wanted to spend time with Marco, to hear his distinctive laugh, to exchange a few words of Latin, to see the wrinkles around his eyes when he smiled. But Suren succeeded in keeping us apart.

As we rode, I constantly thought of Marco. I remembered stroking his warm shoulder when he was wounded. I recalled the feel of his hand as we had stood on the stepping stone in the Khan's garden at Xanadu. Once, I had caught a glimpse of his chest, and it had been covered with curly hair. I wondered what that hair would feel like under my fingers.

We were as far from the lavish court of Khubilai Khan as I could imagine. The strict rules of Mongol court behavior seemed to fade with each mile we rode.

Finally, we came to a village of Tibetans. Our journey would not take us deep into the heart of Tibet, to the monasteries and temples my father spoke of reverently. Instead, we would skirt that huge mountainous land, passing through several of its poorer villages. Gautama Buddha himself had come from a mountainous country south of Tibet, and the red-hatted lamas of Tibet had brought their enlightened ways of Buddhism to the Mongols, converting my father and my grandmother, the Empress Chabi.

As we wound down the mountainside to the Tibetan village of mud houses, large dogs rushed at us, barking.

Villagers came out to greet us in a spirit of friendship, offering their homes for us to stay in. They were poorly clad, wearing handspun wool or the skins of beasts, and their smiling faces were splotched with dirt. I wondered how they could live in such an inhospitable climate, since I saw few signs of agriculture and no fertile grasslands for their herds, lumbering beasts that looked like huge hairy cattle.

That night we did not sleep in our tents but in the homes of the villagers. A toothless woman saw Suren and me and mimed eating from a bowl. We followed her into a small house, wondering what food these poor people could spare for a group of travelers far more numerous than the population of their village.

The house was dark and windowless and had a rancid smell of yak butter. It took a moment for my eyes to adjust. We sat on low wooden stools near the fire.

The old woman put into my hand a small cracked bowl filled with a warm oily liquid—yak-butter tea. It was a long way from the fresh, milky *airag* I was used to. It had a foul, bitter taste. But its warmth calmed my stomach. I smiled at the woman, and she smiled back. She stirred a pot on the fire and offered us thin porridge. Suren went out to our mules and returned with a side of fresh venison. Her eyes bulged when she saw it. Thanking him profusely, she cut a piece of it and stirred it into the porridge. These Buddhists refused to kill animals but did not refuse to eat meat.

After dinner, Suren quickly fell asleep. But I bundled up in my warmest cloak and headed out for the stream that ran through the village. It was late in Eleventh Moon, and after sunset, a still cold descended from the peaks above. I tucked my hands under my arms as I walked, welcoming the clear, cold air on my cheeks and in my throat.

This place was as remote as I could imagine from the festive bustle of the capital, high above the flatlands of Khanbalik. Reality was skewed; what was impossible elsewhere seemed possible here. I wasn't sure what I wanted of Marco, but I longed to talk to him in private.

The thin air of Tibet, and the magical quality of that village, distorted my thinking. I knew very well that a closer friendship with Marco could destroy my standing in the military. Yet I was not thinking about that. Right then I just wanted to be alone with Marco.

The moon was as large and clear as I had ever seen it, a brilliant silvery white, with patterns visible on its pale face. Its light made the landscape glow with an otherworldly clarity. I walked upstream, around a bend, where the huts of the village were just out of sight. I could not even smell the smoke from the wood fires in the village. I wondered briefly about wild creatures, remembering the gleam of the big cat's eyes. But I pushed aside all thoughts of dread and safety.

I leaned back against a boulder and stared at the stream, which reflected a moon that bobbed and changed shape with the rushing water. The Tibet sky, I noticed, had twice as many stars as ours, and each shone more brilliantly than those we saw at home.

I heard footsteps behind me. I sensed the fragrance of spices before I saw him. Somehow, I had known that Marco would come.

He, too, was wrapped in a thick coat and walked with his hands tucked under his arms. He still favored his left arm, though it was no longer in a sling. With his fur-lined hat, he could have passed for a Mongol, but I recognized his step.

Marco stopped when he saw me, then approached wordlessly. He leaned against the same boulder, an arm's length away. It seemed that he, too, had been looking for a way for us to talk alone. We had more to say than we could put into words.

I broke the silence. "Surely the stars are not this brilliant in Venezia?"

He looked above us and soaked up the spectacle. "I have never seen them so brilliant. This land is blessed." I could see his breath as he spoke.

There was comfort and familiarity between us, but also a pulsating tension.

"Marco, tell me. Why did you come on this journey?"

"I swore to your Great Khan that I would tell no one, except Abaji. But it will become clear soon enough, once we arrive in Carajan."

"You can tell me."

"I am loyal only to the Great Khan." He was lightly mocking my own protestations of loyalty that day in the garden.

"You know I would not betray you," I said, echoing his tone.

He cocked his head but did not mention that I had already betrayed him once. I smiled reassurance, and he chose to trust me. "There is a medicine, in Carajan, which is powerful enough to heal the illness that afflicts the Great Khan's feet. To cure gout."

I smiled. Clever Marco. He had figured out a way to make the Khan grateful to him. "And he has sent you to purchase it? You will heal our Great Khan?"

He laughed in that familiar way. "It is made from the gall of a dragon."

I thought he had mispronounced a word. "A dragon? You told me once they were mythical creatures. Superstitious people, you said, think they breathe fire."

He smiled a delicious smile. "In Carajan, in the mountains of southwest China, dwells a creature men call a serpent. In fact, it is not a serpent but a kind of dragon. One that does not breathe fire. The medicine comes from its gallbladder."

"And how will you obtain this medicine?"

"They sell it in the markets of Carajan."

"The Great Khan could have any man buy this medicine and send it back. One of his most trusted generals is governor of Carajan."

"He asked me to capture a dragon and bring it back to Khanbalik alive, so he can have a continual supply."

I laughed. "Even I know you cannot milk gall from an animal. You have to kill the animal to get it. You will need at least one male and one female, to reproduce. I cannot imagine how you would transport two dragons back to Khanbalik."

He paused. "Will you help me?"

"Capture a dragon, with rows of teeth in its jaws?"

"Yes, but without slaying it."

I laughed again. "I can think of nothing I'd rather do."

"Tell no one."

So this was the secret he had been harboring. Marco was full of surprises. We were alone in the moonlight, yet he made no move toward me. His manner was upright and controlled, but I sensed he was reining himself in for my sake.

I reached my hand toward his arm, which was trembling. I slipped both arms around the bulk of his waist. He hugged my shoulders as tightly as our fur-lined cloaks would allow. He put his hand behind my neck and tilted my face up to his. His eyes seemed dark and deep, roaming over my features. My nose tingled with the spicy scent of him. Inside my cloak, my body pushed hard toward him, resisting the layers between us.

His face drew closer, and I could feel the bristly softness of his beard against my cheek. Suddenly, his lips were on mine, soft and wet, and his mustache tickled my upper lip. A wondrous tingling sensation flooded through my body.

For a long moment, I luxuriated in the unexpected, glorious feel of his touch. Then the urgency of his embrace, the full moonlight, the sound of the rushing stream brought me back with a jolt.

I pushed him away. "What was that?" I asked.

He seemed chastened. "We call it *bacio.* What is the word in your language?"

I shook my head. "We have no such word. People do not do this."

"I meant no offense," he said.

The *bacio* was strange but also delicious. I wanted to try again. I began to move toward him.

"Emmajin! Where are you?" Suren's yell sounded frantic.

"Stay here," I whispered to Marco. Suren must not see us together alone. I headed back toward the village. Just as I reached the bend, my cousin rushed toward me.

"Emmajin! Thanks be, you're safe. Where have you been!" he grabbed my arms and looked me over.

"Taking a walk, that's all."

"Are you all right?"

I adopted a commanding tone. "Of course!"

Suren looked past me and saw Marco still standing by the rock. My cousin looked at me, eyes full of questions and accusation. "It's freezing. Come back now."

As I walked back with him, I could sense his anger mounting. He led me to a military *ger,* secured the tent flap, and stirred the fire while I sat cross-legged on a sleeping fur. He added some wood to the fire, then knelt, facing me.

"What were you doing?" His eyes showed concern and disappointment.

I sat straight. What right had he to question my doings? "Talking to Marco."

"Marco. What did you have to say to Marco at this time of night?"

I did not deign to answer.

"Emmajin." He sat next to me, less accusing. "Be careful. Others are watching."

The firelight flickered on the white walls of the *ger.* I looked away. I could still feel the *bacio* on my lips.

"It's my fault," Suren said. "I will never leave you alone again."

It would have been pointless to argue. I knew he was right. To risk harming my reputation in the military was like stabbing my own foot with a dagger. I could not explain to myself this forbidden attraction.

"Suren," I said, with as much authority as I could, "do not fear."

23

To Carajan

After that night, Suren would not leave my side. He slept inside my tent. Even when I went to relieve myself, he stood guard. The other soldiers did not notice. If Marco noticed, he did not show it. He kept his distance, but I could feel his eyes on me. Suren's watchfulness made Marco seem more forbidden, more desirable. Just one glance from him made me feel connected. It was too late for Suren to pry us apart.

Within a few days, we had passed out of Tibetan territory and into the province of Caindu, a verdant, forested land with mountains, not quite as steep, but still arduous. At every village, people came out, trying to sell us turquoise stones and freshwater pearls. I bought a string of them, to give to my sister.

After ten days of riding, we came to a huge river, called the Brius, or Long River in Chinese. It was the second great river of China and ran all the way to the ocean. Even here, thousands of miles inland, it was wide and swift. We crossed it by ferry.

On the other side, at last, was the province of Carajan—a large mountainous region with seven separate kingdoms, each of which had a distinct tongue and a unique style of clothing. We had to hire local guides who understood Chinese, requiring two translations. No one in this part of the Empire understood Mongolian.

Finally, fifteen days after crossing the river Brius, we arrived at our destination, the city of Carajan, sometimes called Da-li. We first spotted the city from a mountain pass to the east. At the crest of the pass, I looked down on a deep mountain lake reflecting pink clouds in the late afternoon. On the far side, Da-li, an ancient walled city, overlooked the large lake, climbing a gentle slope. This mild southern climate was not too cold, even in midwinter. But it had been raining, so I was soaked.

Standing in my short stirrups to take in the view, I grinned at Suren, who was next to me. The weariness of travel disappeared from my body. "I'll race you there!" I took off on my horse and Suren followed. We galloped like madmen straight downhill. We soldiers had not been traveling in formation since entering the mountains.

The palace at Carajan, a stone structure by the lake, was surrounded by high walls and turrets with curved roofs. The buildings inside, small and fanciful, were painted with bright designs well suited to the lush mountain greenery. The servants wore black garments decorated with strips of bright cloth. The women wore many necklaces and earrings, and the men had gold teeth in their smiles.

When we rode into the courtyard, we were met by

Nesruddin, the governor of Carajan and commander of the Mongol army garrison. Nesruddin, a Muslim, had won renown as a valiant soldier. A tall man with wide shoulders and huge girth, he wore a round brimless hat, pure white, perched in his thick dark hair, which he did not shave. He spoke Mongolian with only a slight accent, since he had spent part of his childhood in Khanbalik. He had a broad, ready smile and seemed genuinely pleased to greet us.

Nesruddin welcomed Abaji with open arms and invited Suren and me to join him at a banquet that night. It was the first time since our journey had begun that Suren and I were treated as royalty. It was an indulgence not offered to other soldiers, but I did not refuse. We were given spacious rooms in his palace, with servants who drew fresh hot water for baths in our private chambers. I let the maidservants scrub my head and hair and body, and I soaked in the tub. It felt wonderful to be a princess again.

At dinner that night, I realized that Nesruddin had also chosen to treat Marco Polo as an honored guest, when he had learned that Marco was traveling on the Khan's business. Like us, Marco had been given a private room at the palace. At the head table, Nesruddin served us as much meat as we could eat.

Nesruddin did not mind talking to Abaji in front of us. In fact, he was eager to talk to us about the threat from Burma, the country just across the mountains.

Burma, which he called the kingdom of Mien, was a small but wealthy land, with towers of gold and silver in its noble capital, Pagan. Its king despised the Mongols. He often inflicted ravages on the people of Carajan, harassed our border troops, and mistreated Mongol envoys. Nesruddin's spies told him that the Burmese soldiers were massing on the border, preparing to invade. Burma claimed the right to rule parts of Carajan, because many local villagers belonged to tribes that spanned the border.

So far, Nesruddin had been able to amass only twelve thousand Mongol horsemen, hardly enough for a large-scale attack against Burma. Most Mongol troops were fighting far to the east, on China's coast. Nesruddin was itching for a fight.

Abaji peppered Nesruddin with questions. How many more troops would be needed? How long might it take to conquer Burma and then India?

"It will not be easy," Nesruddin said. "The Burmese use elephants in battle. Our Mongol army horsemen are not trained to fight against elephants."

Nesruddin had sent many missives to the Great Khan begging for enough troops to invade that rich realm and subdue that troublesome king. He took our arrival as a sign that the day would soon be at hand.

"A battle is certain. The only questions are where and when."

I hoped it would be soon enough that I could take part.

24

Dragon Village

Five days later, before dawn, we set off on our dragon hunt. Marco had gone to the local market, accompanied by one of Nesruddin's men, and bought all the dragon gall available, using gold entrusted to him by the Great Khan. Apparently, dragons were plentiful in this region. Still, he needed to find a pair of live dragons to take back to the Khan. Nesruddin knew of a village headman who was knowledgeable about the dragons, and he offered to send a guide and porters with Marco to the village. When Suren found out that I wanted to go, he insisted on going, too, to protect me from Marco.

Even with horses, it took all day to get to the village on winding mountain trails. The winter air was not too cold, but it rained slightly during the trip, and we had to walk most of the way, leading the horses first up a steep hill, then down into a ravine. The village stood next to a river, where a stream entered it.

When we arrived at the village, the headman, Master Li, told us dragon hunting was always done at night. "These serpents live in rivers during the heat of the day and come out at night to hunt. We'll lay our traps in late afternoon, then check the traps early tomorrow morning. My second son here is an expert and will lead you. Do you dare come with us?"

It seemed absurd, hunting dragons, yet I could see the thrill in Master Li's eyes. He had gold-tipped teeth, wrinkles, and the look of a man who enjoyed his life's work.

After a meal of brown-rice porridge with strange blackened eggs, Li described the dragons for us, through an interpreter. Li was a stocky man with muscled arms and legs—not how I had imagined a dragon slayer would look but perhaps better suited to the real-life task.

"The biggest dragons are ten paces in length, longer than this room. They slither along the ground, not higher than this." Master Li held his hand a few feet off the floor. "They drag their bodies using small legs with sharp claws, like a hawk's. In bulk, they are this round and thick." Li pointed to a large cask in the corner of his house. "The bigger ones are ten palms in girth. The head is huge, and the eyes are bigger than a pomegranate. The mouth is large enough to swallow a man whole."

The headman's son, known as Little Li, showed us a dried dragon's head. I had been skeptical, but this head proved the existence of such a creature. It was fierce-looking, as long as his two arms could reach, and flat, with bulges on top where eyes had once been. Huge jaws were lined with great pointed teeth. Its skin was horny and hard. I could imagine its huge body slithering along the ground and chomping my legs off.

Suren reached out and tentatively touched the creature's scales and protruding teeth. His eyes were round with wonder and horror. "What do they eat?" he asked.

Master Li smiled. "They are meat eaters, like you Mongols. They eat what they can find: fish, frogs, birds, monkeys, and squirrels. The bigger ones seek out the lairs of lions and snatch their cubs, without the sire or dam being able to prevent it. Sometimes they even devour full-grown lions or bears."

Suren's eyes shone with awe as he stroked the dried creature's long snout as if it were a pet. I had not expected him to be so taken with this mission.

Master Li smiled proudly. "I am the best dragon hunter in all of Carajan, and my son here is second best." I noticed that Master Li wore gold rings on several fingers.

Marco leaned forward. "Tell us how you capture this creature."

Master Li smiled a gold-toothed grin. "Alive or dead?"

"Alive."

"We will show you both tonight, dead and alive. Come with us and you will see."

I was overjoyed to be included in such an adventure. Dressed as a soldier, in a bulky coat and hat, I hoped to pass for a man. These people lived far from Cathay, and their language was different. Unsure of their attitudes toward women, I stayed silent.

I was told that the people in this village tribe looked much like the Burmese, across the border. Their skin was browner than most Chinese, and their eyes rounder. They wore bright-colored clothing and might easily pass for Burmese.

Master Li opened a cloth-wrapped package, revealing six sharp blades of steel as long as a hand could stretch. They glinted in the firelight. Li held one up and offered it to Marco, who took it carefully. "Feel the blade."

Marco put his finger on the swordlike edge. "How can such a small blade kill a beast ten paces long? How can you get close enough?"

"Time to set our traps. Follow me." Li carefully wrapped the blades.

Bundled in warm coats, we followed the stocky dragon hunter and his son along a trail by the stream toward the river. We wore boots, but the villagers went barefoot, making it easier to walk on the muddy trails. Several boys followed us, prancing and singing hunt songs. Capturing a dragon was a village event. As the late-afternoon sun sank behind the mountains, we walked on a trail through the jungle to a place where Li had spotted a dragon a few days earlier.

"See?" Li pointed to marks on the ground, and we crowded around to look. A large furrow in the soil cut across the path and made a trail through the woods. Something large and menacing had passed here not long before.

"It will come back the same way tonight," Li continued. He gave orders to several villagers, who began to dig deep holes along the dragon's trail, some close together, some far apart. Master Li lashed his sharp blades to the ends of sturdy stakes. Then he buried them in the holes along the trail, with the blades sticking out slightly aboveground, glittering wickedly. The villagers filled the holes and covered the blades with soil.

The dragon master spoke in a near whisper, as if the creatures could hear him. "When the beast returns tonight, he will strike against the iron blades with such force that they will enter his breast and rip him down to the navel. He will die on the spot."

"Why do you bury six blades?" Suren wanted every detail.

"We never know exactly where the beast will crawl on his return. Sometimes we plant six blades and the creature misses them all. That could happen tonight."

"How do we capture them alive?" Marco's eyes shone in the flickering torchlight.

Li's son shook his head. "Much more difficult. Come." Little Li was wiry and monkey-like, with long arms and a broad grin.

We followed Little Li to the riverbank, where we could see five-toed footprints of some heavy creature in the mud. There, several villagers were assembling a trap made of bamboo stakes, a box frame long and wide, with fishnet of sturdy rope covering the sides. One end, near the water's edge, had a trapdoor. The other end had a hook for bait—a live chicken, sacrificed for the Great Khan. Several smaller dead birds were scattered near that end, in the hopes of luring more than one creature to feed.

Marco and Suren examined the trigger mechanism with interest. I was bursting with questions but did not dare open my mouth. I wished to experience the thrill of this hunt by watching.

Suren did not want to leave when the traps were set, although it was getting dark. "Can we stay here all night and watch?"

Little Li, only a few years older than Suren, smiled and shook his head. "The dragons would smell us and would not come out of the water. Or else eat us."

Before returning to the village, the headman made everyone gather in a circle. Then he spoke in his own tongue, making gestures toward the ground, toward the sky, toward the people. It appeared to be a ritual, and we didn't ask for a translation until after it had ended and we were walking back to the village.

Our interpreter explained. "He talked to the Great Dragon, emperor of earth and sky. He asked permission to kill one dragon. He said you will take gall from dragon back to make the Great Khan well. He asked dragon to bring good luck."

After the hunting party returned to the village, Suren was lively and talkative. He seemed to have forgotten both his worry about me and his distrust of Marco. "What does the dragon's meat taste like? Can we eat some tomorrow? Does it make you strong?"

Little Li appreciated Suren's enthusiasm and patiently answered his questions until the interpreter grew tired and stopped translating.

After a simple, spicy dinner, we were shown beds in the back room of Master Li's wooden house. Suren slept next to me, but my thoughts hovered over Marco, sleeping close, just beyond him. Finally, long after midnight, I slept.

Before daybreak, Master Li shook us awake. He pointed toward the sky, and I could hear the caws of birds. "Are those vultures?" Suren asked.

Without pausing to eat, we left the house. The other village men were armed and ready. Master Li gave us each a huge knife and a basket. He told us to stay quiet as we followed him.

As we drew closer to the trap in the jungle, the sounds of

birds grew louder. A little light outlined the mountains to the east. Master Li indicated we should wait while he went ahead. He held a long stake with a blade attached. I strained to see what he was doing. He stopped and looked at something, then poked it several times and shouted back at his men. We dashed forward.

Suren and Marco got there just before I did. A bloody, hideous sight and stench struck me as I reached the creature. It indeed looked like a dragon, long and scaly and low to the ground, flatter than I had expected. Birds had already plucked out the eyeballs. Its back was covered with hard scales and horny knobs. Half its length was a huge long pointed tail. Its fearsome head was as big as the dried one we had seen the previous day.

A villager immediately began to drain the dragon's blood into a leather bag. "Dragon's blood is good for fighting infections," Little Li told us.

Then Master Li flipped the beast over onto its back. A gash was ripped from its neck to mid-belly. Bile rose in my throat and I had to look away for a moment. Master Li took a knife and cut the creature open the rest of the way. With expertise, he immediately found a small pear-shaped organ, the gallbladder. He held it up, still dripping. He handed it to Marco, who accepted it as if it were pure gold.

This gall was the precious medicine that might cure the Khan's swollen feet.

The village men dropped their knives and baskets and began dancing around the dead dragon with joy. Marco placed the gallbladder into a small bamboo container he had brought, and held it high for all to see.

"For the Great Khan, may he live ten thousand years!" he shouted in Mongolian.

Suren and I shouted back, "May he do so!"

That was the easy part of our mission. Capturing live dragons would be far harder.

25

Dragon Hunt

Little Li gestured for us to follow him down to the river, where we could hear men shouting. The muddy path sucked my feet every time I lifted one.

At the river's edge, the trap had worked better than expected. Little Li said we had brought good luck from the Emperor. In the trap were six juvenile dragons, all about the length of a span of two arms, fingertip to fingertip.

Although smaller than the dead beast we had just seen, they were far more frightening. They were thrashing and biting each other, ripping at the rope, trying to escape. Some had damaged the skin on the sides and tips of their jaws, exposing the bone.

Though they were young, I could see how powerful their jaws were, filled with sharp teeth. One had a chicken in its mouth and flailed its head side to side to rip it apart.

Little Li told us to stand on a bank overlooking the scene. Then he strode to the trapdoor. His fellow villagers fell back in respect. He tossed off his coat and I saw bulging muscles in his wiry arms.

In one move, he slit a small opening in the net, grabbed a dragon by the tail, and pulled it swiftly out of the trap.

I grabbed Suren's arm when I saw the live dragon outside the net. A villager tossed a thick wet cloth over the creature's head. Little Li pinned it down by straddling its hindquarters, grabbing the base of the neck with one hand and the base of the tail with the other hand. Quickly, another villager wrapped a thick rope around the creature's snout, stopping its snapping. A third villager dragged the bound creature back by its tail. It was done before I could breathe again.

Little Li stood back for only a moment before making another swift cut in the rope netting, grabbing another young dragon by the tail, and dragging it backward out of the trap. The dragons in the trap directed their snapping and thrashing at Little Li. I wondered how long the netting would hold.

A villager again tossed a wet cloth onto the dragon's head, but this second creature seized the cloth in its teeth like meat and whipped its head from side to side, as if trying to kill it. The next thing I knew, another man tossed a wet cloth onto the dragon's head. It was Marco. Little Li straddled the creature's hindquarters and grabbed it in the same two spots. Someone handed Marco a rope and he wrapped the creature's snout tightly closed. How had Marco found the courage to do such a thing? He was grinning.

Suren struggled out of my grip and jumped down the embankment to help with the next creature. It seemed wrong to let amateurs do this work, but he managed to help Little Li subdue a third small dragon.

Two of the creatures had escaped from the trap and slithered back into the river. Only one remained. Little Li wiped sweat from his forehead and stood panting, catching his breath before the final capture. Then he looked up at me.

I shook my head. I had not traveled all this distance from Khanbalik to lose my arm or leg to a sharp-toothed creature that could easily be captured by someone else. The villagers grinned at me with gold-tipped teeth. Suren was panting from exertion.

"Don't do it," he said. Yet he had obviously enjoyed the thrill of it, and his arms and legs were intact. Even a foreign merchant could do it. This chance would never come again. I had killed a lion.

I moved slowly down the embankment, everyone's eyes on me. Little Li's grin grew bigger. Suddenly, I realized they all knew I was a woman.

A villager handed me a wet cloth, far heavier than I had imagined, and stood by with a long rope. Inside, I was quivering. I could not do this. I handed the wet cloth back. The villager looked at Little Li for guidance.

Little Li put the rope into my hands instead. I followed him to the far side of the trap, near the remaining dragon. With more space, it scuttled around inside. Little Li had to move quickly. Once, he cut the netting in one spot only to watch the creature run to the other side of the trap. It was remarkably fast for such a long, low animal with tiny legs.

Finally, Little Li was quick enough, cutting the netting and grabbing the tail. The creature snapped around to bite his hand, but Little Li was too fast. He pulled it straight out and fell on its back, grabbing it behind the neck. The villager tossed the wet cloth onto its head. Little Li seemed to be wrestling with the creature, which was snapping its jaws under the cloth.

Slowly, I approached the thrashing dragon. The villagers were shouting at me. How was I to get this rope around its snapping jaws? The others had made it look easy. I formed a loop and tried to toss it over the creature's snout, but it fell short. A villager was trying to show me with his hands how to do it. Marco and Suren were shouting directions. Little Li was having trouble controlling the creature.

I tried to wrap the rope around its snout but was too timid. The rope fell to the side. *Stupid girl,* I thought. *How can you fight an enemy if you cannot defeat this animal?*

The third time, I went in more boldly, wrapping the rope solidly around the dragon's snapping jaws, once, tightening, then twice, tightening again, then three times, securing it with a knot. I could see myself in action from above, as if my mind had left my body. A villager took the ends of the rope and made a firmer knot, and the others shouted their approval and praise.

It was not the kind of valor I had expected to need in the battlefield. But a rush of pride and energy swept through me, and I whooped with delight.

Both Suren and Marco beamed with pleasure. The villagers began their victory dance, and we joined in. I had never felt such joy. Would victory on the battlefield feel like this? No wonder men craved it.

26

Fire Rats

The next night, we went dragon hunting again and captured four more live dragons, for a total of eight.

Working together, with the villagers, Marco and Suren and I were like three brothers, laughing and joking, in high spirits. I did not realize how much tension had existed between the two of them until it broke. Unlike during the summer in Xanadu, when Suren had held deep distrust and suspicion about foreigners, he now seemed to relax into his true nature in the presence of both Marco and Little Li. This far from Khanbalik, away from the pressures of living up to others' expectations, sturdy Suren could be himself.

At last I could talk openly and easily with Marco. The three of us talked endlessly about how we could get the fearsome creatures back to Khanbalik. The villagers could not tell male from female, and most of the creatures would probably not survive the long journey. We would need to take as many as possible. Little Li promised to make the journey with us, to ensure that at least some of the dragons would arrive alive. From that remote mountain village, he must have been thrilled at the prospect of visiting the capital and meeting the Emperor.

Suren selected a long, sharp tooth from the adult dragon killed by the blades. With Little Li's help, he bored a hole into the tooth and threaded it with a leather thong. Then he hung the tooth from his neck. "For good luck and protection," he explained.

Marco and the village headman kept the interpreter busy, discussing details about how to get the live dragons all the way to Khanbalik. Little Li rounded up a few men from the village to feed and care for them. The biggest difficulty would be transportation, since horses would be too skittish to transport dragons, and carts would be too bumpy. Marco's eyes shone with zeal as he talked, and Suren was no less engaged. I sat back and watched them with pleasure.

On our last night, the villagers treated us to a big feast. Eating with their hands, they formed balls of sticky rice and dipped them into several dishes with strong fishy flavors and tart tastes that were new to me but strangely delicious. As we were finishing our meal, I heard a bang even louder than those that had frightened Principessa. We all jumped, and I nearly choked.

Little Li laughed. "Fire rats," he said. He led us toward a crowd of village boys shouting with delight. There I saw what indeed appeared to be a fire rat scurrying around on the ground, its tail aflame, causing people to jump to get out of its way. Suddenly, it exploded with a huge bang, and everyone screamed.

"What is it?" asked Marco.

"We do this every year, at New Year's, to scare away the evil spirits." Little Li picked up a small section of bamboo tube and showed us some powder inside it. He poked a piece of rope into it, sealed it, and dipped the end of the rope into the fire. When the rope caught fire, he placed it on the ground. It began to scurry like a rat with its tail aflame. The "rat" exploded with a huge bang.

"What is inside?" Marco asked.

"Fire medicine. They can fly like arrows, too. Watch!"

Little Li mixed three types of powder—yellow, white, and black—then stuffed it into another bamboo tube, which he tied to a long stick. Then he planted it lightly in the dirt. I noticed a thin rope trailing out the bottom of the tube, along the ground.

Little Li took a burning stick and lit the end of the thin rope.

"Stand back!" he insisted. The fire moved slowly up the rope. Some women put their hands over their ears, and the boys jumped with delighted anticipation.

Suddenly, the stick boomed, then shot straight up into the air, like an arrow with a burning tail, trailing acrid-smelling smoke.

"Aaaaah!" we all cried out, admiring the arc of light it traced in the night sky. The stick shot down to earth a few hundred paces away and broke apart as soon as it landed.

"But how does it work?" Marco asked. I admired his curiosity.

Little Li laughed. "I show you!" he said. This time, he let Marco mix the powder and prepare the bamboo tube. Marco punched a hole in the bottom, placed a thin rope inside, and poured the powder into the bamboo. He stuffed paper into it to keep the powder from falling out and made sure one end of the rope trailed out from the open end. Then he turned it upside down and strapped it to a straight stick.

"That's it? So simple?" Marco asked.

Little Li laughed again, a gap between his front teeth showing. "Here!" he said, pointing to the ground. Marco poked the stick into the ground, but it fell over twice before he could get it to stand straight, with the heavy bamboo tube strapped to it. Marco lit another stick in the fire and touched it to the end of the thin rope.

This time, we all knew to stand back. The fire hit the bottom of the bamboo stick and the powder inside. Again, a noise crashed against our ears as the little stick shot up into the air, tracing a graceful arc of light and smoke.

"What is this 'fire medicine'?" Marco asked. Little Li showed him the three ingredients: common black charcoal, a foul-smelling yellow powder called sulfur, and a white mineral called saltpeter. The key ingredient, saltpeter, was something Marco had not known of before. Nor had I. It was a white powder, like flour.

Little Li took a handful of the white powder and tossed it into the fire. The flames turned pale purple and smoke billowed. Little Li laughed at how easily amused we were.

"Where can I get more of this?" asked Marco, his eyes blazing with interest. Marco stayed up late that night, talking to Master Li and Little Li about fire medicine. He wanted to know the exact proportions of the ingredients and the dangers in mixing them.

We left the next morning, leaving the young dragons in the care of Little Li, who promised to find a way to get them to Nesruddin's palace in Da-li. As we headed back to Da-li, we talked nonstop about the best way to transport them to the Great Khan in Khanbalik.

By the time we returned to Da-li, Suren's distrust of Marco had vanished.

Marco said he planned to go to the market in Carajan City and buy large quantities of saltpeter, which, Master Li had told him, was common and cheap in this warm southern climate.

Marco and I had not had one moment alone, but I felt closer to him than ever.

27

To Battle

When we reached Da-li, after an absence of six days, I expected everyone would be eager to hear our tales of dragon hunting. With eight live young dragons to care for and transport, Marco could no longer keep his mission a secret, although he warned us not to reveal that his purpose was to cure the Great Khan's ailment.

But in Da-li, everyone was too busy to listen to our stories. The moment we entered the city gate, I could see that the populace was in an uproar.

A passerby told us the king of Burma was headed toward the border region of Vochan with a huge army. Apparently, he had heard about the buildup of Mongol troops and decided to defeat them before the Great Khan could send a bigger army. Impudence!

General Nesruddin had begun organizing his troops for battle. He had only about twelve thousand horsemen, against a Burmese force rumored to be huge, so he needed every soldier he could get. Abaji had traveled with only twenty trained horsemen plus us thirty recruits, but he offered our services for the battle.

I couldn't believe my good fortune. Less than four months after joining the army, I would fight in my first battle. My muscles tensed, eager for action. Of course, I knew nothing of war, only the fast heartbeat I had felt listening to the tales of old storytellers in the safety of the Khan's court. I assumed I, too, would survive to tell great tales. Only the unknown died in battle.

I felt no fear. I was confident that the greatest army on earth would easily defeat these upstarts from a small, little-known kingdom to the south. The Mongol army conquered all.

The day we left for Vochan was like none other in my life. I packed my things on my horse as I had many times, but it seemed I was outside myself, watching. Every sound was magnified: the whinnying of horses, the slap of saddles landing on their backs, the creaks of the leather belts being pulled tight under horse bellies, the mud sucking my boots, the flapping banners, the high-energy voices of men heading off to battle. Suren could not stop talking, but I found myself almost silent, in awe.

We rode out of the city gate in rows of ten, one squad per row, wearing our full leather armor, a sword on the left, a bow on the right. Two full quivers on our backs held twenty lightweight long-distance arrows and twenty short-distance ones, with heavier tips. Our plan was to return to Da-li after the battle.

Although twelve thousand was considered a very small army, to me it seemed huge. I could not see the front of the line or the back. Each of us was also equipped with a mace and a dagger. I hated the mace, a crude weapon, a spiked ball on the end of a stick, a blunt force requiring no skill or training. But we were ordered to carry it.

We rode five days westward through the jungled hills toward the town of Vochan in the border province of Zardandan. Each night, we slept on the ground along the narrow road, and Suren kept close to me. The evening after we left, it began to rain, and the downfall continued most of the five days—a cold, continuous rain typical of winter in these parts. We were soaked, but the dreary weather could not dampen our spirits.

Marco joined us on the journey to Vochan, though he was no warrior. Nesruddin encouraged him to go so he could tell the story of the victory to the Great Khan. Marco had purchased a gray mare, to replace Principessa. He rode, I heard, near the rearguard. I did not see him during our journey, but I wondered how he was faring in the rain.

When we arrived at Vochan, we pitched our tents on a plain, a large greensward surrounded by hills on three sides. On the fourth stood a great wood, thick with trees. The rain stopped, and we spread out our belongings to dry. My boots were caked with mud. The warm baths and clean beds of Nesruddin's palace now seemed a distant memory.

Nesruddin commanded us to rest and renew ourselves. He used the time to give his colonels instructions for the upcoming battle. The king of Burma was known to employ as many as one hundred elephants in battle. Even the experienced soldiers among us had never faced elephants. I could not imagine how the Burmese could get the giant creatures over the mountain passes from Burma to the Plain of Vochan.

Marco stayed in Nesruddin's large tent with him and Abaji. I envied Marco for his having the chance to listen to the two generals strategize before the battle. But I also pitied him because he had to camp with such a great host of Mongol horsemen but was not equipped or trained to fight. What would he do, watch from a nearby hillside?

Two days after we arrived, we saw great clouds of dust and heard the thundering of the enemy troops arriving at the distant end of the Plain of Vochan, about a mile away. The sound vibrated ominously in my body. The enemy poured over a low hill, thousands upon thousands, mostly foot soldiers but also horsemen. We jumped to arms, but soon it was obvious that the Burmese troops were making camp there after their long march over the mountains. The proximity of the enemy made my blood churn. How dare they invade the Khan's Empire?

Where the Burmese pitched camp, at the far end of the plain, it looked as if they had built a city. We could see and smell the smoke from their campfires. They were preparing for battle the next day.

In late afternoon, the distant thundering grew louder. The enemy's elephants were arriving over the low hill. I was amazed by their sheer number. Marching twenty abreast, they advanced onto the plain, row after row after row.

All twelve thousand of us Mongol soldiers watched in shocked silence as the massive army of elephants crested the hill and advanced. The ground under our feet shook from their stomping. If their intent was to instill fear, they succeeded. I tried to control the dread swelling in my gut, but I had never felt so overwhelmed.

By the time the thundering stopped, more than two

thousand elephants, all equipped for war, had marched onto the Plain of Vochan. How the king of Burma had achieved such a feat was a mystery. I could not believe that so many of these giant creatures existed in the world.

A scout returned, and I crowded with other soldiers to hear his breathless report. "They are large and fearsome, the largest beasts in the world," he said. "Each one carries on its back a fortress of wood, well framed and strong, full of archers. At least twelve, maybe sixteen, on each elephant. All well armed."

I quickly calculated. The archers on elephant-back alone far outnumbered our twelve thousand, and that was only one-third the number of troops the king of Burma had brought to Vochan.

All told, there were indeed sixty thousand Burmese troops. They outnumbered us five to one.

Clearly, the king of Burma was planning the battle to end all battles. We had been caught unawares, with the greatest strength of the Khan's army a two-month march to the east. There was no time to get reinforcements.

Many of us would not survive this battle. I looked at those around me, whom I had come to know well. How many of us would be trampled to death by elephants, felled by archers, or cleaved in two by swords?

Valor, I repeated to myself. It will take valor to face them. But another voice in my head kept repeating a different word: *folly.* I tried to suppress that thought.

Standing next to me on the Plain of Vochan, Suren spoke so low no one else could hear. "You and I must leave this place at once."

I couldn't believe he would say such a thing. "Why?"

"I have strict orders, from the Khan. You are to return to Khanbalik alive."

"What?" I was incensed. "You want to flee before the battle has begun?"

"No, I don't. But you are a woman and cannot die on this battlefield."

I laughed nervously. "Those are the Great Khan's orders?"

"Yes. I have sworn to protect you."

The Khan had allowed me to join the army, but he expected me to flee from battle. Suddenly, Suren, with his broad, kind face, seemed like the enemy. "I'd rather die here than have it told that I fled in fear."

It was as if Old Master were inside my head, shaping my words. He had molded my beliefs as a child so fully that I saw myself as part of a legend, conscious of a role I was acting. The thought of fleeing did not tempt me.

I could see conflicting intentions on Suren's face. He had not chosen this assignment. I touched his shoulder. "Together you and I will tell the Great Khan about our first battle. I will assure him that you tried to stop me."

He smiled uncertainly. But I held my ground.

That night, each company of one hundred met with its commander to receive its orders. Todogen told us that the battle would commence at first light the next morning. Although we were far outnumbered, our skills in battle were unsurpassed, and our archers the best. Even our horses were skilled in war, sturdy and brave.

We had never faced thousands of elephants, but we were not to let them intimidate us. Elephants, Todogen told us, were poor fighters and served merely to inspire fear. When we saw them advancing, we were to hold our ground and begin the battle with no dismay. The elephants' thick skin was not impervious to metal-tipped arrows. Our arrows flew farther, so we should be able to take down many of the creatures before we were within range of the Burmese archers.

We were to advance straight at the enemy. Each of us had to kill five Burmese soldiers, plus another five for every one of our comrades killed in battle.

Todogen stood tall and shouted his final command: "Remember the words of the Great Ancestor, Chinggis Khan, 'In daylight watch with the vigilance of an old wolf, at night with the eyes of a raven, and in battle fall upon the enemy like a falcon.'"

As he spoke, I could feel thrills of anticipation up and down my back.

That night, after dinner, Marco found me sitting by a fire. "Emmajin Beki. I wish I could convince you not to go into battle tomorrow."

I laughed. "If I sat on the side, that would make a sorry legend."

Marco was serious. "I don't care about the legend. Many will die."

I nodded. "I know. Too much blood. I could be killed. But I will not." Certain that I would be protected by the valor of my ancestors, I didn't think of how many of them had been killed in battle.

Marco pulled out a blue silk scarf and handed it to me. "In Christendom, soldiers take these to battle, given by their loved ones."

I laughed. "The ladies give them to the men, though, right?" He did not smile. As I took the scarf, a strange, unsettling premonition swept over me. Would Marco find the scarf on my corpse? I quickly tamped down that thought. "This will bring me luck?"

"Yes."

"Then I will take it into battle." I wished I had brought the Tara amulet my father had given to me. I wished I had reconciled with him before leaving home.

"Emmajin. I . . ." I could tell that Marco wanted to embrace me, but there were too many soldiers around. We could not show any emotion.

I took his hand in mine and held it longer than I should have, wishing I could experience one more *bacio.* "No need for words. I will see you tomorrow night."

28

The Battle of Vochan

That night, I could not sleep. I did not think it would be my last night on earth, but I knew it might. Would death be painful? I thought of my mother, my sister, my father, the Great Khan. It was possible I would never see any of them again. Mostly, though, I thought of Marco, of all the possibilities I had secretly dreamed of with him. Why had I hesitated?

Beside me, Suren lay awake, too, tossing. At one point, I reached out and put my hand on his arm. "Suren." He turned toward me. "It will be a good outcome."

He nodded.

We arose well before daybreak and donned our armor. I wrapped Marco's blue scarf around my neck but tucked it out of sight. We were each given a chunk of mutton and told to fortify ourselves, but my stomach was unsettled. A light breeze was blowing across the plain, and small high clouds glowed red in the morning sky. The rising sun etched the hilltops so clearly the rest of life seemed blurred.

We mounted and stood in formation, twelve thousand horsemen of the great Mongol army, in our brown leather armor. Baatar was skittish, so I patted his neck, trying to calm his nerves and mine. He had carried me from Khanbalik to the jungles of Carajan and now to the battlefield at Vochan.

We recruits were four rows back, since Nesruddin wanted his best archers and most experienced warriors in the front line. I wished I could have been in front, but it was, after all, my first battle. The strategy was to attack with a constant barrage of arrows, one unit replacing another as our arrows ran out.

My squad, under Suren's command, was near the woods at the right side of the plain. Across from us, a row of armed elephants, several hundred abreast, stretched from one side of the plain to the woods on the other. I could see, even from a distance, that the Burmese soldiers wore uniforms of red.

Seated straight in my familiar saddle with its silver ornaments, on the golden palomino stallion I had ridden almost every day for four years now, I kept my mouth in a firm line. Our orders were to keep still. But my mind raced. My life had been too short, too inconsequential to end on this day. If I survived, I decided, I should make my life count, do something that mattered.

The Mongol way was to begin each battle in total silence, allowing the enemy to advance first. I watched as the front line of Burmese troops moved forward, advancing toward us. At first, it seemed just a line of red; then I could hear the grinding of horses' hooves.

When the enemy was close enough to hear, our war drums broke the silence. That was the signal. All of us Mongol soldiers, as if with one voice, let out war cries meant to terrify the enemy. Shouting amidst such a host made me feel invincible.

Our front line surged forward, then the next rows, and finally mine, advancing with order and discipline. Baatar seemed eager to join the battle. So much dust was kicked up around me, I could no longer see the far end of the plain, but I could feel in my bones the roar of hooves advancing toward us.

Those first moments shimmered with pure exhilaration. We advanced across the plain in a long row of horses, just far enough behind the row in front to allow visibility. Wind whipped my cheeks, and the slanting rays of the rising sun put the horses and men around me in relief. I could smell horses and wet earth and fear and bloodlust. I grinned at Suren, galloping next to me. He waved at me with a huge smile. *Now, Suren,* I thought, *do you wish we had fled the battlefield like cowards?*

Finally, I could see the elephants advancing straight at us. Decked in red, they bellowed like trumpets. It seemed as if a mountain had detached from the earth and was rolling in our direction, an avalanche of red boulders.

Suddenly, something went wrong. When our forces were near to the enemy and nothing remained but to begin the fight, the horses in front of us skidded to a halt. We had only seconds to slow our horses before we smashed into the row in front. Those behind plowed into us.

We riders floated astride a teaming mass of horseflesh. The horses screamed in dismay, trying to turn to the side to escape. They did not fall, as there was no room. Baatar's great head was wrenched to the side. I saw terror in his wide brown eye and could feel the lurch of pain in his body as a horse lunged into his backside. I looked desperately for a way to steer him free, but horses and riders engulfed us.

The horses in the Mongol front line had taken such fright at the sight of the elephants that they had swerved and turned back.

All was disarray. No amount of experience in warfare could prevent our horses from retreating. Our horses were caught, unable to go either forward or back. The elephants were lumbering straight at us, with only a short distance to cover before they would trample our fine Mongol steeds. Red-uniformed archers rode in the fortresses on the elephants' backs, and when they came into range, they began to shoot.

I took up my bow and shot at one of the elephant-back towers. But the archers were half hidden behind wooden walls, while we were exposed, below them. Baatar was surging beneath me, trying to get out from the mass of horses, in any direction. The elephant towers were advancing, bobbing atop the huge creatures.

It was nothing like mounted archery, in which I galloped at a steady pace past a stationary target. All my well-honed skills seemed for naught.

Arrows whizzed past my ears and over my head. One shaft came so close to my left side that I automatically swerved to the right. I heard a horrific crack and turned to see a white-feathered arrow deep in the throat of the soldier next to me. It was my commander, Todogen of the big ears. Blood spurted from the wound and he fell sideways.

But the horses were too close together for him to hit the ground.

Suren, on my right side, saw it, too, and there was terror in his eyes. My chest was so tight, and the dust so thick, I could scarcely breathe. Todogen's sudden death, a few feet from me, sent a shock through my system. One arrow could do it. My armor covered only my chest and abdomen.

I pulled another shaft from my quiver and shot straight at the archers in an elephant-back fortress. Now I must kill five more enemy soldiers.

Suddenly, twenty Mongol horsemen rushed around the teeming mass of horses to the front line, riding bravely toward the elephants. I could see only one close-up, and he held what looked like a thick lance with a flame at the tip. He ran directly at one of the elephants and tossed the burning lance in front of its feet. Then he swerved to the side and kept going. My breath caught in my throat when I saw him hit by an arrow.

A thunderous explosion in front of the elephant rocked me. The elephant stopped so suddenly that several archers were thrown off its back. Its eye widened in fright. The creature hesitated, then turned and ran toward the woods.

Beyond it, I heard another huge explosion, then another. The horsemen had hurled burning bamboo stalks in front of elephants. I remembered the fire rats we had seen in the village. The same explosions were happening across the front lines. The blasts scared men, horses, and elephants, Mongol and Burmese alike.

But most of all, the noise terrified the elephants, who a moment earlier had seemed invincible. Their trumpeting noises switched to high-pitched shrieks, horrible, ear-piercing sounds. Panicking, they turned and ran in many directions. Most ran off the battlefield and into the protection of the forest. No driver could control them.

Baatar surged against his reins and struggled to get away from the terrible noise. Our Mongol troops scattered, and I headed for the woods. There, several Mongol soldiers had jumped off their mounts and were tying their horses to the trees.

"Tie up your horses!" Suren shouted. "Aim at the elephants' flanks!"

The order made no sense. Leave my horse and go on foot in the midst of battle, when the enemy troops were advancing on elephants? We would surely be trampled. But I obeyed. All Mongol soldiers seemed to have the same orders, since they were streaming to the side, toward the woods. Our horses were too panicked to be of use.

Shooting from the edge of the woods, we sent scores of arrows high up into the flanks of the elephants rushing past us. It was easier to aim on foot than on a frightened, bucking horse. My confidence returned with each shaft I shot. Several hit the mark.

We plied our bows stoutly, shooting so many shafts at the panicking elephants that the closer ones had arrows sticking out their sides like needles on a pine branch. Burmese soldiers were falling off the elephants like red autumn leaves.

"Aim at their vulnerable parts," Suren shouted.

My next arrow hit true, on a bull elephant's hanging parts. The creature fell to one knee and the tower on his back tipped, throwing off several archers. With its tower tilting crazily, the beast regained its footing with a loud bellow.

Then the creature turned and headed for the woods,

stomping on soldiers in its path. It headed straight toward me. Out of arrows, I had just enough time to slip behind a tree, but it trampled over several of my comrades as it plunged madly into the forest. I feared for Baatar, tied up a few trees behind me, unable to run.

Other elephants followed, clomping with a tremendous uproar. I grabbed the trunk of the tree and held on tightly. The ground beneath me was shaking, and the noise so deafening that I could not let go.

The elephants rushed blindly wherever they could, dashing their wooden fortresses against the trees, bursting their harnesses, and smashing everything that was on them. The Burmese soldiers inside fell screaming to the ground. I pulled out my sword and slashed one that fell near me. The blood spurted up and covered my leg and I could see the look of horror in his face. I felt a rush of disgust I had not felt when killing with arrows.

These soldiers were small brown-skinned men, shorter and slighter than Mongols. Some looked like Little Li, who, fortunately, was far from this mayhem, back in his village. On the ground, one on one, the Burmese were not frightening. In fact, they looked like our friends in the village of dragon hunters.

29

The Battle Rages

When the explosions stopped, the battlefield was in confusion, with elephants retreating or rushing into the woods. Many Mongol soldiers were still on horseback, clearly no longer certain what to do.

"To horse!" someone shouted in Mongolian. Suren repeated it from somewhere behind me. I found Baatar alive but panicked. Relieved, I put my hand on his flank to calm him, then mounted. Those of us who had not lost our steeds emerged from the woods on horseback.

I could see, across the field, that the Burmese cavalry was regrouping to my right. The remaining Mongol horsemen were regrouping to my left. The elephants were no longer a fighting force. It was time for the more traditional battle to begin.

We regained our formation and charged the enemy. Those with arrows left took the front line. They mowed down the first rows of Burmese horsemen with far-reaching Mongolian arrows. I was several rows back, feeling vulnerable with an empty quiver.

As we drew closer, Burmese shafts whizzed past my ears. One hit me full in the breast, but I pulled it out, thanking the weaver who had made the special silk. Had the arrow landed a few inches higher, at my neck, I would have died. Tossing that arrow aside gave me a feeling of invincibility, and watching the Mongol soldiers around me aroused what bravery I had left. Retreat was not possible, anyway.

Our front line of horses hit their front line. For a short time, I managed to stay on horseback, although many men were knocked off and fell to fighting on foot. In the confusion, I didn't even know which way to look for the enemy.

I felt a hard thud on my right arm and realized that a mounted Burmese soldier had hit me broadside with his sword. With my left hand, I reached for my mace and swung with all my strength. The spiked ball whacked the enemy on the face and knocked him off his horse. My right arm stung, bruised, but I could still use it.

Suren maneuvered his horse close to mine and wildly swung his mace at the enemy. One Burmese soldier charged at Suren, holding his sword straight ahead. I raised my sword and struck his down so that it only grazed Suren's horse. Suren shot me a grateful, frightened glance and tried to move his horse to shield me.

In that moment of distraction, another enemy came at me with his sword and knocked me clean off my horse. Baatar bolted toward the woods, and I was left to fight on my feet, sword in right hand, mace in left, a small dagger still at my waist. Many soldiers lay wounded on the ground, and the horses trampled them.

Even as I continued to fight, I saw arms and hands and legs and heads that had been hewn off or blown off by explosions. One enemy came straight at me with his sword. I used mine to hack off his right arm. It took great strength. Bright red blood gushed from the wound like a waterfall.

I had no time to wipe my sword before turning to another enemy, clearly enraged by what I had done to his comrade. I hit him on the neck and he fell. The din from the swords and horses and shouts was so loud that, as Marco would have put it, God might have thundered and no man would have heard it.

Suddenly, I noticed that I was surrounded, not by enemy troops, but by Suren and three men from our squad of ten. How they had found me I knew not. They all had their backs toward me and were fighting furiously with sword and mace. For a moment, I stood still, too far from any enemies to reach them. Suren, whose soft side I knew so well, was wielding his sword with skill and fury.

I saw it coming before Suren did. An enemy soldier, still mounted, charged him from the left, aiming straight at his neck.

"Suren! Look out!" I cried.

Suren quickly turned his head, just in time to see the sword coming, but he could not raise his sword quickly enough to parry. The tip of the heavy broad sword penetrated his throat.

I screamed.

I charged at that Burmese soldier with full force and fury, landing a blow from my mace on his leg so that he flew off his horse. The horse kept going, and Suren's attacker lay floundering on the ground. I raised my sword and hit him hard on the side of his head, stunning him. Then I pointed my sword straight down at him and thrust it into that same vulnerable spot in his throat. A gush of blood spurted up. I took my mace and smashed him in the face for good measure. The hatred pounded in my ears and killing him felt good. It was battlefield justice. *One less foreigner to fight!* I thought.

I turned to Suren. It was too late. He was lying on his back, eyes open to the sky, blood gushing from his neck. My treasured cousin, who had taken so seriously his task of keeping me alive and safe, was dead.

Blood rage overtook me. Fueled with fury, I became a mindless killer. I swung my mace and sword at all men in red, knocking them off their horses, slicing off arms, hacking at necks, smashing faces, slaying mercilessly. I hated them all. They had invaded our country, attacked our great army, and killed my cousin.

I felt satisfaction, elation each time I killed. The red of their blood was brighter than the red of their uniforms. I wanted the whole plain to be covered in their blood. The coppery smell of it lifted me, and my arms amazed me with strength I didn't know I possessed. I swung and slashed, mowing down all who moved. I felt stronger, taller, better than I had ever felt in my life.

I had no sense of time and lost track of how many enemy soldiers I killed. They say we continued fighting until midday. Finally, the Burmese king's troops turned and fled. We gave chase. I ran after them, still swinging my mace, hitting them from behind.

For Suren! I said to myself each time I hit one. *For Suren!*

It was as if each Burmese soldier was responsible for killing my beloved cousin. Killing five enemy soldiers for each of ours seemed like it was not enough. I wanted to kill them all.

Finally, a Mongol soldier grabbed me to prevent me from pursuing any further. "Stop!" he said. "We have won."

I turned, my heart still full of hatred, and swung my mace, nearly hitting him. Suddenly, I realized that he and I had run much farther than any of the other Mongol troops, who had stopped fighting. The Burmese soldiers were retreating in disarray.

The battle was over. We were victorious. Flush with triumph, I thrust my bloody sword into the air. The soldier smiled. When I sheathed my sword, I noticed that my hand was trembling. We headed back toward our troops. Now I had to find Suren.

The scene revolted me. Soldiers in black and red scattered across the battlefield, wounded or dead, many trampled by horses or elephants. Squashed faces, flattened bodies. Legs and arms and heads blown off from corpses. Dead or thrashing horses. Elephants lying on their sides in huge pools of blood, squealing. Moans and screams from piteously wounded men. The smells of blood and horses and filthy bodies and excrement. The sharp, acrid taste of despair.

I saw the head of a Mongol soldier I had met during our five-day journey from Carajan, his eyes staring at the sky. Eerie screams came from a quivering mass of wrinkled elephant. I looked for Baatar and saw a horse the same golden color lying on his side, his guts spilling out. But it was not Baatar.

The stench of death caused bile to rise in my throat. I vomited, heaving again and again. I wiped my mouth, covered my nose, and plunged into the writhing bodies. I had no idea where Suren might be but kept searching.

"Regroup at the tents!" someone commanded. I did not obey this order.

I wandered far longer than I should have, looking into the faces of the dead and wounded Mongol soldiers, who were broken and bleeding. The vomiting made me light-headed and I stumbled. I saw one man pull an arrow out of his ear and grab his head in pain. I glimpsed a young Mongol soldier, still alive, holding his hands over a bleeding gash in his abdomen. Each of these soldiers had a family who loved him, somewhere.

Again I vomited, though there was nothing left in my stomach.

I pushed on, still searching. One Burmese soldier tried to grab my foot. When I pulled it away, I looked into his eyes and saw a haunting, pleading look. His leg had been nearly hacked off. He was begging for help using words I didn't understand. Perhaps I had cut off his leg. I could not tolerate his anguish. I tore my eyes away and stumbled on.

"Emmajin Beki. Come," someone said. But I refused. Where was Suren?

Finally, I found his body, with its deep throat wound. His spirit had already fled. He was lying in a pool of blood. A drop of that blood was mine, given freely to my *anda,* my blood brother.

I had to get his body out of there. I tried to pick him up, but he was too heavy. So I dragged him. My hands were so weak I kept losing my grip.

A Mongol soldier confronted me. "Leave him. We cannot help them all."

"This is the Khan's eldest grandson, son of the crown prince Chimkin," I said.

He looked at me in surprise, hearing my woman's voice. Then he picked up the body and heaved it onto his broad shoulders. "Come," he said. "Are you injured?"

Now that I was not swinging my sword, I could feel the deep soreness in my upper arm, and my whole body trembled. "No," I said. But I was spent. I followed him back to camp, trudging through the mayhem.

On our way, we passed a company of Mongol soldiers heading toward the woods. They told us they had been ordered to capture as many of the elephants as possible. The Khan would be pleased.

One side of the camp had been set up to treat the injured. We headed for the other side, where the survivors were meeting and regrouping, exchanging news of who was lost and who had fought valiantly. The mood was jubilant.

Abaji and Nesruddin rushed toward us. They appeared ruddy and uninjured, but both looked stricken when they realized that Suren was dead. They lay his body flat on the ground so that it would not stiffen in an awkward position. Abaji closed Suren's eyes. "Thank Heaven you are not injured," Abaji said to me.

I stared at Suren's body, then sank to my knees next to him. His hand was cold. His death was my fault. If I had left with him, as he had insisted, he would still be alive. Driven by dreams of glory, I had not thought my decision could endanger him.

Someone brought a sleeping fur and lifted Suren's body onto it. I reached into my clothing and pulled out the blue scarf Marco had given me. It had kept me safe. Now Suren needed it, for his journey to the spirit world. Somewhere, unseen to me, he was being welcomed by the Great Ancestor himself.

I started to cover his neck wound with it and discovered the dragon's tooth, hanging on a thong around his neck. So much for that good luck charm. I cut the thong and replaced it with the blue scarf, covering his neck. I wanted to toss the dragon's tooth away, but instead, I tucked it into my waistband. It had been precious to Suren, the symbol of an adventure he had loved.

"Keep his arm flat at his side," someone said. "You don't want it to stiffen at that angle." I lay his arm flat but wrapped my fingers around his hand.

Suren had saved my life, but I had failed him.

"I saw her. She fought valiantly," I heard someone say.

"Of course," said Abaji. "She has the Great Ancestor's blood in her veins."

"She killed over a hundred soldiers, wielding her mace with fury and chopping off heads," someone else said. I could hear the admiration in his voice.

"She brought us good luck," said another.

It was the praise I had longed to hear. But I was not in the mood to be celebrated as a hero. What was valor compared to the loss of life? Suren and I would not return together to Khanbalik and boast of our exploits on the battlefield. Hundreds of other Mongol soldiers still lay out in the field, dead or dying in agony, never to return home.

Again, bile rose in my throat, but I choked it down. I was beyond tears.

Suren had been part of my life since my earliest memories, always there, ever eager to learn with me, to compete with me, ever good-tempered, ever smiling. I had shared countless meals with him. I had learned swordsmanship with him. We had been comrades-in-arms, sharing a dream. Now his dreaming was over.

But what of me? I had tasted battlefield victory. And it was bitter.

30

After the Battle

For a long time, I knelt at Suren's side. Behind me, men crowed of their battlefield prowess. With ardor, they recounted heads they had severed, arrows that had pierced an eye or a nose, elephants and horses they had slain. Their mirth rose and overlapped like flames of a newly stoked fire.

They cheered the joy of victory, a thrill I had always longed to feel. But I felt empty. Inside me was a huge hole, dark and deep.

". . . the foreign merchant," I overheard someone say.

My head bobbed up and I listened through my black fog.

"Yes, killed. He didn't even fight."

The news hit me like a bolt of lightning. Marco was killed, too? I turned quickly to the men behind me. "How?"

The soldier laughed. "The fool. When the battle was nearly over, he went to the woods to see the elephants and was trampled."

I could barely sputter out the words. "Marco Polo? The Latin?"

"Beard like fire. Strange eyes. They say he was a storyteller."

I couldn't breathe. A lifetime of unrealized possibilities flashed before my eyes and faded.

Marco. I remembered how intensely he had held me by the stream near the Tibetan village. How he had wrapped the rope around the snout of the dragon. I thought of our walks in the Khan's garden in the heat of summer. I recalled standing next to him, teaching him Mongolian archery skills. I remembered how he had listened to Abaji's stories of Mongol glory. He could not be dead.

I squeezed Suren's hand and stood up, my knees stiff from kneeling. I shook off a moment of dizziness. If Marco's body was out there, I had to find it. Already some soldiers were stacking up corpses, which would be burned. If I did not move quickly, I might never see his body.

Baatar picked that moment to find me in the chaos. How, I would never know. I hugged his neck and buried my face in his mane, coated stiff with sweat and blood. He whinnied, and I felt sure I saw relief in his eyes. I had no time even to find water for him. I mounted him and rode across the battlefield. Soldiers were busy dragging the dead to the side and carrying the wounded to camp.

I headed for the edge of the woods, where most of the elephants had entered. A few elephants were being led out by our Mongol soldiers. Moving slowly and silently, the beasts no longer seemed threatening.

Human bodies were strewn about, both in black and in red. I held my hand over my nose and searched. Once,

I thought I saw Marco's body, underneath that of a Burmese soldier, but when I pulled the enemy's body off, I saw that it was a Mongol soldier I had met on the road. The Burmese soldier on top of him still had his fingers wrapped around his sword, covered with precious Mongol blood. I kicked him.

Nearby, a badly wounded Burmese soldier was moaning. I stabbed his throat. Now I understood why the Mongols refused to take prisoners or treat injured enemies.

The winter sun dipped below the tops of the hills, and the light began to fade. I kept searching, feeling increasingly frantic. Suren was dead, and Marco was, too. No one else meant as much to me. I had no reason to hope that Marco was still alive in these woods. But if he lived, I would find him and make sure he was treated.

Marco Polo. I knew, now and too late, that I loved him. If he was alive, I wanted him close to me, always. If he was dead, I could not go on.

I was not able to find Marco's body anywhere. Fires had been lit. I could smell roasting mutton. My stomach grumbled, but how could I eat? How could the sun set?

I searched for Abaji. He would know if Marco had died. I found Abaji sitting by a fire, a mutton rib in his hand, listening to Nesruddin talk about the battle.

"There you are!" Abaji said. "I sent a man to search for you."

My throat constricted but I forced it open to speak. "Marco?" I asked.

Abaji gestured to his left with the rib. There, sitting by the side of a tent, writing furiously on parchment, was Marco Polo.

The tightness inside me burst. He was alive!

I stood before him, soaking up the details: his reddish curls, matted with sweat and glowing in the firelight; his bushy beard; his high nose; his thick eyebrows, drawn together in concentration. His moving hand, his breathing body.

He stopped writing and looked up. A smile of relief lit up his face. "Emmajin!" He dropped his ink brush and paper, stood up, and embraced me in a way no Mongol man ever embraces a woman in public. I was so relieved I didn't care. He spoke into my hair. "I was so afraid for you, during the battle. I searched and searched but could not find you."

I buried my head in his chest. "They told me you were dead."

He laughed. "Oh, no. I'm alive. And you are, too. Thanks be to Deus." He squeezed me more tightly against him. I was too choked up to speak.

Finally, he pulled back and looked into my eyes. "Abaji has been telling everyone about how valiantly you fought. Everyone praises you. Sit here, and tell me your tale."

I stared hard at him. "Suren is dead."

His face darkened. "Yes, I know. He died a hero's death."

I nearly gagged. To Marco, the battle was nothing more than a story. He would gather the facts and prepare a good tale for the entertainment of the Great Khan. The battle of Vochan would go down in history, and his would be the official version.

A surge of anger flared through me. Marco had not fought. He had stood to the side and observed. He had done nothing to ensure the victory, yet the Khan and his men would shout, "Good! Good!" as if he himself had laid his life on the line. Suren was dead, and Marco wanted details, like a vulture picking at carrion.

"Emmajin Beki?" He could see the shadow covering my face. I pulled away from his touch. "I loved him, too, you know," he said.

I looked away, remembering how Marco and Suren had seemed like brothers just a few days earlier, sharing the excitement of dragon hunting. I had never seen Suren so happy.

"You fought well," Marco said, as if to soothe me. "There is much to celebrate."

I whipped around and stared into those green eyes, which seemed empty again. "No. Suren lies dead. And you did nothing." Suddenly, this man, dear to me a moment before, seemed like a court fool.

He dropped his arms to his sides, looking at me sadly.

"You just watched from a hillside as we fought." I spoke with venom in my voice. "Or were you in your tent, writing?"

Marco looked stricken.

Abaji lumbered over to us. "Emmajin." He, too, tried to touch me but I pulled away. "Emmajin. You have not heard."

"What!" My voice cut like a saber across a man's throat.

"It was Marco's idea. He has no military training, but his idea helped us win."

"What idea?" Whatever it was, I cared not.

"He brought the fire medicine to use against the elephants. Those explosions."

I looked hard at Abaji and then at Marco.

"We owe him thanks. We could not have won otherwise."

The explosions that had frightened the elephants. The fire rats and the powder Marco had collected in the dragon village. Yet I could not believe that Abaji was giving credit to Marco for our victory. We did the fighting and killing.

Seeing my anger, grief, and disbelief, Marco looked at his hands.

"But you, Emmajin Beki!" Abaji continued. "I hear you killed one hundred enemy soldiers." One hundred. I had never said that number. Later stories expanded it to one thousand. But it was not valor or glory that had driven me. It was anger and retribution. Ugly actions driven by ugly motives.

"You must be hungry." Abaji seemed eager to soothe me. "Have some meat."

I could not eat. Blood and mud caked on my hands. I went to the stream and washed. My hands came clean, but the stains of battle were embedded in my clothing and my heart. I went to my *ger* and sat a long time. Suren was dead. Marco and I were alive. I had proved I could fight like a man. But there was no thrill in it.

PART III

Return to Khanbalik

31

New Possibilities

I did not dream of the horrors of battle that night, although I have many times since. But halfway through the night, I heard Suren calling my name. I woke up saying, "Yes? What is it?" thinking he was sleeping next to me, as he had during our latest journey. Even in the darkness, though, I could sense that he wasn't there.

Images from the battle flashed through my mind. I tried to shut them out and remember Suren's face at peace. "What shall I tell your father and the Khan?" I pleaded, ever more desperate to hear him answer. "Suren!" I nearly shouted. My heart was barren and my eyes were dry. I could feel his spirit there with me. I knew well that angry ghosts often haunted those they had quarreled with, but I had never quarreled with Suren. I wanted to tell his unsettled spirit to leave and find peace, but I didn't have the heart to.

The next morning, at first light, we buried Suren's body. This far from home, we could not wait for the lamas to declare an auspicious day. As a prince of the Golden Family, he was placed in a coffin, with his sword by his side, a rock under his head, and Marco's blue scarf around his neck. His grave was unmarked, but I tried to remember the spot—the slope of the hill and a large rock nearby. Abaji stood by my side, out of respect.

It was raining, and I could not help thinking about that wooden coffin rotting in the wet soil, far from home. It seemed wrong to leave his body there. I wore the dragon's tooth on its thong under my *del,* next to my heart. It felt heavy and burned my skin.

When we returned to camp, we had to walk between two fires, to drive evil spirits away and prevent further misfortunes. The fires sizzled in the rain, and men worked hard to keep them going.

The other dead soldiers were too numerous to be buried. And we could not follow our nomadic Mongol custom of "casting out" the bodies in remote, dry areas for the wild dogs and vultures. Their bodies had to be burned, to allow their spirits to rise directly to Heaven. A group of men took pains to lay out the bodies of the Khan's soldiers in close, neat rows, heads pointing north, in preparation for cremation when the rain stopped. It was much quicker to kill hundreds of men than to care for their corpses.

I was glad not to be assigned the hideous task of collecting and burning the bodies. Instead, I was directed to help care for the wounded. I knew nothing of such work, but others had been doing it throughout the night and taught me how. I dipped cloths in water and cleaned superficial wounds. I wiped cool cloths over the faces of the feverish. I tightened tourniquets around arms and legs to minimize blood loss.

Some of the soldiers had burns or limbs missing from the explosions of the fire medicine. Overnight, half the wounded had died, and more died during the day. We could do little to save them. Their moans and screams lacerated my heart.

During the day, I saw Marco several times, in the tents of the wounded. He brought out the precious medicines he had bought in the market of Carajan and explained how to use them. He had traded almost all the goods his father had retained for those medicines, and now he was offering them to help save our soldiers.

Seeing Marco doing such important work calmed me. But there was no opportunity for us to be alone. Part of me was glad of that, because I did not trust myself.

My feelings had shifted. Losing Suren and nearly losing Marco had made me rethink what was important to me. Before I had met Marco, all that had mattered was my ambition to join the Khan's army and to achieve glory in battle. Now I had achieved those goals, but they were empty vessels. Glory on the battlefield had come with a price too high to bear. Without Suren at my side, even the grandest of victory parades would mean nothing.

"Water!" A Mongol soldier waved his bandaged stump to get my attention. I dipped a bowl into a bucket of water and brought it to him.

With the clarity of a lightning strike, I realized that I could never fight in a battle again. After all my bravado in front of the Great Khan, I would have to go back before him and ask to be released from the army. The thought made me shiver.

If I did not continue as a soldier, what would I do? Who would I be?

My heart in turmoil and confusion, I sank into despair.

* * *

A few days later, we left Vochan and began the five-day ride through the mountains back to Nesruddin's palace in Da-li. Of the twelve thousand Mongol army soldiers who had set out, eight thousand had survived. Of the thirty young recruits who had left Khanbalik in Tenth Moon with Abaji, just sixteen remained. Todogen was dead, and only one of the three sergeants was left. The empty spaces between us hung heavily.

During the journey to Da-li, the soldiers kept talking of the battle, each telling what he had seen. They mourned lost friends but were jubilant about the victory. The farther we traveled from Vochan, the more epic the proportions the tale took on. The number of enemies killed increased daily, but the horror and bloodshed disappeared behind such words as "the battle raged furiously with sword and mace" and "right fiercely did the two hosts rush together, and deadly were the blows exchanged."

The tales began to sound more like the familiar words of Old Master and less like the battle I had witnessed and fought. I realized that tales, even true ones, do not reflect truth in its fullness. In fact, all of the storytellers' tales of battles were trickery. They pumped up men's spirits so they would go eagerly into battle, when the reality of battle was unbearable. Soldiers who had killed men could live with themselves only if they believed the storytellers' versions of battlefield glory.

As I rode each day under the winter gray of the mountain skies, I thought about the future. Marco and I had never spoken words of love to each other. And certainly we had never discussed the possibility of a life together. But despite my anger at Marco, I realized that he was precious to me now. Suren's death had taught me how vain it was to put my desire for glory above my love for others.

I looked forward to arriving at Nesruddin's palace, hoping I would find time there to relax with Marco. Now that my feelings toward him had changed, I needed to think about what my choices might be. I wished I could come up with some way to keep Marco with me. It was tempting to imagine running off with him. But where would we go? To Venezia? His father and uncle had remained in Khanbalik, and they would be punished, possibly executed, if Marco ran off with a princess from the imperial court. The Khan's power extended throughout his Empire. We were near the border and could slip outside the empire quickly, but across the border was Burma, territory of the enemy.

Could Marco and I get married somehow? I laughed silently at the image of my father, Prince Dorji, and Marco's father, Niccolo Polo, toasting each other at a wedding banquet. It was impossible. Granddaughters of the Khan were valuable property, to be offered in marriage only to men of allied clans as a reward for loyalty and service. Marrying me to a Latin merchant and storyteller would be like throwing a diamond into a dung pile. I hoped that battlefield glory would give me the right to refuse any more marriage offers. But no one in the royal family would accept Marco as a suitable mate.

Besides, as much as he meant to me, I cringed at the idea of becoming Marco's wife. That would mean moving out of the Khan's court and into the cramped rooms Marco shared with his father and uncle. I would no longer be the Great Khan's granddaughter but the wife of a merchant. Marco would not stay in China forever. I would have to go to Venezia when he was ready. As attractive as Venezia sounded, I had no desire to leave the center of the world and go live in a waterlogged city so far outside the realm of the known that it took more than three years to get there. I would be as foreign there as Marco was here.

Traveling with Marco would allow me to see the world. But it would mean leaving my homeland forever. I imagined the life of a traveling merchant: stirring pots over campfires, plodding along on camelback for days on end, living among uncivilized barbarians who could not speak my language.

A merchant's wife—it reminded me of the famous Tang poem "The Lute Girl." In it, a woman sadly plucked her lute, remembering the days of her youth, when all admired her musical skills. When she grew older, she was forced to become "a trader's wife, the chattel of a slave, whose lord was gold."

No, marrying Marco was out of the question. But what could I do, an unmarried princess, granddaughter of the Khan, veteran of the battle of Vochan? My brain hurt as I pushed it for answers.

32

Precious Medicine

Finally, the day before we reached Nesruddin's palace, I found a chance to talk to Marco. During a steep uphill climb, I deliberately slowed my horse and dropped behind the others, to the back of the line, where Marco was riding with a servant.

"I hope you are not too tired, Messer Marco," I began as his horse pulled up next to mine. I could not bring myself to apologize for my outburst after the battle, and the intervening days had made me more eager to see him.

In a short meeting of our eyes, I could see both pleasure and concern in his. "Thank you. I am not too tired, Emmajin Beki." The soldier behind me was not close enough to hear, but close enough to see our manner of speaking.

I had to work to keep my voice even, as if discussing the weather. "Will you be returning with Abaji to Khanbalik?"

"I must take the dragons back to the Great Khan. I am hoping that Little Li will travel with me, to take care of them. That will mean a slow journey. General Abaji has told me he wishes to return quickly."

My heart fell. I wished I could travel back with Marco, but I knew that General Abaji would never allow it. "General Abaji plans to celebrate the New Year in Carajan before returning home," I said. "But . . . after you return to Khanbalik? What then?"

He looked sad. "My father's plan is to begin our journey home in the late spring."

I rode in silence, as if I'd heard a death sentence. While I had known that Marco planned to return to Venezia, I had just realized that it would mean losing him forever. In a few days, I would leave Carajan and might not have a chance to see Marco again. "Of course you must return to your homeland," I said.

He lowered his voice. "But I hate to face my father with empty saddlebags. He will be furious."

"What do you mean?" I had never asked him about his trading.

"My father gave me half his profits, what little he had left after giving our greatest treasures to the Khan, and asked me to buy goods on this trip. I spent most of it on rare medicines in Carajan, items not available in the capital, small and easy to carry."

"That sounds like a wise purchase."

"Yes. But now they are gone."

I remembered seeing him go from tent to tent when we were caring for the injured after the battle. "You gave them to the soldiers."

"Yes." He looked at me intently.

"And now you have no gold to buy more medicine in Da-li?"

"That is correct."

"What will you tell your father and uncle?"

He twisted his mouth. "I have been pondering this every day."

Caught up in my own problems, I had been oblivious to his. "Marco," I said. "I will see what I can do."

Back in Da-li, the following evening, Nesruddin invited us to a banquet to celebrate our victory. I sat next to General Nesruddin, with all the sergeants of ten and commanders of one hundred. The *airag* flowed freely, and the food was delicious: spicy rice noodles, ham, snake, stewed fish, bamboo shoots, and mushrooms. The flavors and spices danced on my tongue as if I were eating for the first time.

After dinner, talk turned to the battle of Vochan. Every man present told his view of the battle, except Marco. So Abaji stood and told the story of how Marco had gotten the idea of using fire rats and bamboo lances filled with fire medicine to frighten the elephants. The men shouted, "Good! Good!" Marco smiled humbly, and I realized that he hid his brilliance and acted the fool so as not to appear threatening.

When Abaji had finished, I stood, feeling uncertain. Women seldom spoke at banquets. All eyes were on me. Steadying myself with my hands on the table, I looked across at Marco, then at Abaji and Nesruddin.

"I am not a trained storyteller," I began, my voice cracking. "Still, there is something else you do not know about our

Latin friend. After the battle, many soldiers were wounded. Messer Marco gave to our wounded troops his precious medicines that he had bought with his own gold."

A ripple of approval rose from the gathering.

My voice grew more confident. "I saw this with my own eyes. One young soldier was in great pain. He took Messer Marco's medicine, stopped moaning, and later recovered. Messer Marco gave freely, sacrificing all he had. Now he has nothing of value to take back to Khanbalik to trade. This, too, is heroism."

"This is true?" asked Nesruddin. Marco waved his hand as if it were nothing. "Remark on this!" the general continued. "A foreigner has contributed to the Great Khan's cause. For a merchant, merchandise is like blood. Yet he gave it freely!"

"Good! Good!" shouted Abaji, and others followed.

"I will see that you are compensated," said Nesruddin to Marco. And he did. As the Khan's highest representative in the province of Carajan, Nesruddin was empowered to spend the Khan's gold. On behalf of our generous Khan, he gave Marco enough to replace all the precious medicine he had bought and to buy other goods as well.

I was glad I had helped Marco. But it was bittersweet. Helping him buy goods would enable him to return to his homeland.

33

Under the New Moon

Soon it was time to celebrate the New Year—Tsagaan Sar, the White Festival. We stayed at Nesruddin's Palace in Da-li to enjoy the biggest holiday of the Mongol year.

Despite our victory and the festivities, the Mongol holiday traditions filled me with sadness. Suren's absence darkened every activity. We greeted one another with *khadag*s, the blue ceremonial silk scarves we Mongols present with both hands as a gesture of goodwill. Each of them made me think of Suren with unbearable pain. I was sure I would never again feel pleasure on this holiday.

On the evening of the second day of the New Year, when most people of the palace had aching heads from too much *airag,* or sore bellies from too much meat, I found time to talk to Marco alone. He was standing on the ramparts overlooking the huge ear-shaped lake that lapped at the palace walls. This time, there was no moon, as New Year's Day is always on the day of the new moon. The stars seemed brighter, reflected in the lake water.

"Do they see the same stars in your homeland?" I asked, startling him as I came up behind him.

When he saw it was I, he smiled. "It's strange. The stars look exactly the same, and so does the moon. This is the only thing here that reminds me of home."

"You are eager to go back," I said, standing near him.

He turned toward me. "Thank you for your help," he said. "Still, I wish I could find some way to stay." Even in the darkness, I could see that his eyes burned with sincerity.

"There is no way. You know that," I said, wishing it were not true.

He looked over the lake. "Yes. Of course. I understand."

"Far from home, we are free to think different thoughts," I said.

"And you will return home soon, to the palace." He continued my train of thought. "I hope I have not offended you in any way." His voice became more formal. It saddened me.

Side by side, we stared out over the water awhile. His arm was two hand widths away from mine. My heart was full of sorrow. I felt sure we would never be alone again. "Princess, you remember, in Xanadu," he began, "I told you about courtly love, when a low-ranking man admires a lady from a distance."

So he had been thinking of me. "A lovely tradition," I said.

"Do you recall," he said, "the day you shot down the eagle?"

We had not mentioned the incident since that day. "Mmm," I said.

"You proved, so clearly, that your archery skills were as

good as any man's," he said. "But what moved me was something different. You had a heart for that magnificent eagle."

In the dark, I blushed, ashamed that he had noticed this weakness. Yet his voice was gentle and calm, not accusing.

"That eagle died quickly," I said.

"That eagle soared majestically before it fell," he responded. "That was the moment I knew I loved you."

His words, so direct, stunned me. He loved me. He had loved me all this time, all these months. He knew that with certainty.

By contrast, my love for him had not come at a single moment. It had grown over time, from scorn and distrust, through curiosity, to something deeper, a certainty that my life was not worth living without him. I knew that now, with just as much certainty. Yet my life was not my own. It belonged to the Khan.

Marco was looking at me, hoping for a reply. "After the battle," I began. The words stuck in my throat. I swallowed a lump and went on. "Someone told me you were dead."

He moved to comfort me, but stopped. "You seemed angry at me that day," he said.

"I was angry. But not at you."

"We have one more night," he said. He had heard in my voice what he needed to hear. We had one night to act on our love, before I had to return home to the court.

I remembered his kiss, the passion of his embrace in Tibet. On this night, even the maid in my chamber would be away, celebrating with her family. No one would know if Marco came to my room. Night after night, I had dreamed of this opportunity.

But it felt wrong. Suren's concern rang in my ears.

A heavy weight in my heart felt as dark as the new moon. It was not the right moment for joy. As much as I had wanted Marco, for so long, my heart would not allow it now.

"I don't know what to say," I replied. "The sky is so dark without the moonlight."

Marco could see I was holding back. "The stars are distant, but beautiful. I will always admire them."

Suddenly, I wanted to cry. Nothing would ever be right in my life again. I thought of Ai-Jaruk going off to battles with her father and returning home to an empty bed. Her story had seemed happy when I had first heard it. Now it seemed tragic.

"I must go now." I could barely choke out the words. I turned and walked quickly to my empty bed.

34

News

On the third day of the New Year, we set off from Carajan. With a heavy heart, I left with Abaji and the remaining soldiers.

Before our departure, Little Li and some men had brought the eight young dragons from their village to Da-li, carrying them in baskets suspended from poles balanced on their shoulders. In a courtyard of Nesruddin's palace, they constructed wooden pavilions and secured them on top of the elephants. Inside were special pens to hold the juvenile dragons in shallow water. Each dragon had its own pen, to protect them from snapping at one another. It turned out to be the perfect solution to the problem of transporting the dragons over long distances. Marco was bringing back a little of the magic of Carajan.

During my two-month journey back to the capital, I kept wishing I could be with Marco, traveling through lowlands with the elephants and dragons. Night after night, I regretted my decision not to go with Marco that night of the new moon. I let my mind wander, imagining what might have happened.

I also agonized about my future. What could I ask of the Great Khan? I could not become a military commander. I no longer wanted to fight in battles, and I certainly did not want to conquer Marco's homeland.

General Abaji, I knew, would recommend to the Khan that we attack Burma as soon as possible, to exploit the king of Burma's weakness after his loss at Vochan. Abaji wanted to raise an army in Khanbalik and return quickly. But I would not take part in that battle. The future seemed like a blank wall that I was racing toward every day.

Shortly before we arrived in Khanbalik, early in Third Moon, a small party of horsemen headed by my cousin Temur came out to greet us.

Temur seemed older, with a deeper voice and a hint of a mustache. He wanted to hear about Suren's death before others did. He acted sad, but Suren's death made Temur the Khan's eldest grandson. If his father, Chimkin, succeeded our grandfather, as expected, Temur might someday become Khan himself.

Temur nearly burst with his own news. "General, you have heard the good news? Our troops have taken Kinsay."

This news sent a lightning bolt through my body. Kinsay was the capital of the Southern Sung dynasty, center of power for southern China.

Two soldiers who were riding close enough to hear cheered. "A victory in Kinsay! All China is ours!" Our army had been fighting in southern China for fifteen years. Now the Khan's empire stretched to the sea in the South and the East, adding hundreds of thousands of subjects in the world's wealthiest country. It was a huge victory, the biggest Khubilai Khan could achieve.

"I was there," Temur said with pride, "with the army as we marched into Kinsay. It was a glorious moment."

"Was the fighting fierce?" I asked.

Temur shook his head in dismay. "Our great general had conquered so many of their cities that the rulers of China knew it was pointless to resist. The mother of the boy emperor conceded without a battle. Our troops rode into Kinsay with no opposition."

This news hit me hard. Suren had died in a battle that had not gained new territory for the Empire. Yet the glory would go to Temur and the army that occupied Kinsay.

We dismounted to hear the rest of the story. Temur told it with verve and gusto, as if it reflected his personal glory. I found myself leaning toward him, eager to hear every word. So were the other soldiers.

All winter long, Temur told us, the Great Khan had received news of victory after victory, as General Bayan Chincsan and the Mongol army conquered twelve major cities in southern China. Everyone had been expecting a huge battle at Kinsay, with great loss of life, because they had expected the Chinese to defend their capital to the last man. Then came a messenger with the great news: Kinsay had fallen without a battle.

The empress of South China, mother of the six-year-old boy emperor, had called in an astrologer when the Mongol forces had surrounded Kinsay. The astrologer reminded her of a forecast her late husband, the emperor, had been told as a young man: only a man with one hundred eyes could rob them of their kingdom. Back then, the forecast had been seen as good news. But when the empress learned General Bayan's name, which, when said in Chinese, sounds like "hundred eyes," she surrendered and handed over the imperial seal.

Full of confidence, Temur seemed mature and articulate. With his slim body and handsome, wide-set eyes, he looked more the part of a crown prince than Suren had. I could see in their eyes how much the other soldiers admired Temur. Still, his manner was arrogant. He was too eager to step into Suren's empty boots.

"Good news indeed!" Abaji slapped his thigh. "When is the victory parade?"

A pang shot through me. I had envisioned returning to Khanbalik as part of a victory parade. Now I was returning with a straggling group of soldiers, victors of a distant battle. Our hard-fought win on the plain of Vochan, against such great odds, paled in comparison to the conquest of all southern China. Would the Khan value our victory?

"General Bayan is on his way back from the South, bringing the empress and the young boy emperor. They should arrive in ten days or so."

"Good. So we will arrive in time for the parade—and for the beheading." Abaji's voice sounded eager.

I shivered. A Chinese queen and her young son would now face the wrath of the Khan of all Khans. Their execution would send an essential message, I knew, a warning to all who dared to resist Mongol conquest, including the kings of

Burma and Zipangu. Sparing the enemy's rulers was not an option. It would encourage others tempted to resist.

But to me, at that moment, the public execution of a woman and child in the streets of Khanbalik seemed barbaric.

35

Reentry

Khanbalik was brimming with a sense of pride in Mongol greatness. From the moment we rode into the capital under the huge arch of the south gate, with its curved blue roofs, I could feel the exuberance. Scattered crowds near the gate had been waiting for the arrival of General Bayan with the Chinese empress and her son. People surged forward to look at us, soldiers traveling under the Khan's banner. It was hard to keep riding in formation, and Baatar shied and whinnied.

"General Bayan!" a man shouted in Mongolian, and more men moved forward.

"No, not yet!" one of Temur's soldiers responded. "General Abaji, returning from a victory in the Southwest."

"General Abaji, returning from the South!" someone shouted. The announcement was echoed in Cathayan, and a cheer rose around us.

Everyone seemed to realize that we were living at a

historic moment. It had been sixty years since Chinggis Khan began the conquest of China by sacking the northern Chinese capital of Yenjing, which later became Khanbalik. For decades, we Mongols had controlled North China. Now, with the conquest of Kinsay, his grandson Khubilai Khan had unified all of China, north and south, under Mongol rule. A new era was beginning, full of the promise of harmony.

General Abaji rode down the main avenue of the capital in a stately manner. Temur followed him, holding high the Khan's white horse-tail banner. The rest of us followed in formation. The half-grown trees lining the sides of the avenue had been wrapped in silk strips of yellow and white, contrasting with the vivid spring green of the buds on their branches. Banners of red, yellow, blue, and white fluttered from the roof tiles topping the walls that lined the street.

The atmosphere was festive. Men, women, and children, Cathayans, Mongols, and foreigners mingled along the sides of the avenue, watching and pointing, raising their children to their shoulders, cheering and laughing.

"It's Prince Temur!" one boy shouted.

"Temur! Temur!" others echoed in joyful voices. "Returned from the South!"

Finally, I was entering the city of Khanbalik in a victory parade, but without Suren. No one recognized me or shouted my name. Our triumph at Vochan had not won me celebrity. Instead, they cheered this man who had marched into Kinsay without a fight. After the horrors and losses of battle, I still did not get to enjoy the victory parade that Suren and I had desired so ardently. It felt like an insult to Suren's memory.

I had hoped the Great Khan himself would greet us, but he was on his annual spring hunting trip. Abaji gathered us just inside the palace gate, praised us for our service to the Khan in battle, and instructed us to return to our families for a rest of twenty days.

I dismounted, handed Baatar's reins to a servant, and headed to my parents' courtyard. Everything looked different to me. The great audience halls of the palace seemed larger and grander. But after seeing Nesruddin's smaller, elegant palace by the lake, the Khan's palace seemed ostentatious.

After months on the road, eating simple meals with my companions around open fires, riding with the wind in my face, wearing the same uniform day after day, the everyday luxuries of court life seemed excessive. On the road, we had talked of war and peace and the future of mankind. Here, people talked of minor spats and spread rumors of concubines who flirted with guards. My cheeks had grown ruddy from exposure to the elements, and here women rubbed lotions on their cheeks to keep them smooth.

As I walked toward the back of the Khan's palace, no one greeted or recognized me. A hard spot around my heart began to throb.

When I entered my home, my mother rushed out to greet me. She grabbed both my hands as if I were still a young girl. The top of her head reached no higher than my nose. She leaned back and examined my face, my arms, my body, looking for wounds.

"Were you injured, my daughter?" she asked.

"No, not at all." I squeezed her hand. "But . . . Suren . . ." Suddenly, I was weeping like a girl with a gaping wound that would never heal. It was the first time I had cried after Suren's death. Here, at home, it was safe to mourn.

Small as she was, my mother embraced me, just above my

waist, and laid her head against my shoulder. She hugged me so tightly that my breath came in gasps. Her hair, flattened with a fragrant oil, exuded the flowery scent I remembered from childhood. I, too, hugged her so tight I thought I might squeeze the breath from her.

Drolma seemed happy to see me, but the gulf between us was wider than ever. During my absence, my parents had arranged a marriage for her, with Jebe, son of the general who had dismissed me.

"General Aju said I was exactly the kind of daughter-in-law he wanted," Drolma told me with pride. I was bursting to tell stories, of the lion I had killed, of the dragon hunt, of the battle. But they didn't want to hear of my adventures. Drolma only wanted to tell me the latest court gossip.

That night, I slept in my old bed with my sister. I retired early, overcome with six months' worth of exhaustion. What had been the point of trying so hard to be a soldier, to fight like a man and keep riding day after day? Here I was, back where I had started, like a maiden who had never left her father's *ger*. I had still been able to smell the pungent wind of the farmlands and the sweat of the army on my outer clothing. But once I'd taken my army clothing off and lain down under my sister's quilt, all I could smell was her perfume. My body felt tired and heavy, yet my mind was swirling. I felt sad, bitter, lost.

The next morning, my mother handed me a square of silver. It was the Tara amulet from my father that I had cast aside nearly a year ago.

"Your father heard about Suren's death. He wanted to make sure you were carrying this, from the goddess of mercy, to help you in your grieving."

This time, I accepted the amulet. I needed whatever compassion was offered.

"He is at the monastery," Mama said. "Go talk to him."

After all I had been through, I was in urgent need of answers, and I no longer felt certain that my father's choices had been wrong. For the first time in my life, I felt a pressing desire to learn from his wisdom.

36

At the Monastery

After resting a few days at home, I made the journey to the Buddhist monastery. It was a half day's ride from Khanbalik, situated on a hillside overlooking the plains.

I was not sure what I wanted to hear from my father. I needed to fill this painful hole inside me, to find some meaning in life after the loss of Suren. I had to decide about my future, about the army and Marco. My father had never provided such wisdom for me before, and I was not sure I could speak honestly to him. But I sensed that he had deeper thoughts than he had ever expressed to me.

As I entered the front gate of the monastery, I breathed in the fresh mountain air, scented with the sweet smell of burning incense. This was one of the oldest Buddhist compounds in this part of Cathay, built almost a thousand years earlier. Each of the temples was spacious and imposing, with wise-looking Buddhas—past, present, and future—carved of wood. I wandered through a series of courtyards with twisted pines and cypress trees, stone monuments called stupas, and rock formations. The atmosphere was one of quiet serenity and humble contemplation.

I saw a monk and asked him where to find my father, Prince Dorji. He understood Mongolian but did not speak it. He took me to the Hall of Guanyin, the goddess of mercy.

There, a nun, with head shaved bald, was kneeling and praying on the stone steps, facing the statue. She was wearing simple gray robes and chanting a stream of foreign words. I guessed they were Tibetan, since the sutras were written in Tibetan. The air was thick with the smell of incense.

The monk cleared his throat and waited. The nun seemed totally absorbed.

Finally, she stopped chanting, paused, stood up, and walked toward me. Her looks surprised me. She was young, with a smooth, broad face, round like a moon. She seemed vaguely familiar, but I had never talked to a nun.

"Yes? How can I help you?" She spoke clear Mongolian. This was odd. I had heard of Chinese and Tibetan nuns, but had never known a Mongolian to become a nun.

Only after the move to Khanbalik, during my childhood, were Mongols introduced to this foreign religion of Buddhism. By tradition, Mongols worshiped Eternal Heaven—Tengri—and Mother Earth. We built *ovoos* in sacred spots in nature and circled them, tossing stones onto them to ask for good fortune. Ours was not an organized religion with temples and texts. Some Mongol tribes were Christian, such as that of Khubilai's mother, but few had adopted the Buddhist or Muslim religions. My grandmother Chabi was an exception, a Mongol who had become a devout Buddhist.

When I told the nun my name, she smiled and examined

my face carefully. "Ah, Emmajin! Follow me," she said. She led me through a gate to another courtyard. At its center was a deep pool, surrounded by mulberry trees just beginning to bloom.

Inside a nearby room, my father was sitting cross-legged on a low bench, looking at some long, thin books laid out on a table. The pages were covered with curly connected letters arranged in neat rows. I could not imagine how they made sense.

Just seeing him, with his heavy-lidded eyes and deep under-eye shadows, brought back my feelings of bitterness. He had left my mother to fend for herself at court and showed no interest in me at all. What wisdom could I expect from him?

My father's eyebrows rose, but he did not stand or approach me. Instead, he pointed to a low bench just opposite him. I sat there with my legs crossed. My father had shaved his head bald, too, and wore a simple monk's maroon robe.

The nun poured some boiled water into a bowl and handed it to me to drink. She sat near the wall, watching like a chaperone.

"I hear you fought in a battle," my father began. "I'm glad to see you alive."

"But Suren," I began. I choked, unable to continue.

He shook his head in sorrow. I was glad I would not have to explain. "Such a fine young man. You two were so close."

I didn't know what to say, and my words tumbled out. "I just wish I could . . . The battle wasn't what I expected. Bodies everywhere. Even horses killed! And Suren . . . I saw . . . I never thought . . . I was so angry. I wanted revenge. Once I killed an enemy soldier, I couldn't stop killing."

A flash of pain surged across my father's face, but he waited for me to finish.

"It all seems so pointless now," I continued. "How can I go on without Suren?"

I had thought he might be angry or say *I told you so,* but he seemed sad. "Suffering is a part of life. I am sorry you had to learn this so young."

He began to speak in a calm, flowing voice. He told me that he had been a soldier, too, when he was my age. I had not known this. My father had joined the army at the age of sixteen, as the eldest son of Khubilai, who was then a minor prince of the Golden Family. In the army, he had come down with a terrible disease. He could not move and could barely breathe. Many others died of this disease, but he recovered. He had had to learn to use his arms and legs again, which was why he limped.

As he spoke, the tension in my shoulders began to ease. "I was told you fell from a horse," I said. Such a fall is the ultimate shame for a Mongol.

His lips formed a grim line. "I did, later. I tried to ride too soon, before my legs had regained full strength. That fall made it harder to learn to walk again."

My heart filled with sympathy.

"For years, I hunted for answers. I wanted to know why I had suffered from this disease. Why I could not lead a normal life like my younger brothers. My mother, the Empress Chabi, was the only one who seemed to understand."

My mother, in a moment of bitterness, had once blamed the Empress for taking my father away from her. Now I knew why. My father would never have become a Buddhist if not for his mother. But she had helped him in a moment of turmoil.

"And what of the family you left behind?" I asked him.

"I knew you would be well cared for at court."

I looked away. It was not a sufficient answer. Growing up, I had felt fatherless. Suren's father, Prince Chimkin, was always nearby, but he did not take my father's place.

My father continued. "I tried to quiet my heart, to put aside the difficulties at court. But I see now that I also lost much joy. The joy of watching you grow up."

My heart lurched. The sorrow in his face had deepened.

"You lost Suren," he said. "I lost you."

I watched as his eyes teared up. His loss, unlike mine, had been by choice. We sat in silence a few moments. My bitterness softened.

"So Buddhism does not have all the answers," I said at last.

He tilted his head, giving my comment serious consideration. "No one has all the answers. But it's important to keep searching. There is much wisdom in these sutras. Back when I was at court, my heart was in distress. I did not see the world the way other men did. Fighting wars cannot make the world a better place."

He stopped to check my eyes, as if to see whether I was truly listening. I nodded.

"Every life is worthwhile. Every sentient being, including animals. Even those of the enemy soldiers you killed on the battlefield."

I looked away, remembering. Some of the dead horses had had frozen expressions of fear. Some of those Burmese faces had looked like Little Li. At the time, I had hated them all. Did any of them have cousins, like me, who were mourning their deaths?

"The Burmese attacked us," I said, only half convinced. "They sent a huge army, with elephants, over the border. This battle was their fault."

He shook his head. "Someone always gives a good reason for war. Sometimes it even has a positive outcome. I would not want to be the Great Khan, making such decisions."

I could see his point. I had wished so hard that I had been born a boy, the eldest grandson, possible heir to the throne. To have men kowtow to me! I had never understood how my father could give up that honor. Now I was glad I would not inherit such responsibility.

"The Great Khan," I began. "He has talked of sending an army to invade Christendom." I wondered if my father had heard about Marco Polo.

"The Khan knows that Tengri, Eternal Heaven, has commanded him to complete the conquest of the world," said my father. "He senses his grandfather, Chinggis Khan, looking over his shoulder, expecting him to finish the work begun by our ancestors. But the Khan has begun to change his emphasis. He is spending more of his time finding ways to wisely rule the lands we already control."

"Do you think he could be convinced not to invade Christendom?"

My father looked as if he was trying to figure out my motives. "Christendom? Why Christendom?"

I did not have the courage, or the right words, to explain about Marco. "I don't want to fight in any more battles. I wish I could stop them somehow."

He laughed gently. "You don't sound like a soldier in the Great Khan's army."

I shook my head. "I am not sure what to do next. I don't want to stay in the army. But I do not want to get married. Please."

My father's eyes glowed softly. "There is another path. You could become a nun, like my sister here, Miaoyan." He indicated the young nun sitting by the wall.

I looked at her in surprise. I had not recognized her as one of my father's many younger sisters. I did not know her well, and without her braids, she looked different.

"Aunt Miaoyan Beki," I said to her, bowing my head in respect.

She smiled and nodded.

"Miaoyan came to me, about a year ago, just as you have come today. She asked many questions. She became a nun just five months ago."

I felt as if two walls were closing in on me, one on each side. I had not come here to enter a nunnery.

My father reacted to my look of consternation. "I will not force you. This choice must come from your heart."

Miaoyan spoke up in a soft voice. "Emmajin Beki. This life is right for me, I know that with certainty. But living here has many restrictions. You should take your time before deciding if it's right for you."

Their suggestion jarred me, since it was so at odds with the way I had lived my life. But in my despair, it seemed tempting to retreat to this peaceful place. I would miss Marco, but we had no future together. Perhaps I could say good-bye to him, then enter the nunnery with my heart at peace.

I promised my father I would think about it. Miaoyan

said I could stay that night with her, at the nunnery nearby. It was too late to return home that day, anyway.

After leaving my father, I went, alone, to the Temple of Guanyin. As I entered the temple, my eyes went straight to the large, central statue of the goddess of mercy. In this Chinese manifestation, as Guanyin, she had a look of gentleness but seemed remote. On an altar in front of her were an incense burner, several plates of dried fruit, and some metal religious objects.

Guanyin was not really a goddess; my father had told me that. She was a bodhisattva: an ordinary woman who had meditated and studied Buddhism deeply enough to enter Nirvana, the highest state of enlightenment. But instead of entering Nirvana, she had returned to earth, to help the rest of us become more enlightened. That sacrifice was the ultimate in compassion.

Butter candles burned steadily in the quiet.

As my eyes adjusted to the semidarkness, I began walking around the temple, trying to think clearly after the conversation. On a side wall in one nook was a brightly painted mural. Clearly, it had been added recently, to give a lively Mongolian flavor to what was otherwise a serious Chinese temple. At first the colors seemed too bright. But then I looked at the detail.

With a start, I realized that I was face to face with Tara, the Mongolian version of Guanyin. I pulled the silver amulet out of my sash; yes, the images were almost the same. But on the mural, nearly life-sized, Tara seemed alive.

This Tara looked young, with a plump face of smooth jade-white skin, arched eyebrows, a slim and graceful figure. Adorned with jewelry on her ears and neck and wrists, she sat on an open lotus, holding a blue flower on a long stem. Her expression was sweet and consoling.

Tara had an extra eye, set sideways, in her forehead, and also an eye on the palm of each hand and the sole of each foot. Each one was a thick black line, but nonetheless recognizable as an eye. Seven eyes altogether. Ever vigilant, she could see all suffering in the world. Her eyes were gentle, not judging. Yet she could see right through my rough exterior, past my bold name of Emmajin and my status as a soldier, into my soul.

As her eyes locked onto mine, I felt my turmoil melt like butter in hot sun. Her compassion flowed into me, through my eyes, down my throat, into the deepest parts of my body. The amulet glowed warm in my palm.

A beam of clear thinking shone into my mind. I could not flee from the world and become a nun. It was not in my nature. I needed to go back out into the world and do whatever I could to save Christendom and Marco. To make future battles unnecessary. To build a bridge between our people, the Mongols, and those from faraway lands.

I knew this suddenly, standing before the image of Tara, born of tears, whose compassion for living beings was stronger than a mother's love for her children. She had come back into the world to help people like me. She was in my father; she was in Princess Miaoyan. She was, from that moment, in me.

Breathing deeply, I lost track of time. In that place, I was not a warrior—not even a granddaughter of the Khan—or a princess who loved Marco Polo. The boundaries between me and the world around me faded. I was becoming something new, something I could not quite figure out, yet it filled me with calm.

37

Chabi's Wisdom

The next morning, I took leave of my father. I explained that I needed time to figure out what I would do, but I doubted I could become a nun. He blessed me and sent me back into the world. The tension between us had melted away.

As I was leaving, I noticed a short, wide woman dressed in elegant silks—my grandmother Chabi. Although her moon-shaped face was not beautiful, she emanated regal dignity.

"Honored grandmother," I said, falling to my knees to kowtow.

"No need," she said. "You are returning to Khanbalik today? Ride with me."

Like all the grandchildren, I was a little afraid of my grandmother. She was the highest ranking of Khubilai Khan's four wives. She seldom spent time with us or her daughters-in-law, who also feared her. She seemed stern, and I expected a lecture from her. *Become a nun. It's your only choice*, I imagined her telling me. As far as I knew, Chabi had never stepped out of the role expected of her as Empress.

To my surprise, my grandmother insisted on riding her own horse. Other royal women rode in closed carriages, suspended from poles carried on porters' shoulders.

Chabi sat erect and confident in her wooden saddle, which was covered with gold and silver medallions. She gestured for me to ride just behind her, near the front of her traveling party, which included armed guards. I didn't want to discuss my decision and was relieved when she kept silent as we rode together single file down the hillside.

Once we reached the flat land, the Empress gestured for me to ride next to her. "Do you see, girl, the contrast in greens?" she said. "That fresh, light green of the new leaves on the broadleaf trees against the darker color of the evergreens?"

Startled, I didn't know what to say. She had an accent from her native tribe, the Naimans, who were once our enemies. Her marriage had sealed our alliance with them.

"Notice the dappled shadows on the road, so clear in this bright sunlight. And do you see? The blue of the sky is deeper back there, above the hills, than it is overhead. Look at the red-brown of the earth. These are the natural colors of our world."

It was not what I had expected her to say. I examined my surroundings. True, this early-spring day was achingly beautiful. The sun warmed my arms. Each color grew more vivid after she mentioned it.

"The sun rises each day, even after we have lost a loved one," she said.

So she knew of my suffering. I looked away. Suren had been her grandson, but she could not possibly feel his loss as deeply as I did. Still, I appreciated her compassion. We rode on in silence.

"In a few days," she said after a while, "the young emperor of China will arrive in Khanbalik, with his mother and grandmother."

"Will they be executed immediately?"

The Empress gazed into the blue sky. "That decision is up to the Great Khan. I have spoken to him about this matter. I hope he will change his mind and not kill them."

I couldn't believe her words. "But they resisted our troops for so many years. Thousands of our soldiers died. Won't the Khan need to punish them?"

"The boy emperor had no part in these decisions. His grandmother, the Empress Dowager, chose to spare the lives of her people by surrendering without a fight."

"But . . . won't our people insist on an execution, to celebrate our victory?"

Chabi sighed. "One day, our dynasty, too, will come to an end. How would you want our descendants to be treated?"

It had never occurred to me that our dynasty would come to an end. We Mongols, the strongest and the best, ruled the world because Tengri had decreed we should. The Khan's destiny was to complete this conquest. How could his empress even imagine the day when Mongol rule would end?

"The Khan seems to like foreigners," I said. "That worries many men at court."

The Empress sighed and looked to the horizon again, her bulky body swaying gently with the amble of her horse. "Many men at court do not understand the Great Khan. I knew him as a young man. He was as impetuous and battle-hungry as the next warrior. Like you, he killed many enemies in battle. But over the years, he has developed a different way of thinking."

It was hard to imagine my grandfather as a young man. I had always known him as old and fat, barely able to walk.

"Yesterday's enemies are today's subjects," she continued. "Some of them have years of accumulated wisdom, stored in scrolls. Some have centuries-old religions, ways of understanding Eternal Heaven that go beyond our Mongol lore. That is why the Khan invites men of different religions to debate in front of him. He believes men from every country have wisdom to offer."

"Some say . . . ," I dared to interrupt, almost afraid to speak yet not willing to remain silent. "Some say he has become too . . . too much like the Chinese."

Chabi laughed. "Yet he has killed more Chinese than most Mongols. As he ages, the Great Khan is not more Chinese, but wiser. He is not rejecting his Mongol heritage but expanding upon it. He has allowed the Chinese to return to farming, instead of taking over their land for pasture. He has stored excess grain for famine years."

I had never thought of the Great Khan as benevolent.

"The Great Khan no longer sees the world as a conflict between Mongols and foreigners, us against them. He can already envision a world at peace, unified under one ruler. Eternal Heaven has granted the Mongols a mandate to rule the entire world. Should not we use all the wisdom Heaven has given the world?"

I was struck dumb. This vision was much wiser and far-reaching than any I had imagined. Since his youth, the Khan had changed and grown in his thinking. I suspected that Chabi had influenced him.

"So one can be loyal to the Khan," I said, "to our Mongol heritage and our right to rule forever, and still . . ." *Love a foreigner,* I wanted to say but did not dare. She would be shocked to know of my love for Marco. "And still respect foreigners?"

"Absolutely," said my grandmother. "To be loyal to all humankind does not mean giving up your loyalty to your people."

I rode in silence awhile, trying to understand. In my experience, loyalty to my people directly contradicted this wider vision of compassion for others. These ideas were grand and appealing, but they didn't help me as I tried to decide what to do about Marco.

"Tell me, Emmajin," said my grandmother. "You wanted to join the army and fight a battle, and now you have succeeded. Will you remain in the army?"

I squirmed in my saddle. "The Khan honored me when he allowed me to join the army. I understand that."

"But now," she continued, "what do you want most in your life?"

"My father wants me to enter the nunnery."

"But you wish to return to the world, to do good, like Tara."

If I had said these words, it would have been presumptuous. But when Chabi said them, they seemed right. "Yes. I would like to do something different, somehow. To make a difference."

She smiled. It was a tiny smile in the broad expanse of her face. "Women do not usually make a difference in the world."

I looked at her. She was a woman who made a difference, through her influence on her husband. "I can try."

She smiled and nodded approval. "I hope you can become a messenger of peace."

Peace. The word sounded different when spoken by a Mongol empress. After the terrors of battle, I found it appealing.

38

The Emperor of China

"Attention! Stand by for the entrance of the defeated!"

The Khan's small audience hall, filled with joyful chatter, went silent. We all turned to the front door, where the sunlight silhouetted three small figures. The deposed Chinese emperor—a little boy—entered the Khan's hall with his mother and grandmother. They walked in soundlessly, on slippered feet. Both women hobbled with tiny steps, because their feet had been broken and bound when they were children—a Chinese aristocratic custom that Mongolian women regarded with disgust.

I had quietly entered the hall through the back entrance to witness this historic moment. The Khan had invited all his sons and grandsons and his highest officials. My father was not present, but Chimkin stood near the Khan, as did Temur. I stood behind them, out of sight. The Khan, with his massive bulk, high on his wide throne, was ready to receive obeisance from a small boy whose bow would acknowledge Khubilai Khan as Emperor of all China.

Together they stood before the Great Khan. I craned my neck to see their faces, which were grave. The grandmother, once known as the Empress Dowager, had been the real power behind the throne in southern China. Her face was lined with defeat. Her back was hunched and she leaned on a cane. Next to her stood a beautiful young woman, not much older than twenty, willowy and graceful, looking devastated. Beside her, no longer holding her hand, stood the boy, who was six. Until recently, he had been called the Emperor of China, a title he had inherited at four, when his father had died. He looked frightened but did not fidget. The historical might of China had come down to these three frail figures.

All three wore robes of silk, but not their imperial robes. In China, by tradition, only the emperor wears robes embroidered with dragons, and only empresses wear robes with the symbol of the phoenix. That day, the Great Khan's yellow robe was covered with imperial dragons, showing that he was now Emperor of all China, north and south. Seated next to him, Chabi wore a robe covered with phoenixes.

The Great Khan had returned early from his hunting trip, to welcome General Bayan after his victory in the South. General Bayan had entered the city in a victory parade, with large cheering crowds. Temur had ridden in that parade. I had stayed in my room, not wishing to witness the glory heaped on General Bayan and his men. The victory feast would be held a few days later, at the Khan's hunting camp.

Now, the day after the parade, the Great Khan had called

all forty-seven of his sons, from all his wives and concubines, to witness his treatment of the deposed imperial family of China. I was not invited but no one stopped me at the rear door.

I had heard rumors that despite Chabi's pleas, the Khan planned to execute them. Far too many of our great Mongol warriors had died because the Chinese had resisted for nearly twenty years. To let these former monarchs live would strengthen the hopes of those who still planned to resurrect the Sung dynasty. Two of the young Chinese emperor's half brothers had escaped farther south, and our troops were pursuing them. The Khan needed to send a strong message that such resistance would be futile.

On low tables displayed before the Khan were the trappings of Chinese imperial power, seized after the occupation of their capital, Kinsay. Jewel-encrusted crowns, imperial robes, jade tablets of authority, jewelry, and other treasures were piled high. Most precious was the Sung dynasty's official seal, a block of jade adorned with the carving of a dragon, which the Empress Dowager had submitted to General Bayan the day our troops entered Kinsay, as the symbol of her surrender.

A man's voice rang out: "Kowtow to your ruler, the Great Khan Khubilai, founder of the Yuan dynasty, Son of Heaven!"

Behind the princes, I stood on the tips of my toes to see the three of them fall to their knees and drop their foreheads to the ground. This act showed their humble submission to the Great Khan. It was the ultimate symbol that they accepted him as rightful ruler of all China.

Then they stood up. The grandmother struggled to

stand, leaning on her cane. They kowtowed again, then a third time. It was painful to watch the elder empress. She had shown bravery by refusing to abandon the capital even when her counselors had advised that she take the imperial family and flee to the South.

At the third kowtow, the three of them, grandmother, mother, and boy, remained with their foreheads to the stone floor.

The Great Khan held the power of life or death over them. With one word, he could order their execution, a public beheading.

The Khan remained seated, high on his throne. His voice rang out, loud and clear. "The Sung dynasty has come to an end. Our Yuan dynasty, which I declared five years ago, has inherited the mandate of Heaven."

All those present broke out in cheers. "Long live the Khan of all Khans!"

From the crowd, I sought out the round face of Empress Chabi. She was seated next to the Great Khan. Her face was somber. She did not cheer. So I did not, either. Had she been able to convince her husband to change his mind?

The Khan raised his hand to quiet his men. "Rise!" he commanded.

The three stood up and faced him.

How would it feel, I thought, to know that you would die before sundown? The grandmother seemed resigned, the boy confused. I could see raw terror on the beautiful face of the young mother, whose lip quivered.

"Boy, step forward."

The child looked at his mother, then stepped toward the Khan of all Khans.

"You can no longer call yourself an emperor. But henceforth you shall be known as the duke of Ying."

A murmur of surprise rose from the sons as the words were translated into Chinese for the prisoners. Not only would there be no execution, but the Khan was prepared to treat these people as royalty. Temur seemed especially agitated.

"You may keep your servants that you brought north with you. You may not return to Kinsay, ever. I will provide residences for you, here in Khanbalik."

As the translation rang out, the young mother shut her eyes as if in relief. Her dynasty was dead, but she would live, as would her child.

The Khan continued. "I hereby grant pardons to all your officials who submitted to our rule. We will treat your scholars with respect. We will provide support to southern China's widows, orphans, and childless elderly. Our troops will not plunder your cities or your land. These are now our cities, our land. We will bring prosperity back to them after years of war."

The murmurs stopped. The Khan had stated his will, and no one could openly oppose it. Clearly, the Khan wanted his sons and grandsons to witness his benevolence and generosity. I wondered if any of them knew that his wife had convinced him to make this decision. Perhaps he would now be known as Khubilai Sechen, Khubilai the Wise.

But what of my fate? Would the Khan be generous with me? Since my talk with Empress Chabi, I had been formulating a plan. Finally, I knew what I wanted to ask for. If the Khan could show mercy to the rulers of a huge country that had warred against us for decades, surely he could be kind to

Christendom, a weak, distant land that had never attacked us. Inspired by his benevolence, and the wisdom of Chabi, I was starting to envision a role I might play in ensuring peaceful cooperation between Marco's homeland and the Mongol Empire. Once again, it would mean making a request of Khubilai Khan to allow me to do what no woman had ever done.

Maybe our ruler, wise and far-thinking, would grant my wish.

39

Face to Face

Late that afternoon, a servant rushed into my family's compound, where I was resting. "Empress Chabi wishes to see Princess Emmajin."

After changing into my best *del,* I nearly ran to the Empress's private chambers. I was filled with hope. I had been mulling over my plan, refining it and rehearsing what I would say. This would give me the chance to tell my grandmother about it and see if she would help me convince the Khan. I needed an answer soon, before I had to report back to Abaji.

My plan was ambitious, bold. I needed a strong ally.

But that was not to be. As it happened, I was not to meet with just the Empress. From her chambers, a servant led me into a part of the palace I had never entered before—the Great Khan's private courtyard, his personal residence.

As I waited for the servant to announce my presence, I was breathing hard. What could this mean? I heard the

Great Khan's voice within. My heart jumped. Perhaps Chabi had arranged an opportunity for me to speak to my grandfather about my future.

Quickly, I had to think of a new plan. I would have no chance to enlist Chabi's support. Still, I needed to make the most of this opportunity. I had rehearsed these words, and now I would be able to to speak them.

Chabi's advice came to me: *Return to the world. Make a difference.*

I tried to call up the calm certainty I had felt in the monastery. I would be face to face with the leader of the largest empire in history. When I was a child, he had indulged me. But now I was grown, a soldier, and must do whatever he commanded. I silently asked Tara for strength and clear words. I fingered the amulet in my sash.

When my name was called, I threw back my shoulders and entered the Khan's private sitting room. The Khan sat in a wide wooden chair, with Empress Chabi at his left. I was relieved to see her gentle moon-shaped face.

Between them was a small table for porcelain Chinese-style teacups, each with its own lid. Chabi gave me a small smile and nodded encouragement.

I kowtowed, despite the informal setting. The Khan ordered me to rise and sit next to him, on his right. Close-up, he looked ruddy and well, after two months of hunting in the open air. His feet were propped on silken cushions but did not seem swollen.

A servant poured boiled water over dried leaves in our porcelain cups. This drink, tea, was a kind of fragrant water the Chinese loved. Not many Mongols liked it. Bayan had probably brought some fine tea leaves back from the South.

"Well, my child, you fought well at Vochan." The Great Khan began with a statement, not a question. In this setting, he used the informal language of family.

I nodded, showing the proper humility.

"General Abaji told me you killed hundreds."

I winced but nodded acknowledgment. It was high praise, the kind that would once have made me feel elated.

"I had doubted that a girl could rise to the occasion. In fact, I thought it impossible."

Finally, I found my voice. "I hope I proved myself worthy."

The Khan smiled. "I look forward to hearing the full story about the battle. I have asked that Latin, Messer Marco, to tell it to me and my men."

My heart jumped. "Has he returned?"

His narrow eyes scanned my face, as if he was trying to read my thoughts. "Not yet. He will arrive within a few days. I hear you helped him capture live dragons."

Remembering the scene made me smile. But my smile faded, since Suren was so closely associated with those memories. I swallowed. "Messer Marco believes that medicine made of dragon's gall is valuable."

My grandfather smiled. "He sent some ahead, with General Abaji. I have tried this medicine and feel some relief already."

I tried not to glance at his feet, since I knew he was sensitive about them.

"I am pleased with the Latin. I have given him the honor of telling the story of the battle of Vochan. If he does well, I plan to reward him with another assignment, to send him south, to Kinsay. He can report to me about conditions there."

Marco would not be pleased with such an assignment. He wanted to go home. In fact, my new plan required him to return to Christendom.

"I believe that . . ." I stumbled over my words. I had not planned to discuss Marco's future with the Khan. "That Latin is a mere merchant. He, his father, and his uncle wish to return to their homeland, laden with goods to trade. If he pleases you, the best reward might be to grant him the goods they need and let them return."

The Khan's intense look jabbed into my face. "Nesruddin has rewarded him well. You wish for him to leave?"

I did not want to make my request in the context of Marco's future. "I . . . I think . . . he wants to go home."

"I have a question for you, Emmajin Beki. I assigned you to report on the foreigner, not to befriend him. Abaji tells me you became too friendly with him."

I sputtered. What else had Abaji seen or reported to the Khan?

The Khan kept me off balance. "I trust you kept your virtue, as a princess of the royal family."

I looked him straight in the eye, glad I could reassure him. "Yes, I did. Of course."

"And what of the Latin's behavior? Did he act honorably toward you?"

I straightened my back. "Indeed, he did. His actions are the most honorable. Did Abaji tell you of his intelligence, how he helped to win the battle, using fire medicine?"

"Yes. Most admirable." The Khan still examined my face.

"Messer Marco also showed generosity. After the battle, when many of our Mongol soldiers lay gravely wounded, he offered precious medicine to help our soldiers."

The Khan's thin eyebrows rose. "So I have been told."

"His action showed bravery, even heroism, though in a quiet way."

"I am glad to hear it. I had some concerns, sending him to the South in your company. Clearly, you admire him. And trust him."

I tried not to blush. The Khan's concerns were justified, and I had trouble concealing that. My grandfather was known as a good judge of character, and I feared he could see right through me.

"Still, I did not summon you to discuss the future of Messer Marco. I wish to discuss your future, Emmajin."

I swallowed hard and rehearsed my words again in my head.

But the Khan seized momentum. "General Abaji is willing to have you remain under his command."

"I am honored. I have great respect for General Abaji." Now was the time to speak up. Still in awe of the Khan, I scrambled to recall the words I had rehearsed.

"I understand Suren's death affected you sorely," he said.

That familiar pang pierced my gut. "I am sorry I could not prevent it," I said.

"Have you had enough of battles?"

The right answer was no; my heart said yes, but I could not find my voice.

The Khan heard much in my silence. "Do you wish to leave the army?"

My eyes flitted to Chabi. What had she told him? Her face was impassive.

My highest dream had been to join the army. How could

I leave it after just one battle? I hung my head in shame. "Yes," I said quietly.

"I have had an offer of marriage for you," the Khan continued before I could collect my words. "This is an attractive offer that would be of service to our family. My daughter Yurak, married to the king of Togtoh, has a son who will soon be of marriageable age. This is an alliance I wish to strengthen."

My breath caught in my throat and my eyes shifted to my grandmother again. Is this what she had planned? If the Khan had made up his mind, it was over for me.

"Once, you told me you did not wish to marry," he said.

"That remains true," I said. I was supposed to add, *but I will do whatever the Great Khan commands,* but could not bring myself to do so. "But I . . ."

"You wish to make a difference?" So Chabi had spoken to him.

"Yes!" I said, with more enthusiasm. "Since the Khan entrusted me—"

The Khan cut me off. "Your grandmother has suggested a role for you, and I agree. You are aware of this Chinese boy who dared to call himself Emperor of China?"

I nodded, wondering what this could have to do with my future.

"This boy's mother is young, like you. Your assignment is to become her companion, to teach her the ways of the Mongols. You did well civilizing that young Latin. The Empress believes you could civilize this Chinese woman as well."

I was shocked. They had thought this through, and he

had made a decision. Chabi's eyes shone with pride and satisfaction. Was this what she had meant by being a messenger of peace?

"Your Majesty honors me," I said, the right words. "But I . . . I had another idea." How could I dare suggest a different assignment? And yet I had to speak now.

The Khan's eyebrows rose again. "Tell me," he commanded.

I swallowed hard. "Last summer, Your Majesty entrusted me with the task of spying on the Latins, Marco Polo and his father and uncle. I gathered much knowledge about their homeland's kings and armies. I even learned a few words of their language."

The Khan and his empress remained silent.

"The most important thing I learned is that Christendom is weak, a group of small countries with no strong central government or army. But it has many smart people and much potential. There is no need to send our army to invade it."

There! I had said it. The Khan narrowed his eyes with suspicion. I knew he would think that I was siding with the foreigner. I went on, needing to speak my piece.

"I am but a woman, and not skilled in great matters. But perhaps you could send me, as your emissary, to their leader, the Pope . . . with a letter from you. My very presence, as a granddaughter of the Khan of all Khans, could convince the Pope that the countries of Christendom should be friendly subjects."

The Khan's head jerked back at this remarkable idea. Yet his first reaction was not to reject it, as I had feared. "I have already deigned to communicate with their Pope," he said. "I sent him a letter, through the Polos, ten years ago."

"And their Pope wrote back, expressing a desire for peace," I said. "It should not be hard to convince their leaders to cooperate with us. If you were to send me to Christendom, as your envoy, I could convey your goodwill and establish friendly relations with the Pope and his people. Sending a member of the Golden Family would be a stronger message than sending a letter with merchants. Marco and his father could tell the Pope of the Great Khan's power, wealth, and wise rule. Perhaps the Pope would agree to join the Mongol Empire by sending gifts of tribute, with no need to engage in battle."

It was foolhardy to give unsolicited advice to the Khan of all Khans. But I felt strongly about traveling to Marco's homeland as an emissary of the Great Khan. I could meet the Pope of the Latins, who was, after all, a man who knew Marco and his father. Then he could send the one hundred Christian scholars the Great Khan had requested. Perhaps I could visit Venezia, to see its streets of water. Back in my own chambers, I had imagined the entire journey. It had seemed possible, this plan of mine.

The Khan frowned. "You would travel with this foreign family? The Khan of all Khans does not entrust his granddaughter's virtue to foreign merchants."

I tried to keep my emotions from my face. "We would travel with an armed escort, of course."

His frown deepened. "No one sends a woman to do such work."

"I watched my best friend die in battle," I said. "I wish to serve you in a different way, to bring your wisdom to others in this world."

He rubbed his thin beard.

"Perhaps this is the plan of Eternal Heaven, the reason that you chose me to learn Latin," I said.

The Khan of all Khans seemed taken aback by my idea. He frowned at me while he contemplated its implications.

"Tengri," I said, "appointed you to fulfill the Great Ancestor's mandate, to unify the world. But not every country needs to be conquered. Even the Great Ancestor promised leniency to those foreigners who cooperated."

The Khan's eyes flashed at the gall I showed by interpreting Eternal Heaven's commands to the Son of Heaven.

An endless moment passed. I looked at Chabi, who was regarding him steadily. Couldn't she see that this was a much more important way for me to make a difference than civilizing the Chinese empress?

Finally, the Khan responded: "This is not part of my plan. But I will consider it."

My heart flooded with joy.

"But it is unlikely. The khan of the Golden Horde in Russia and the Il-khan of Persia expect me to send troops to aid in the conquest of the Holy Land and Christendom. A promise to the Pope might disrupt those plans."

I shuddered. How could I stop those plans, which I had set in motion?

"As for you," continued the Khan, "my preference is that you accept the assignment I gave you."

I was beaten. I bowed my head. "The Great Khan is the wisest of all rulers," I said. "Whatever you decide, I will obey your commands."

The Khan continued, as if aware of my disappointment. "However, I will allow Marco Polo to return to his homeland, if he so requests."

"As you wish," I said. "May I make one more small request? I would like to hear Marco Polo tell the story of the battle of Vochan."

"Granted," he said. "I will give you my final answer by then. You may go."

40

Search for Marco

Now that I knew that Marco would be returning to the capital soon, I could not wait to see him. I had been thinking of him, without pause, since leaving him in Carajan. His lopsided smile, that distinctive laugh, that scent of cloves and spice. I wished he had the wings of a dove so that he could fly back to me.

If the Khan refused my request, I would have to say good-bye to Marco forever. But if he said yes, I would need his ideas. I had to find a way to tell Marco about what I had proposed to the Khan. Marco was clever. Maybe he would know how to change our fates.

A few days later, at midmorning, my sister asked if I knew about the dragons from Carajan. The word "dragon" made my heart leap.

"Are they at court?" I demanded.

"They say some foreign men presented them to the Khan

this morning," Drolma reported. "Could that be your foreigner, back from Carajan?"

My foreigner. I ran to the Khan's audience hall in the public part of the palace. A crowd of onlookers had gathered in one corner of the great courtyard. I could tell by the shrieks and murmurs that the dragons were at the heart of it.

Eagerly, I pushed in. Sure enough, I caught sight of a gold-toothed grin and heard Little Li speaking in accented Mongolian. "Careful! Not so close! They bites!" I guessed that Marco had taught him to speak Mongolian during their journey together.

I worked my way through the crowd until I reached the front. Little Li tossed a live mouse into one of the cages, and the dragon caught it in its long mouth, full of jagged teeth. A huge gasp rose from the crowd.

I looked behind and around Little Li but did not see Marco. "Little Li!" I called. "Where is Messer Marco?"

He smiled when he saw me. "They was here, Marco with father and uncle," he called back. He pulled a child's hand away from a dragon cage. "Could you get these people to stand back, lady? They no understand."

"Stand back!" I shouted in Mongolian in my sternest voice. The women and children immediately pulled back, but the men looked up in curiosity, not used to obeying a woman's voice. "The dragons will bite you if you get too close."

I pushed my way through the crowd around the four cages, to stand near Little Li.

"Did Marco leave court?"

"Oh, yes. After the big meeting. Great Khan very happy." Little Li picked up another mouse by the tail and tossed it into a cage. The dragon snapped at it, missed, and chased it before snatching it. The crowd gasped and cheered at this show.

"Please, I have to know where Marco went."

"That way," he said, pointing toward the palace's main entrance.

Marco had been in that very courtyard, with his father and uncle, and I had missed them. I ran through the gate, to the outer courtyard. This place was full of petitioners waiting to see the Khan. There were so many men—Mongols, Chinese, and foreigners—it was hard to pick out any one individual in the milling crowd, although I was sure I would recognize Marco's reddish curls. I saw no sign of the elephants.

I rushed on to the main palace entrance and questioned the guard. He remembered seeing the dragons come in, but he had not noticed three foreign men leaving.

I felt light-headed. I ran out of the palace, onto the square, then along the avenue leading to the city's west gate. I wished I had thought to get my horse. It was hard to push through crowds of people on foot. A cramp tore through my side, and I stopped to steady myself against a wall. I had to see Marco, as soon as possible.

When I arrived at the city's west gate, a guard stopped me and would not let me exit. He had his orders: women from the palace were not to leave the city without a male escort. When I told him I was a soldier, he smiled in disbelief.

I stood at the gate a long time, watching people go into and out of the city. Everyone seemed to be carrying a lot of goods, either on donkeys or hanging from the two ends of a pole carried on their shoulders, as Chinese do.

Marco, I thought. *Please. Come now. I'm here.*

"Emmajin Beki? Is that you?" A man's voice came from behind me. I whirled around, filled with hope. There stood a tall, big-bellied Latin with pure white hair and beard. It was Marco's uncle.

"Messer Maffeo!" I exclaimed. "Where is Marco?"

The old man smiled broadly under his huge beard. "He met with the Great Khan this morning, with great success."

"Where is he now?"

"He was on his way back to our rooms."

"Can you take me there? I must see him!"

He paused. "The foreigners' section is not fit for a royal princess."

"I command you."

Maffeo Polo's brow wrinkled with concern but he bowed his head. He offered me his arm in the Western way, and I took it. We walked out of the city and into the foreigners' quarter. Seeing me with a male escort, the guard did not stop me.

I had thought the streets of Khanbalik were chaotic, but they were nothing compared to the ragged alleyways outside the city gate. Dirty, half-naked children ran about. Toothless beggars thrust their hands into my face. Poor women sold scraggly vegetables on blankets. Young women waved at men to lure them into brothels. I saw men with beards, hook noses, dark skin, and leering grins. The stink of urine and garbage was everywhere. Was this how foreigners lived just outside the greatest city in the world? I had seen nothing like it in my six months of travel.

Maffeo kept a firm grip on my elbow and steered me around aggressive beggars and vendors. Fortunately, he soon ducked into a wooden doorway and shut the door behind us. We stood in the murky, stinky hallway of an inn for foreigners. Several men lounged on pillows on the floor, smoking a long pipe. Maffeo led me into a small empty sitting room. It was clean but simple. I sat down hard and took a moment to catch my breath. My senses had all been assaulted at once.

The old man sent a servant to fetch Marco from his room. I wiped the grit from my face and smoothed down my braids. *Stay calm,* I told myself. But how could I? I had not seen Marco for more than two months. Would he be distant again in this setting?

When Marco arrived, his bearded face and green eyes were the most welcome sight in the world. He had an eager look that matched my own feelings.

My whole body leaped toward him. It was unseemly. I had not planned it. But months of separation from him had made me hungry to touch him. A look of surprise and pleasure crossed his face before he folded me in his arms. Along with that smell of spice, I breathed in love and trust and confidence. How had I ever thought he was frightening?

Nothing else in life mattered more than being with Marco now. I did not know what would happen. But at that moment, I knew that we could not be separated again. He would help me find a way.

Marco's uncle—so different from mine—quietly stepped out of the room and closed the door.

After a long embrace, Marco pulled back and examined my face. "You've changed."

I smiled. Yes, after talking to my father, and to Chabi, and even to Tara, I had changed. I was calmer, more confident. Of course Marco would notice.

"Did you hear?" Marco grinned. "The Khan's medicine is working!"

I nodded happily. "I saw him, too, recently. His feet are not so swollen."

We sat down in the Chinese chairs. "The Khan said he was pleased with me. Right in front of my father and uncle. He promised us excellent goods to take home."

"That's the news you've been awaiting. Your father and uncle must be thrilled," I said.

"They are." Marco's face turned serious. "But I've made up my mind. You said there was no way for you and me to be together. I understand that. Even so, I cannot leave you here. I will not return to Venezia. I have told my father and uncle already."

I could see in his somber eyes his determination to stay here with me.

"Wait," I said, remembering how I had pushed the Khan to let Marco return home. "You haven't heard my idea." I told him about my conversation with the Khan and my request to have him send me as an ambassador to the Pope.

Marco leaned toward me as I spoke, as if drinking in every detail. His eyes misted when he heard my proposal. "You would be willing to leave Khanbalik? And travel all the way to Christendom, to make sure that your homeland and mine can live in peace?"

"That is my highest dream," I said.

"I am astounded." Marco sat back. "What of that plan to invade Christendom?"

"The Khan is still in discussions with his kinsmen in Persia and Russia." It was wrong of me to divulge such information, but I wanted to be completely honest with him this time.

Anguish showed on Marco's face. "I wonder if the Tartar troops will get there before we do." I knew he was imagining his beloved Venezia in ruins. After witnessing a battle, that image was even more vivid in my mind.

At that moment, though, instead of feeling despair, as I had so often, I could think only of hope and possibilities. There had to be some way we could prevent the Khan from sending our army to Marco's homeland. "The Khan did not reject my plan. He said he would consider it. We need to think of a way to convince him."

Marco's forehead furrowed. "I have done everything I could," he said. "With every word I have said to him, every action I have taken, I have tried to prove to him that we Latins are a friendly people, not a threat to the Empire. We're not like the Burmese, who sent an army to invade your country."

I moved from my chair and sat on his armrest, wrapping my arms around his shoulder. Normally, Marco had such an easy laugh, a ready smile, a clever idea. This time he was relying on me.

"We must think clearly," I said. "We need to make a plan."

He sat back and smiled at me, though his face was still sad. "I wish that the Khan would send the army to Burma instead of Christendom. It's a much richer land than Christendom—and closer."

I nodded. He was right. That made more sense.

"Maybe," Marco said, "after the Khan hears my story about the battle of Vochan, he will decide to do that. After all, he would want revenge on the king of Burma for attacking the empire and killing his beloved grandson."

Revenge. The word jumped out at me. This plan was attractive, but it did not seem right. Saving Christendom at the expense of Burma? It was hardly compassionate. "Remember the people of Little Li's tribe, in the dragon village?" I said. "They looked a lot like the Burmese."

Marco nodded, chastened.

Thinking of the dragon hunt reminded me of Suren. I felt his dragon tooth, hot on the skin of my chest. I pulled it out.

"Suren," said Marco, shaking his head in sadness.

"Suren," I said, fingering the smooth surface of the tooth. "You know, I think the happiest moments of his life were hunting those dragons, with you and Little Li. You were like brothers."

Marco smiled with his eyes. "He loved that."

"Suren would not have wanted the Khan's army to do harm to your people."

"Did he say that?" Marco asked, his green eyes wide.

"No, he never questioned the Khan's orders. But he would be horrified if our people attacked your homeland."

Marco nodded.

"Yes," I said, trying to think as I spoke. "It would be a testament to him, a lasting legacy, if we could find a way of living together in peace."

Marco looked skeptical.

"Marco, you always have good ideas. What can you do to convince the Khan to send me to Christendom as his ambassador?"

Marco shook his head in wonder. "I will do anything I can to help. I can tell the story of the battle, and I will, in a way that makes you look strong and heroic—which is the truth. But you are the one who needs to show the Khan that you can do this, that you can be forceful and persuasive as his representative. You must say something dramatic and convincing."

He was right. But words had never been my strength.

Before I left, he held me close. His lips touched mine in a *bacio* that I had long anticipated. His gentle touch convinced me that somehow we would find a way. I didn't want to leave him. I promised to see him at the Khan's hunting camp after he told his story of the battle.

All the way back to the palace, that night, and the next day and the next night, I thought until my head hurt. This idea seemed even more improbable than my request, a year earlier, to join the army. But it was the only way Marco and I could be together.

I hoped that Chabi was persuading the Khan about my future. But it was up to me to prove my worthiness for this assignment. If I did not, Marco might have to return to his homeland without me, whether he chose to or not. One day I might hear that a Mongol army—one the Great Khan did not directly control—had destroyed Christendom. That image made me shudder.

41

The Khan's Hunting Camp

My breath caught in my throat. On horseback, at the top of a rise, I looked out over a sight I had heard about but never seen: the ocean.

The water stretched along the horizon, as broad and endless as a Mongolian steppe, but blue-gray and glinting in the late sunlight. It was in constant motion—not like grasses in the wind, but like an earthquake, heaving up and falling back, crashing against the beach in white-capped waves. I searched the distance for the far shore and could see none. It was like no lake I had ever seen—roiling and alive, stretching to the end of the earth. I couldn't believe anyone would ride on a boat of wood and trust such a seething mass of water. Baatar tossed his mane and whinnied, as if threatened.

The Great Khan's hunting camp sprawled along the seaside at an area called Beidaihe, Northern Dai River, not far from the Chin Emperor's Island. It was the largest encampment of tents I had ever seen, a sea of white dots stretching from the water's edge over hill after hill to the horizon. The Khan's imperial flags fluttered lazily. Guards stood on duty around the perimeter of the camp. Within, the mood was high with the excitement of the hunt and the thrill of being away from home. It was a great escape for the men of the court, most of them military men. The end of this two-month hunting season was the highlight of each year for them.

The smell of fresh meat cooking over fires wafted up the hill and drew me down into the camp. Bare-chested men, their arm muscles bulging, wrestled in the warm sand. A pack of men howled and chased each other across our path. One man, his jaws working and his chin greasy, looked up at me from a fleshy bone he held in both hands.

Here in the Khan's hunting camp, steaming in their male juices, with no wives or children around, men could boast of the hunt, overeat, and burp, free of the restrictive rules and majesty of the court.

The only women other than me were those who had been brought for the pleasure of the men. They were laughing, loose-haired women. I had heard of such women and seen a few on the road, but I had never seen so many flaunting their bodies openly in one place.

My cousin Temur had escorted me from Khanbalik, two days' journey to this hunting camp by the seaside. We traveled with a small group of his friends from the army, sons of young officers, and a maid from the court to attend me. I had heard tales of the rowdiness of the Khan's hunting camp, but I did not know until we arrived how unusual it was for a royal woman to visit it. Not only was I out of place here, among the Khan's men, but I realized I had no desire to be part of this man's world. I was certain they didn't want me here, either.

I was happy to retreat to my own tent with my maid, as well as two guards. Even after six months with the army, I was glad to have the guards. I had no idea where Marco was staying and did not dare wander about the camp on my own to find him.

During the journey, and alone in my tent, I took time to think. Confused and worried, I wanted to be prepared and not act on impulse.

That evening, I felt sure, my fate would be decided. Perhaps my grandmother had spoken to the Khan and he had already made up his mind. Perhaps not.

This would be my last chance to state my case. Marco would tell his story about the battle of Vochan and praise me as a hero. I was no longer proud of killing all those men and horses in battle, and I hoped he would not exaggerate my role. But if all went well, his story would validate the Khan's decision to let me join the army, and help me appear worthy in the eyes of his men. As one who had helped achieve victory, I would have a voice worth hearing.

Fingering the dragon's tooth, I thought about Suren. That night would be his funeral oration, shaping the way Suren would be remembered. Saddened, I wondered what advice he would give me if he were here. What legacy would he really want? Suren was a loyal Mongol soldier. He represented everything that was finest about Mongol ideals.

I needed greater strength than the memory of Suren could give me. I took out the Tara amulet, which fit easily in my palm.

Tara, Tara, I thought. *What should I say?* She looked out of the amulet, her sweet face emanating compassion. I felt certain she would approve of my taking a message of peace from the Khan to Christendom. I wished she could speak to the Khan through me.

Compassion. I remembered the faces of the Burmese soldiers I had killed. The soldiers of the Burmese army were good men like Suren, obeying their king. How had I looked to them, hacking and slaying? Questions of war and peace were beyond me. The Khan of all Khans, at the age of sixty, had far more wisdom than I did about such matters. But whatever small role I could play, I wanted it to be for peace.

I could not solve the problem of Burma. But distant, weak Christendom, and its leaders, might be open to a different resolution. Exchanging letters could not solve all the problems of the world, but it might work in the case of Marco's homeland. How fine it would look to Marco's people if the Khan sent not an army but a maiden!

Marco and I could be partners in this effort. He could explain my mission to the Pope, in their language. As a representative of the most powerful ruler in the world, I would be welcomed and treated well.

But how could I prove to the Khan that I was mature enough, skilled and articulate enough, to be taken seriously as an ambassador? How could I convince him that I wanted to do this not for my own glory, or simply to spend more time with Marco, but for a greater purpose, a mission of which Tara would approve?

In one hand, I held Suren's dragon tooth, still on its leather thong. He had won it by bravery, not on the battlefield but in service to the Khan's healing. It was also a symbol of his friendship with the foreigners Marco the Latin and

Little Li, the villager from a tribe near the border with Burma.

In the other hand, I held the amulet. I had once scorned Tara but now treasured her as a symbol of my aspirations. I looked closely at her picture. In her hand, she held a large flower. She was known as the Great Protectress, yet she did not carry any weapons.

Next to me, beside my sleeping fur, were my bow and arrows. I ran my finger along the smooth surface of my bow. It had served me well in battle. It was the symbol of my status as a Mongol warrior. I had worked hard to be accepted as a soldier. But I could not stand for both war and peace. Whatever came to pass, I would no longer fight with weapons. Instead, I would pour my fighting energy into something more worthwhile.

I wanted to show the world that we Mongols were not just fierce fighters, the conquerors of Chinggis Khan. We had evolved into wise rulers, heirs to his grandson, Khubilai the Wise.

Looking at these objects, at last I figured out what I needed to do.

42

Becoming a Legend

That evening was Marco's big opportunity to tell his best story to the Khan.

The Khan and his men gathered outdoors, in a grassy meadow not far from the sea, on a warm spring evening that felt like summer. The Great Khan sat on a wide wooden throne-chair halfway up the hill, behind a coarse plank table loaded with freshly cooked meat from the hunt. Everyone else sat on the ground, grabbing meat off platters passed by servants, eating with their hands, licking juice off their fingers, tossing bones onto the ground, drinking *airag* from greasy silver cups.

The meal was an orgy of excess: the usual venison, but also bear, wildcat, wild boar, and various birds. There was not one fish dish, though we were by the ocean, and there were no unappetizing vegetables, rice, or grain. The meat tasted even better for the smell of smoke and aromas from the cooking fires and the crispness of the night breezes off the sea. Overhead, stars spattered across the clear sky.

Men mingled easily. I wished I could find Marco and sit with him, but I did not see him. I wondered if he was in his tent, rehearsing his story.

Temur introduced me to more of his companions, who peppered me with questions about the battle.

"I hear the Burmese fought with elephants, is that true?" one man asked me.

"Yes, they brought at least two thousand of them!" I said.

The men murmured their amazement.

Temur looked away. "Her role was very small," he said.

I smiled and shook my head. The others would hear the story soon enough.

When it was time for the entertainment, Temur and I sat down near the Khan, on a blanket. On the Khan's right sat Chimkin. Near them sat many of the Khan's other sons, and just below Temur sat a group of princes from his generation. Although an outsider might have thought we were sitting casually on the ground, the strict hierarchy of the court prevailed.

After the feasting was over, I finally saw Marco. When his moment came, he appeared in the area where we of the Golden Family were seated, and he bowed to the Khan.

At a signal from the Khan, Marco climbed up on a table and held out his arms to quiet the crowd. From that place, not far from where I was sitting, he could be heard by hundreds of men. Marco looked stunning in a blue *del* with silver threads. He ran his eyes over us, lingering a moment on my face. He had known where I was all along.

"Great Khan of all Khans, generals and commanders, princes and kings, dukes and marquesses, counts and knights!" He spoke loudly and clearly. I noticed how much improved his accent was after he had spent nearly a year in our land. Still, he had a slight lilt to his voice, softening the harshness of our tongue.

"I have traveled the length and breadth of this great Empire, and I can tell you that there is no city in the world as grand as Khanbalik! No garden as fair as Xanadu! And no meal as delicious as the freshly killed game I have eaten tonight!"

The men cheered and stomped. Flattery works everywhere in the world.

Marco held up his silver cup. "There is no wine as delightful as this fresh springtime *airag*! And no ruler as powerful, as wealthy, and as wise as the Great Khan Khubilai, Son of Heaven, founder of the Yuan dynasty, Great Khan above all Khans, ruler of the Mongol Empire, which stretches from the lands of the rising sun to the lands of the setting sun!" His voice rose in a crescendo to a peak of intensity.

The Great Khan had a big smile on his broad face, under his sloping mustache. His eyes disappeared into thin slits above his ruddy cheeks. The Son of Heaven rose from his throne. Several aides rushed to his side, but he gestured for them to move back. He stood on his own, balancing easily on his feet. The Khan lifted his jewel-studded golden cup, and the music struck up. All the men raised their cups, watching the Khan drink before they followed suit. After they swallowed, they let out a loud cheer: "Long live the Great Khan! May he live ten thousand years!"

Marco began with the story of the dragon hunt. He exaggerated the dangers and played up each moment of bravery. He knew better than to make a hero of himself, and he did not mention my role. But he made a hero of Suren, eldest grandson of the Great Khan. At the first mention of Suren's name, the men fell quiet. Marco made it sound as if Suren, with minor help from local villagers, went stalking the beasts deep in the jungle and captured them with a lasso. When he described the dragons, he did not need to exaggerate their length, their ferocity, their sharp teeth, their spiny scales.

The men cheered at the ending of the story and helped themselves to more intoxicating *airag*. Marco knew his audience and played it like a zither.

Finally, with his audience drunk on dragons and danger, Marco waded into bloodshed. He told the story of the battle of Vochan with such skill that he brought the Great Khan and all his men to suspenseful silence, then whipped them into a fury of cheering. Marco did not need to embellish the story much. He told of the glory of Burma, with its legendary towers of silver and gold, a country rich beyond imagining.

The Burmese troops were menacing, their numbers overpowering, the elephants mighty and fearsome. Marco captured the nervous apprehension before the battle. The Mongol troops attacked with courage. The elephants bellowed; the horses whinnied in terror; the woods loomed dense and ominous. General Abaji showed brilliance with his mid-battle shift in tactics, using explosions to scare the wits out of the elephants. Marco did not mention that he had suggested this tactic.

Finally, Marco came to my role. He portrayed me as tall

and strong, lean and supple, renowned for fine archery skills, braids flying, bow held high as I charged into battle. Then he described Suren as gallant and fearless, strong and determined, stirring up the enthusiasm of the troops with his war cries, advancing boldly into the fray.

Marco's words became more extravagant: "Then might you see swashing blows dealt and taken from sword and mace! Then might you see knights and horses and men-at-arms go down! Then might you see arms and hands and legs and heads hewn off! And besides the dead that fell, many a wounded man never rose again, for the sore press there was. The din and uproar were so great that Tengri Himself might have thundered and no man would have heard it! Great was the medley, and dire and perilous was the fighting. The Mongols hacked and slew so mercilessly that it was a piteous sight to see.

"Then Suren, gallant Suren, with the blood of the Great Ancestor Chinggis Khan pounding in his veins, raised his sword and raced directly at the king of Burma himself."

I smiled to myself as Marco veered off into his "embellishments." We had never come close to the king of Burma, who had disappeared after the battle ended.

"Emmajin the Brave, her braids flying behind her head, saber raised high, whipped her horse and raced behind him. Mightily did that king of Burma fight. Mightily did Suren hack and hew. The dust and blood flew up in a whirlwind.

"Prince Suren knocked the hostile king off his horse. The dastardly ruler plunged his sword into Suren's horse, causing the young prince to fly into the air. The prince fell to the ground, wounding his arm. But he jumped to his feet, sword in hand, and engaged the king in direct combat. Wounded though he was, Prince Suren would have killed the king on the spot. But an enemy came from behind and whacked his legs, causing him to fall."

A few of the listeners cried out, as if in pain.

"The king raised his sword to the sky and was ready to bring it down. But suddenly, the Burmese soldier fell to his death. Princess Emmajin, archer supreme, had felled that evil protector with one well-placed arrow, straight to the base of the neck."

"Aaaah!" Their approval was touching, though for something I had not done.

"The king redirected his sword to her horse, and she, too, fell to the ground. Full of rage, the king set upon her with his heavy sword. He would have killed her in an instant. But Prince Suren deflected the blow. The king's sword hit the ground just inches from Emmajin's head. Suren stepped in to protect her. The king raised his sword and sliced the young prince's neck. The gallant prince dropped to his knees, grabbing his wound, trying to staunch the gush of blood. Prince Suren, beloved grandson of the great Khubilai Khan, sixteen years old, fell in battle, under the sword of a mighty king that fateful day."

Marco paused, his eyes cast down, as if in tribute. The men went silent, too, stunned and horrified. Prince Chimkin looked stricken. A tear glistened in Temur's eye.

"The king was about to plunge his sword into the prince's gut. But Princess Emmajin, full of rage, plunged her dagger deep into his back, just below the rib cage. The king staggered and fell to one knee. His sword clattered uselessly to the ground. Emmajin wielded her dagger, ready to slash the king's throat, as well. But his men crowded in to protect their wounded king. She turned to help her cousin. But it was too late. With a sigh, Suren breathed his last. She knelt by his side, weeping inexhaustible tears."

Hundreds of men sat in silence. Mongol soldiers all, they were moved beyond speech. Tears rolled down my cheeks. The facts were false, but the spirit was true. Listening to his words, I had watched the battle happen just as he described it, and so had all the men. I took a jagged breath, remembering the look on Suren's face as he had died.

Temur reached over and put his hand on top of mine. His face was contorted in grief. As much as they had competed against each other, the brothers had been close.

I was glad Marco did not go on to tell how I had slain dozens of enemies in revenge. Perhaps Marco knew that I did not want the men celebrating that.

"Here she is, soldiers of the Khan: your heroine, victor of the battle of Vochan, granddaughter of the Khan of all Khans, first woman to serve in the Mongol army, warrior of legend, your own princess Emmajin!"

Marco gestured at me, and I stood. All eyes were on me, and the men's cheers sounded like thunder. I took a moment to compose myself. Marco reached his hand to me. I climbed up onto the table and stood next to him. He held my hand high and stood a half step behind me, allowing me full glory.

The Khan's wide face glowed with pride, as if he had believed in me from the beginning. His open approval meant the world to me.

My heart nearly burst. Marco's hand was warm, as if pulsing from the exertion of the battle, and its strength leaped into mine. I felt as though I had lived my life for this moment, for this feeling of pride and recognition, these shouts and whistles of admiration. The cheers lifted me and carried me above the scene so that I was looking down on throngs of valiant Mongol men. They were yelling as if their lungs would burst, raising their fists to the sky, declaring to the universe the endless glory of the Mongol race.

I had not known as a child exactly what I was aiming for all those years, racing on horseback and practicing archery, or even as a soldier, riding across the farmlands and mountains of the great Mongol Empire. But at that moment, I knew.

Thanks to Marco and his skill at storytelling, I had become a legend.

The feeling was wonderful. But I knew that the story was false, as perhaps all true heroes do. These men needed a hero, but I no longer needed to be one.

43

The Khan's Decision

Slowly, I pulled at the thong around my neck, till my fingers touched the dragon's tooth that had meant so much to Suren. I slipped it over my head and held it high so that even the men in the back could see it.

The men quieted. I showed it first to the Khan, then to Chimkin, Temur, and the other men. It took me a few minutes to get up my courage to speak.

"O Khan of all Khans, Prince Chimkin, Prince Temur, men of the Khan's court and army!" I began as firmly as I could. "This tooth once belonged to the dragon Prince Suren killed. Suren wore it around his neck until the moment he died in battle."

The men were silent now.

I was not acting in the effort to control my sorrow. But then I recited my well-rehearsed lines, much as Marco had said his. "On the night before he died, Prince Suren stayed in my tent, as he often did, to protect me. That night, he tried to persuade me not to fight in the battle. 'It's too risky for you,' he said."

This much was true.

"Suren did not expect to die in battle. So he did not speak to me of his dying wish. But I knew him well. I watched how he lived, and what he held dear."

All eyes were on me. Chimkin and Temur especially were staring up at me. At last, I had found my voice.

"This, I believe, would have been Suren's last wish: that we Mongols, who have achieved a greater empire than any in history, find a way forward without war. That we find a peaceful way to our God-given destiny of expanding our empire to the ends of the earth. That I, his cousin, help convey this vision, the wise vision of our Great Khan."

The Khan's eyebrows met in a slight frown. The men, half drunk and eager for war stories, murmured angrily. It seemed they had expected me to ask for revenge. The former Emmajin might have done so.

I thought of the Tara amulet tucked in my waist sash.

With both hands now, I held up the leather thong with the dragon tooth, and the men watched. I loved that tooth, but it was time to pass it on. Temur would need the strength and goodness of his brother, Suren.

I gestured for Temur to join me on the tabletop. Without a word, I dropped the thong over his head, around his neck. He immediately grasped the dragon's tooth, his eyes brimming.

"Prince Suren, your brother, loved this Latin, this storyteller, as a brother. He would have wanted harmony between the Mongols and Marco Polo's homeland."

The silence was deafening. No one, man or woman,

publicly gave advice to the Great Khan. My only hope was that the Khan had not already finalized the orders to his cousin khans to invade Marco's homeland.

Temur regarded me with suspicion. It would take more than a memento from his brother to convince him of the importance of harmony. Still, I hoped, with that thong around his neck and my words seared into his memory, Temur could not in good conscience join any army that planned to invade Christendom.

My uncle was another matter. He was a careful, thoughtful man, well educated and prudent, not one to take orders from a girl. His eyes were wary. From a young age, as the Khan's favorite son, Chimkin had been pressured to live up to the highest expectations, obey the Khan's every wish, and achieve great victories for the empire. Now he had lost his eldest son, a loss greater even than mine. But his future lay in pacifying the West.

From inside my waist sash, I pulled out the feather from the golden eagle I had shot down in Xanadu. I had kept it all these months. Now it had a purpose.

I stepped off the table and faced my uncle Chimkin. I held the eagle feather with my right hand and put my left hand under my right elbow—the Mongol way of offering a treasure or good wish. Eagles' feathers are great portents in Mongolia.

"This feather is for you," I said to Suren's father. "It is a lasting symbol of Suren's strength and his far-sighted vision. He stood for the future, a realization of the Great Khan's desire for the peaceful unification of all nations."

It was, in Marco's words, an embellishment. But Chimkin's eyes misted over when he took the feather from me.

Then I turned to the Khan, my head bowed.

The Khan, no fool, would never let himself be manipulated. But from what Chabi had told me, I knew that his heart was no longer in military conquest but in the new vision of wise rule. My proposal was consistent with that. I needed to do something bold.

Without a word, I reached for my bow and lifted it high over my head, with both hands, so all could see. Then, slowly and deliberately, I lowered it and placed it at the feet of the Khan. I fell to my knees and dropped my forehead to the stony ground. Every man present knew what this gesture meant: I would never again fight in a battle.

No Mongol man would do this; I felt certain of that. To a warrior, it was a weak, female gesture, giving up my power. Yet I knew it took another kind of courage.

Silence spread from us like ripples in the water. Soon I sensed that all the men were looking at the Khan, to see what he would do.

"Rise," he said at last. "You may continue."

I stood before the Khan. It was true that I desired to travel with Marco. I knew I could not be as good as Tara, but I wanted at least to embark on her path of compassion.

Yes, I was heir to the World Conqueror, Chinggis Khan. But I was also heir to many strong Mongol women. I was heir to Empress Chabi, who preferred mercy to justice. I was heir to my father, Prince Dorji, a man who dared to seek a higher way.

My words came out with calm certainty. "I beg you to make me a messenger of peace. I will do with my life whatever the Khan commands." I bowed my head.

After a long pause, the Khan spoke. This time, it was not

in a commanding voice that silenced the men around him. Only those closest to us, including Chimkin, Temur, and Marco Polo, could hear. "Here is my decision," the Great Khan said.

I closed my eyes and held my breath.

"Messer Marco Polo, you have served me well. I would have you stay here and serve me. But if it is your wish to return to your homeland with your father and uncle, you are free to go. You have delivered to me a letter from your Pope. I will prepare an answer to that letter."

Marco bowed.

Then my grandfather turned to me with a solemn look. My heart pounded even harder.

"Emmajin Beki. You, too, have served me well. You fought hard and helped bring about victory in a battle we might have lost. You suffered a deep loss. I can see the spirit of Suren in you. I have decided to send you to Christendom to deliver my response to the Pope. If he agrees to join our empire, there will be no need for warfare."

My heart soared to the stars in the sky. I did not dare look at Marco. Tears threatened, but I controlled them. I stepped forward and knelt in front of the Khan. I put my forehead on his knees.

He placed his hand on my head. I imagined his wisdom and benevolence flowing into me. I wanted to say, *I promise to serve you well.* But the words did not come.

44

At the Ocean

After the Khan was carried away, men surrounded me, touching my arms, as if my glory would flow to them. They asked questions, unable to understand why a warrior would lay down her bow. Most of them had not heard what the Khan had said to me, and I did not explain. They seemed a blur, the voices, the braid loops, the thick eyebrows, the flush of excitement, the warm glow. Chimkin disappeared, as did Marco, for a time.

Temur stood by my side, fingering the dragon tooth. He seemed to bask in Suren's glory. The tension, the envy, I had felt from Temur was gone.

Still, before he left my side, he leaned toward me and spoke quietly. "Thank you for this. But you need to be careful, Emmajin. That foreigner's words are like honey, meant to trap you. Remember which side you are on, where your loyalty lies."

I nodded. He meant well, but he did not understand. Perhaps he never would.

When the hubbub calmed, servants discreetly took the dishes and the bones away. Men milled around, laughing and drinking. The night was warm, and many of the men removed their shirts. They sang crude drunken songs and danced wildly. The hired women hovered in the shadows.

Clearly, it was time for me to leave. I headed for my tent. Along the path, standing discreetly, was Marco, in his blue and silver *del*. As I walked past him, I put out my left hand, inconspicuously, and lightly brushed my fingers over the hairs of his arm. He stepped onto the path and followed me at a distance.

Instead of returning to my tent, I headed straight for the beach, where half-naked men were singing or rolling with the hired women in the moonlight. My boots kept sinking at odd angles in the sand. I veered off to the right, toward a point in the land, where there were fewer people. I walked alone, trying to get my mind around what the Khan had commanded and what my future might look like now.

Marco followed. I did not look at him, but I knew exactly where he was, and was content to know he was following.

The beach narrowed to a rocky strip at the point of land, but the tide was low enough that I could walk around the point. On the other side was a smaller beach, rimmed by trees, quiet and empty. The warm night air was still. The moon, three-quarters full, lit the sky with a shimmering light.

Just after I passed the last couple, I looked back. Marco was no longer walking behind me. I panicked for a moment, then saw him sitting on a rock, removing his boots. He ran across the sand toward me, smiling.

"It's much easier barefoot."

I sat on a drift log, and he pulled off my boots. My toes were moist and rank from spending too much time inside my boots in warm weather. He lifted some sand and dusted my feet with it. It felt cool and soft and refreshing. He rubbed my feet. A jolt of pleasure shot through to every part of my body.

"You did it," he said to me in wonder.

"Now you can show me your homeland," I said.

"Venezia." With his voice, he caressed each of the foreign syllables. He touched his forehead to my foot, as if to say, *Thank you for saving Venezia.*

"Fay-nay-shya," I said. I had often imagined its streets of water and singing boatmen. Now I might see it.

"To Fay-nay-shya!" I shouted. Barefoot, I dashed down the empty beach, away from the others.

He sprinted after me and caught up quickly. He took my hand and angled toward the sea, which was pounding the beach, black and menacing. I tried to divert him. Even the bravest Mongol soldiers fear and distrust water. Venetians, by nature, are drawn to it.

He pulled me to the edge of the ocean, where the sand was wet and soft. My feet sank slightly into it, making footprints. A wave, cold and perilous, lapped at my land-bound Mongolian feet. I pulled away, shrieking, and sprinted along the dry sand, parallel to the water. He ran after me, staying on the wet sand near the waves.

I discovered that it is easier to run on wet sand than on dry sand. It felt good to let loose and gallop. We covered the entire length of the beach, then rounded another small point onto a deserted arc of sand.

Marco caught up to me and took my hand. Again, he pulled me toward the dangerous black void of water. I tugged back. We fell into the wet sand, and a cool wave washed over us, soaking our trousers. I shrieked again, only half afraid now that I saw how confident Marco was in the ocean.

He grabbed both my hands and pinned me to the sand. He hesitated, checking my eyes. The wave moved away. I stopped struggling. His body drew close to mine, lying on the wet sand, and he nuzzled my nose. I opened my mouth and kissed him with all the passion that had been bottled up inside me those many days and months. Another cold wave came up and I jumped.

He laughed and pulled me up to sit beside him. He turned so that our feet faced straight into the water. Lit by the moon, the waves crested with white foam and crashed against my feet. I remembered voices of warning, tales of strong undercurrents ripping people out to sea and certain death by drowning.

I scrambled to stand up, and so did Marco. "You fear not blood, but you fear the sea?" he asked. I looked again at the water. It was calmer here, in a protected cove.

Slowly, deliberately, Marco led me, his hand in mine, into the dark sea.

My mind rebelled, shouting, *Danger! Water!* but my heart chose to trust Marco. Marco, who had elevated me to a legend. Marco, who had showed me a new way of seeing the world. There would be danger, yes. But Marco would be my partner as we tried to build peace between our homelands.

This water felt warm, soft, safe. I could still feel the current, but it was tamer than in the open ocean. Subduing my fear, I followed as Marco pulled me farther into the sea. The water rose above my knees, my thighs, my waist. My body seemed to be disappearing, though I could feel every patch of my skin. I clutched his hand.

He stopped when the water lapped just below our chests. He turned to me in the moonlight, his eyes bright and clear. He caressed my face, embraced me, kissed me, there in the water, in that most dangerous of elements. I relaxed and gave in to him.

He lifted me, and my body strangely floated. I closed my eyes and pretended I was in a dream, secure in his arms. I laid my head against his chest. My legs floated like fishes' tails. My arms clung to him like the weeds in the sea around me.

I tossed my head back and opened my eyes. Marco smiled playfully at me and tugged at my trousers.

"No need to fear the sea," he said.

I smiled back. He gently lifted my legs and wrapped them around his hips. We glided together like creatures of the sea. Our bodies, our destinies, were entwined. Together, we would be heading to the West.

GLOSSARY

AI-JARUK: Also known by her Mongolian name of Khutulun, daughter of Khaidu. She was famous for defeating her suitors in wrestling. Her dramatic story was told by Marco Polo in his book.

AIRAG: Mongolians' favorite alcoholic drink, fermented mare's milk.

ANDA: In Mongolian, closest friend, like a blood brother, with a vow of lifelong loyalty.

BATTLE OF VOCHAN: A battle between the Mongols and the Burmese that took place in 1277, although the exact date is unclear. In his book, Marco described the battle, saying that twelve thousand Mongol horsemen fought a Burmese army of sixty thousand soldiers and two thousand elephants. He did not mention gunpowder, the use of which is fictional here. Vochan is believed to be the city today known as Baoshan, in Yunnan Province.

BEKI: Mongolian for "princess."

BURMA: A country southwest of China, now called Myanmar.

The Mongols conquered and sacked Burma's capital at Pagan in 1287.

CARAJAN: Mongol-era name of Yunnan Province, in southwest China.

CATHAY: Name used for North China during the thirteenth century; it may be a corruption of the spelling of "Khitai," a group of nomadic people from Manchuria who ruled this part of China from 907 to 1125.

CHABI: Chief wife of Khubilai Khan and a devout Buddhist.

CHIMKIN: Khubilai Khan's second son, who became heir apparent. He died before his father, so he never became Great Khan. The Chinese name of Chimkin, sometimes spelled Zhenjin, means "True Gold," and his father ensured that he was educated in Chinese.

CHINGGIS KHAN: Known in the West as Genghis Khan, the Mongol leader who conquered much of the known world during his lifetime, from 1162 (estimated) to 1227, and founded the Mongol Empire. His birth name was Temujin.

CHRISTENDOM: Europe was known by this name in Marco Polo's era. The word "Europe" was not widely used until centuries later.

DA-LI: A city in Yunnan Province, then known as Carajan. The ancient capital of the Nanzhao Kingdom and the Da-li Kingdom, conquered by the Mongols in 1253. Also spelled Ta-li Fu, and known today as Dali.

DEL: Mongolian clothing, a long-sleeved robe that crosses over in the front and is secured with a sash at the waist. Worn by men and women in summer and winter.

DORJI: Khubilai Khan's eldest son, who was passed over as heir apparent. Little is known about him. His name is sometimes spelled Jurji. Dorji is a Tibetan Buddhist name.

DRAGONS: The creatures described here are crocodiles. Marco Polo called them "great serpents."

DROLMA: Fictional younger sister of Emmajin.

EMMAJIN: Fictional daughter of Dorji, Khubilai Khan's eldest son. Born in 1260, the year her grandfather became Great Khan. In 1275, she would have been fifteen by today's reckoning, but she was then considered sixteen by Chinese and Mongolian reckoning. Her name, more properly spelled Emujin, is the female form of Temujin, the birth name of Chinggis Khan.

GER: A round, collapsible Mongolian tent, known in the West as a yurt.

GOLDEN HORDE: The name of the Mongol *khanate* (kingdom) that ruled Russia and nearby lands for nearly three hundred years. The name is believed to have come from the golden, or yellow, color of the tents and flags used by the Mongols to denote imperial status. The English word *horde* comes from the Mongolian word *ordo,* meaning "camp."

HOORAY: English word that is believed to have come from the Mongolian word for "amen," used as a cry of bravado and encouragement (see Jack Weatherford, *Genghis Khan and the Making of the Modern World*).

IL-KHAN OF PERSIA: The Mongol ruler of Persia, subordinate to the Great Khan. The area he ruled included modern-day Iran, as well as parts of Iraq and neighboring countries. The first Il-khan was Khubilai Khan's brother Hulegu.

KHAGAN OR *KHA'AN:* Mongolian for "emperor," "Great Khan," or "Khan of all Khans." Marco Polo translated this word as "Great Lord of Lords."

KHAIDU: A descendant of Chinggis Khan through his son Ogodei, the second Great Khan. Khaidu believed that Ogodei's line should have inherited the right to rule the Empire, so he challenged Khubilai Khan's right to be Great Khan.

KHAN: Mongolian for "king," "commander," or "ruler."

KHANBALIK: "Khan's capital" in Mongolian, this city was built by Khubilai Khan to be the capital of the Mongol Empire. It was formerly known as Yenjing, and then as Peking, and is now known as Beijing. Marco Polo called it Cambaluc, a variation on Khanbalik. The Chinese refer to Mongol-era Beijing as "Yuan Dadu," which means "main capital of the Yuan dynasty."

KHATUN: Mongolian for "queen" or "empress," used for wives of the khan or *khagan.*

KHUBILAI KHAN: The fifth Great Khan, born in 1215, who ruled the Mongol Empire from 1260 to his death in 1294. Commonly known in the West as Kubla Khan or Kublai Khan. During his reign, the Mongol Empire reached its greatest size. For details of Khubilai Khan's life, the author found the best source to be *Khubilai Khan: His Life and Times,* by Morris Rossabi.

KINSAY: Name used by Marco Polo for Hangzhou, capital of the Southern Sung dynasty. Kinsay is a variation on the Chinese words *"jing shi,"* "capital city."

MAFFEO POLO: Marco Polo's uncle, who traveled to China twice, once with Marco's father only and again with both Marco and his father.

MARCO POLO: A young Venetian who traveled to the capital of the Mongol Empire in China, leaving home in late 1271 and arriving in 1275 at the age of twenty-one. After returning home to Venice in 1295, he wrote a book about his travels, becoming the first European to write about China for a Western audience. Many versions of Marco's book exist; the author of *Daughter of Xanadu* relied on *The Travels of Marco Polo: The Complete Yule-Cordier Edition.*

MIAOYAN: A daughter of Khubilai Khan who became a Buddhist nun. At a Buddhist temple outside Beijing, called Tanzhe Temple, there are indentations on the stone where it is believed she knelt and prayed.

MONGOL EMPIRE: Founded by Chinggis Khan in 1206. At its

peak in 1279 the Mongol Empire included all of Mongolia, China, Tibet, Korea, Central Asia, Iran, and Russia. It was the largest contiguous land empire in history, rivaled only by the nineteenth-century British Empire. The Mongols ruled China and Iran for about one hundred years, and Mongols continued to rule Russia for about three hundred years.

MONGOLIA: Homeland of the Mongols, now an independent country north of China. It included parts of China known today as Inner Mongolia.

NICCOLO POLO: Marco Polo's father, who made his first journey to China from 1260 to 1269, and his second journey to China with his son, Marco Polo, from 1271 to 1295. Both times, Niccolo Polo traveled with his brother, Maffeo.

ovoo: In Mongolian custom, a heap of stones that marks a sacred place.

POPE: The head of the Christian religion in Rome. When Marco Polo left for China in 1271, the new Pope was Gregory X, whom his father and uncle had befriended earlier, during their travels.

SOUTHERN CHINA: Before the Mongol era, in 1127, China was divided into two countries, north and south. The north was ruled by the Jin dynasty and the south by the Southern Sung dynasty. Marco Polo called northern China Cathay and southern China Manzi, the Chinese word for "barbarian." It is likely that he learned these terms from the Mongols. The Mongols conquered the Jin dynasty by 1234, and completed the conquest of southern China in 1279, three years after the conquest of its capital at Kinsay (Hangzhou).

SUREN: Fictional eldest son of Chimkin, born the same year as Emmajin.

TARA: Buddhist goddess of compassion, revered by Tibetans and Mongolians.

Tartars: A word used by Europeans, especially Russians, to describe Mongols.

Temur: Son of Chimkin, who later became the sixth Great Khan, ruling from 1294 to 1307. The year of his birth is uncertain; it is either 1261 or 1265.

Tengri: Mongolian for "Eternal Heaven," or "God."

Tolui: Chinggis Khan's fourth son, father of Khubilai Khan.

Venezia: Italian spelling of Venice.

Xanadu: Alternative spelling of Shangdu, the site of Khubilai Khan's summer palace, due north of Khanbalik/Beijing. The name Shangdu means "Upper Capital" in Chinese. Today it is in ruins, located near the town of Duolun in Inner Mongolia. Marco Polo described it in great detail; various translations of his book spell the name "Chandu" and "Xandu." In the famous poem "Kubla Khan," by Samuel Taylor Coleridge, it was spelled "Xanadu," which is the name most widely used in English.

Yangtze River: Main river in central China, known today as Chang Jiang ("Long River"). The Mongols called it Brius, or "Gold River," for its upper reaches, the Jinsha River.

Yellow River: Main river in northern China. The Mongols called it Caramoran, meaning "Black River."

Yuan dynasty: An era of Chinese history when China was ruled by the Mongols. Khubilai Khan declared the Yuan dynasty in 1271, eleven years after he became Great Khan of the Mongol Empire. His heirs followed as emperors until the Yuan dynasty fell in 1368.

ACKNOWLEDGMENTS

After the long process of researching and writing this book, I have many people to thank, starting with my husband, Paul Yang, who suggested that I write a novel about Marco Polo. Week after week, I received great input and advice from my writing coach and teacher, Brenda Peterson, and the many in her class who read and commented on the book as it progressed, especially Leslie Helm, Susan Little, John Runyan, Mary Matsuda Gruenewald, Donna Sandstrom, Jennifer Haupt, Leigh Calvez, Trip Quillman, J. Kingston Pierce, Liz Gruenfeld, Liz Adams, Laurie Greig, Dan Keusal, Leska Fore, Susan Knox, and Sara Yamasaki.

For support and encouragement, I also want to thank my daughters, Emily and Serena, and my friends Rita Vesper, Katy Ehrlich, and Kathy Renner, as well as my fellow Mongolia explorers Jeanne DeMund, and Elton, Bonnie, and Erin Welke. Jeanne and I managed to locate the abandoned ruins of Xanadu, as well as the earlier capital of the Mongol Empire, Karakorum, and the mausoleum of Chinggis Khan. I am also grateful to Steven Yang, who created the map. Many other friends and relatives encouraged me along the way, commented on early drafts, and endured long monologues about why the Mongol Empire mattered so much in history and why we can be confident that Marco Polo really did go to China.

I particularly want to thank my wonder-working agent, Michael Bourret, as well as Jane Dystel and Miriam Goderich of Dystel & Goderich Literary Management, and my terrific editors, Michelle Poploff and Rebecca Short of Delacorte Press, who appreciated and enriched my vision for this book.

For information about the Mongol Empire, I read many books, the most useful of which was *Khubilai Khan: His Life and Times,* by Morris Rossabi. By and large, I have followed the spellings he prefers. Mongolian words and names are notoriously difficult for English speakers to pronounce correctly, so feel free to pronounce them as you wish! Both Emmajin and Suren are fictional, but many other characters in this book were real people. I tried to imagine and re-create them as accurately as historical records would allow. Any mistakes that remain are my own.